Castles in the Air

Castles
in the Air

Mary Hagey

EDITIONS

Cover design by Doowah Design.
Photo of Mary Hagey by Boris Skljarevski.

Acknowledgements
I am grateful to the many people who contributed in various ways to my development as a writer: family, friends, profs and fellow students at Concordia University, editors of literary journals in which my work has appeared, and everyone at Signature Editions, especially my editor, Karen Haughian.
    Four of these stories have appeared previously, in a somewhat different form. "The Long Way Home" in *Prism International*, "Human Interest" in *The New Quarterly*, "Modern Women" in *Room of One's Own*, and "Tooth and Nail" in *Grain*. *Hero, The Buzz Beurling Story*, by Brian Nolan, was my primary source of information on the real-life Canadian flying ace, George Beurling, featured in "Human Interest."

This book was printed on Ancient Forest Friendly paper.
Printed and bound in Canada by Hignell Book Printing Inc.

We acknowledge the support of the Canada Council for the Arts and the Manitoba Arts Council for our publishing program.

Library and Archives Canada Cataloguing in Publication

Hagey, Mary, 1947–
        Castles in the air / Mary Hagey.

Issued also in electronic format.
ISBN 978-1-927426-00-5

        I. Title.

PS8615.A364C27 2012   C813'.6   C2012-906324-X

Signature Editions
P.O. Box 206, RPO Corydon, Winnipeg, Manitoba, R3M 3S7
www.signature-editions.com

For my children, Kim and Steve McIntosh

Contents

HOME REMEDY

"Doesn't this look scrumptious?" gushes a short, stout woman, a cousin of yours, presumably. She casts an anxious smile across the table to where you are, her small dark eyes flitting from salad bowl to meat platter to macaroni casserole. There are nearly a dozen picnic tables arranged end to end and laden with potluck offerings. You consider the claim, scrumptious, and think, Not really. Abundant, surely, but that's as far as you're willing to go. There isn't a black olive in sight. No marinated vegetables, no endive, couscous or quinoa…

"We've been so very fortunate again with the weather," the woman says, searching your face for signs of agreement.

You look within yourself, discover that your stockpile of forbearance has been greatly depleted, especially the weather reserve, but you manage a nod.

"The man upstairs must love us Delaneys," the woman continues, glancing heavenward.

Having been asked by your mother to stake out and claim two seats near the middle, you check to see if there are any in proximity to less irksome individuals, and just as you're about to excuse yourself and venture to greener pastures, your mother appears and says to the woman, "You've found Holly, Agnes, that's good. You girls have so much to catch up on."

For at least two decades you've been trying to train your mother to say women when referring to adult females, so it's most annoying that she's still saying girls, but you offer a defeated smile and reach across the table to shake Agnes's hand, trying all the while to place her. For what seems like hours now, you've done nothing but smile and shake hands. A quick glance at your watch and you see it's been only thirty-four minutes since you arrived at this, the 75th Delaney reunion.

"So, you're Holly McCarthy," Agnes says with disbelief and no joy whatever. "You look totally different without pigtails."

You had, unhappily, worn braids until well into your teens. Leave it to this woman to remind you. You suppose you ought to confess to her that you haven't a clue who she is, but some instinct warns you not to. Agnes seems equally wary. She peers down the table in both directions at the numerous seats yet available, and says, "I should move down a piece... I'm assuming Chris and Nancy will be along and you'll all want to be together...?"

Instead of thanking Agnes, your mother encourages her to stay put, explains that Nancy didn't come and Chris will be supervising either the barbecue pit or the kiddie table this year.

"I see," says Agnes, and you think: *nice try.* "I like your hairdo," she says to your mother. "You look like, oh, what's her name?, the actress, you know, a big star years ago... she took up with that married man, the actor whose wife was in an asylum."

Your mother pats her hair tentatively. "It was Holly's doing. You don't think she got a bit carried away?"

"Oh no," insists Agnes. "It's quite becoming and at least it's off your neck. I wish I could think of the actress's name. You're a dead ringer. Holly, you must know."

And you *do* know, but you tell Agnes you shun popular, show-biz movies — a statement that earns you a worried look from your mother, one that says, *Please don't get on your high horse and trounce all the films everyone loves. People will think you're peculiar.*

"Never mind," says Agnes. "The name will come to me. So, Holly, I heard through the grapevine that you haven't settled down yet."

You think: What an odd thing to say to a forty-six-year-old woman who's settled down — settled down many times, in fact.

Agnes proceeds to summarise her own settled life, her marriage to Garth Timberland, her lack of success in having a family, her husband's premature death. But her account flounders in the presence of Reverend Dick Delaney, your third cousin on your mother's side, your mother being a Delaney originally. "Helen," he says to your mother, taking one of her bony little hands into his two big spongy ones, "you're keeping very well, I see." Glancing in your direction and finding your eyes upon him, he says, "And who have we here? Holly is it? Home for a visit? How *nice*. It was at your father's funeral I saw you last, was it not? Two years ago, or three perhaps? How good to see you under less distressing circumstances."

"Five years," you tell him. "Dad died in '91."

"*Ninety-one*," Rev. Dick says, doubtfully, and goes on to boast of longevity in his immediate family.

"Eighty-two," you tell him, raising your voice. "Dad was *not* ninety-one."

"Eighty-two, not as long ago as that, surely," says the man known most for his troubled youth, troubled until he found the Lord, after which life was all smooth sailing.

"Not 1982. Dad was eighty-two when he died in '91," you say, and you imagine yourself telling him the reason for your visit, just to watch his fake zest fizzle. But why do you have such outrageous fantasies anyway? Why harbour animosity toward someone whose only crime is to be determinedly pleasant, something you were going to strive to be too? You remind yourself to relax, the lump is gone — it was removed at the time of the biopsy. Of course, further surgery is needed. Indeed, a woman has time to lose her mind while she waits to lose her breast. Your oncologist is doing his best to get you an earlier date. "Why not go home in the interim?" he told you. "Family can be a tremendous asset in fighting this disease."

Like most people, you dread your family, even under the best of circumstances, but you do love them in that socially obligatory and biologically programmed way, and there was no denying your need for some distraction. "You're coming *now*?" your mother said when you phoned to tell her of your visit. "It's not that you're not welcome," she hastened to assure you. "It's just that, there's the reunion this weekend and you know the Delaneys are not arty people. You know how impatient you get, dear."

You *do* know how impatient you get, and most of your impatience is, in your estimation, quite justified. "Whose feelings are you worried about, theirs or mine?" you asked.

"This is what I mean."

"Suppose I try extra hard to stand them," you countered. You had no intention of revealing the real reason for your visit, of burdening your mother with apprehension and bringing upon yourself a lot of unsolicited advice.

"Why not come for the Labour Day weekend, before your classes start?" she suggested, and all your well-rehearsed restraint crumbled.

"Oh, no, dear, *no*," your mother said upon hearing the news. "Of course you should come if you're up to it. Have you checked with your doctor?"

"It was my doctor's idea, actually."

"We won't bother with the reunion," she said, which made you feel generous too. You worried that your younger brother, Chris, might feel obliged to miss the gathering, and his family as well.

"I'll come and catch up on my reading while you and the others are at the reunion." You actually looked forward to having the big old house you grew up in to yourself for a day. When your father was alive it had felt like home, but ever since Chris and his family moved back to be company for your mother, and to undertake the upkeep, you've felt like a guest whenever you've been there for a visit.

"If you're here and we're going then you ought to go too, Holly," your mother reasoned, thwarting your plan. "The children would be most disappointed," she added, "and one of them would be bound to mention your visit home and people would wonder, wouldn't they? I mean, it's not as though you're a moody teenager anymore."

So here you sit, moody and middle-aged. But now, mingled with your annoyance is a heightened awareness of being alive. Of course it would be better to be alive somewhere else, but there's something tender and affecting about your mother's contentment just now. Thanks to you, she's seated near the centre. Last year she got stuck near the end of the table and it had felt all wrong, she said, like having her underwear on backwards.

But what's this? You're about to lose your elbow room. A teenager — broad-shouldered and buxom as a Gaston Lachaise sculpture — introduces herself as Sheri-Lynn and fills the spot on your left. The only person still standing is the man of the cloth, who waits for a degree of decorum then proceeds with the blessing.

"Will you be going on that weird diet again?" your mother murmurs to you just as everyone says *Amen*. She means the macrobiotic regimen you'd adhered to following your initial cancer treatment seven years ago — a treatment that was experimental then, and has since been proven risky. There had been those who'd said it was risky at the time as well — to have just the lumpectomy and the removal of the lymph nodes with no radiation and no chemotherapy. But given that the alternatives were not risk-free either, you'd opted for the new and daring approach to fighting cancer, augmenting the treatment with healthful food. "I don't know about the diet," you tell her. "I'm certainly not going to think about it today."

"Don't you just hate it, Sheri-Lynn," Agnes says, "when skinny people like Holly talk about going on a diet?"

Sheri-Lynn's plump rosy cheeks turn rosier. A vision of health, she tells you how lucky you are to be fine-boned.

You try not to think about your fine bones, whether or not they harbour a trace of the enemy. You consider explaining that it wouldn't be a weight-loss diet if you were to go on one, but you don't dare say anything that could lead to telling the whole long story. The fact that your mother would bring the subject up and refer to the diet as *weird* proves she absorbed nothing of your exchange this morning. She'd wandered into your room around six, hairbrush in hand. Thought she'd heard you up, she said, and came to check, make sure you were okay. You were sitting on the floor in the lotus position, meditating.

"Oh, Holly, you've taken *that* up again," she said, as though she'd caught you smoking dope or playing with yourself.

Besides following a macrobiotic diet, you'd taken up yoga when cancer was diagnosed the first time. You'd practised it religiously for three years, then haphazardly for two years, after which you gave it up because it had, in the quietest moments, reminded you too much of the cancer.

"Couldn't you just pray normally?" your mother implored.

This is all your mother has ever wanted of Chris and you: for the two of you to be *normal*. As though such a state existed. So you asked her why sitting quietly on the floor breathing deeply struck her as a cause for concern. "It's not like I hold any absurd beliefs," you said, and then you used *her* belief, the virgin birth of a bloke who walked on water, as an example of absurd. She stood dumbstruck a moment before turning to leave. A tiny woman with cataracts and a frail heart, she'd paused in the doorway to steady herself. "Oh, never mind me, Mom," you said. "Come back. Let me do your hair." And she returned, sat on the little vanity stool, put her head in your hands. Such silvery, baby-fine tresses.

"You had hair like a woolly mammoth," she said, after a bit. "Who'd have believed it would turn out so nice?"

Your hair now is medium-length and held back from your face with decorative combs. You could have had it this way when you were a kid too, but your mother wouldn't hear of it. Whenever you begged for a shorter style, she'd argue that only braids could make your hair tidy. Unless you want it *cropped*, she'd say in such a threatening manner that, imagining yourself completely shorn and humiliated, you invariably yielded to her will.

You've been preparing yourself for the likelihood that you'll lose your hair once the treatment starts, and are determined not to make a big deal of it. Perhaps you'll just cut it all off before it has a chance to fall out. Crop it. Yes, that's what you'll do.

"That's an unusual outfit you're wearing," Agnes says, drawing you back to this supposed real world. "Wherever did you get it?"

You don't regard your outfit as particularly unusual, so you explain that the pantaloons and tunic are standard apparel in Tibet, that you'd drawn up a pattern based on something you'd seen in a documentary.

"Your earrings sure match," she says. "Did you make them too?"

You tell her, no, you bought them in a little shop that sells the work of the mentally handicapped, and she puts in that she never did jump on the bandwagon and get her ears pierced. "Isn't it nice they're able to keep busy?" she says of the artisans whose work is daring and playful, not haphazard, as people like Agnes imply.

You spend a day each month — well, two hours, actually — supervising the threading of colourful beads at a school for those with special challenges. Having survived cancer beyond the five-year mark, you'd felt compelled to do some kind of public service. Your volunteerism had been part of a bargain — with *whom* or *what* you couldn't say, but now that the cancer has returned, you can't help but feel betrayed.

"We were just kids the last time you came to a reunion," Agnes says. "Must be thirty years now since you were here?"

"Hmm," you say, calculating. "I was fifteen — it was the summer after Uncle Neil left for Australia — so that's thirty-one years ago." You'd learned, that last time, thirty-one years ago, that without your uncle in attendance the reunion was a misery.

"Ah ha!" Your mother claps her hands in apparent glee. "Here's proof of what I was saying on your last visit home. You had plenty of freedom as a child. Lots of parents would have forced you to attend the reunions. But no, we allowed you…" She stops abruptly, apparently undergoing second thoughts about trying to score one against her daughter when the poor thing is in such a precarious situation. She changes gears: "But let's not argue. Not that we argue, Agnes. We just have to get to the bottom of things sometimes, isn't that right, Holly?"

"Hmhmm," you say again. The truth is this: you and your mother *never* get to the bottom of things, nor do you try to particularly, not that you wouldn't like to sometimes. But the habit is to tiptoe around the circumference of things, sparring without actually confronting each other.

And now you tune in to your mother's conversation with Agnes and hear her being somewhat less than diplomatic. "I'm just saying that you ought to have brought your father along. A day among family is probably just what he needs."

"*No,*" says Agnes most emphatically, "the doctor was the one to nix the idea." Glancing briefly at you, she explains that her dad has Alzheimer's. She shifts her attention back to your mother. "Even the occasional visitor leaves him quite agitated," she says.

The way she averts her eyes and the way your mother searches her face would suggest that your mother has been paying visits and upsetting the poor man. You can't recall any mention of visits to an elderly cousin in your mother's agenda-like letters and phone conversations. But you don't quiz her, sensing enough tension in the air already. "You come to these reunions every year, do you, Agnes?" you ask to change the subject, and Agnes assures you that yes, oh, yes, she wouldn't miss them for anything. In all likelihood, she was, long ago, one of the many kids who used to take advantage of your diminutive size and taunt you for not possessing the Delaney name.

You take a basket of bread rolls from Sheri-Lynn and pass it along to your mother, your mind drifting back to the reunions of long ago. The park in your memory is greener, lusher. The stream on which ducks putter and dunk is wider and deeper. The tables are covered in a sunshine-yellow cloth — a huge bolt unfurled. You must have had *some* fun to remember it thus.

You think of your uncle, the way he was, handsome, sardonic, restless. Lately, he's been working as a hired hand on a camel farm in the Australian outback, whenever he needs money, that is. The rest of the time he writes articles that are, on occasion, published in small scholarly journals.

"You seem awfully pensive, dear," your mother whispers. "Are you feeling okay?"

"I was just missing Uncle Neil," you tell her, and a funny look crosses her face, one that suggests she's hiding something. "Is he all right?" you inquire, and the way she says, "Why do you ask?" you know something is up. "Is there news?" you prod, and she says *later*, and indicates that Agnes is talking to you.

"I did miss one reunion, in 1978." Agnes's voice is a mixture of reverence and melancholy. "I'd had a miscarriage, you see. I came the year my husband died, but the miscarriage, the loss just hit me so hard."

What to say to this annoying woman who has, nevertheless, suffered two major losses…? God, the agony of trying to live up to social expectations! Why doesn't your mother offer one of her nice sugar-coated platitudes? "I truly can't imagine. You've been through a lot, Agnes," you say, finally, and feel almost winded from the feat.

Agnes assures you that, indeed, unless one has been through a miscarriage, one just can't know. "It's as much a death as any other death," she says, and you feel as though the grim reaper has set a hand on your shoulder.

Agnes says your name, repeats it for no apparent reason, then explains it's a name she's always been partial to. "I know it's an old name but it sounds so modern compared to mine."

"I have my mother to thank. She chose it."

"Holly was my grandmother's name," Agnes says. "Poor soul died when my father was born."

"It's a very common name," your mother states, so firmly Agnes blinks. It seems to you that if anyone is coming across as peculiar, it's not you, but your mother.

"I was just trying to remember what it is you do," Agnes says to you. "Your father did tell me once, so let me just put on my thinking cap. He was a very imposing man, your father, we didn't often speak."

"I'm an art historian," you tell her. "And I teach."

"And she writes," your mother puts in proudly. But Agnes is distracted by a great steaming platter of corn on the cob that's being sent around, so she may not have heard. "Be careful," she warns the old man next to her whose crab-like hands extract a cob. "It's scalding," she tells him.

"Holly has written *two* books," your mother says rather loudly. Her pride is so touching you can't help but wish — for her sake, not just your own — that people were more appreciative of art. You wonder if your mother has actually read your books, beyond the captions accompanying the colour plates. Chris, flipping through one of them, asked, "You mean you genuinely like this scribble and drip? Come on, my kids can do better." It had felt as though your life had been dismissed out of hand.

Is art your life?

When cancer struck the first time, your second book was in its infancy. You remember pleading with God — the one you'd never believed in — bargaining away the many other books you dreamed of writing if only you'd get to finish *Surfaces, Method and Meaning,* because you felt that the surface treatment of a painting, so often regarded as mere style, was the key to interpretation — more relevant than the actual subject matter — and it was imperative that you say so. While you fully intend to finish your third book, to examine and explain the role of anarchistic art, it doesn't seem absolutely vital that you do this time. Actually, there are moments when you doubt the world needs another book of any sort, but perhaps that's just a symptom of depression.

"So, these books you write, Holly, are they art books, are they the *how-to* type?" Agnes asks. "My neighbour recently learned how to draw horses from a book. It's sort of amazing to think that all along she'd had incredible talent and hadn't known it."

"Holly is writing a novel," your mother puts in before you can think of a way to trash the neighbour's so-called talent, and she smiles in a conspiratorial manner at you. Her intent is to silence you, of course, but is it more than that? The notion that you're compiling material for a novel is ongoing fiction that began when you were twelve. Having returned home that summer from a visit with your Uncle Neil, you announced that you were going to be a novelist, and over the years the novel, the idea of it, that is, has taken on a presence. "Now *here's* something for Holly's novel!" someone in the family will say, and they'll go on to tell of some peculiar experience, an unpleasant encounter, a moment of insight they most likely wouldn't have bothered to share were it not for the phantom book.

"You're writing a novel? Holly, that's wonderful," says Agnes. "Is it a romance?"

"No," you tell her. "Definitely not." Your mind lingers on the so-called novel. Suppose you *were* to die; what would happen to it? Would it perish too, or survive? Would it be a comfort for your family to go on sharing suitable material, or would it be too painful?

"Not a romance novel," says Agnes. "Are you down on them, or what?"

"Yes indeed," you say without apology, your distaste extending to romance itself. Your most recent relationship has just been terminated, the two long years of trying to hold it together possibly the source of the stress that may have caused this new cancer — an idea not entirely dismissed by the oncologist.

"Is it a murder mystery?" Agnes inquires. "Those can be awfully good."

"Not really," you say. "Unless it becomes a romance, despite all my efforts, in which case it'll be a murder mystery as well."

You're distracted now by motion at your elbow. "Hi honey-bunch," you say to your littlest niece, Katie, hauling her up onto the bench between you and your mother, mindful of the ice-cream cone she brandishes.

Your mother says, "Well, look who we have here. Are you *supposed* to be here? Shouldn't you be with Carrie and Ben?" To you she says, "She shouldn't be running loose like this," and to Agnes, "Her mother ought to be here. Chris has only two hands," then to you: "Maybe you could accompany her back to the kiddie table, Holly."

"She's fine here," you assure her. "She's not running loose."

"Her mother really ought to have come."

"What's the big deal, Ma?" you ask. "Why shouldn't Nancy have a day to herself?"

"In my day, a mother did her job and that was that."

You bite your tongue, allowing your mother her version of the past. In your version, you were banished from the house — sent to the shop, your father's farm implement business that Chris now runs — to supposedly help your father so your mother didn't have you underfoot while trying to do the laundry, the gardening, cooking, and cleaning — or trying to enjoy her tea, her ear to whatever radio drama she was keen on at the time.

"So what's your novel about?" asks Agnes.

You have to stop to think what kind of novel you might like to write, one day, if given the time. "I'm just mapping out the plot at this point," you tell her, "but I guess you could say it's essentially a study of family dynamics."

"Oh, it sounds too serious for me," Agnes says too seriously. "I like something light, something to take me out of myself." She leans across the table, motioning for you to do likewise. "Roy there, in the blue plaid shirt, he writes limericks. Some of them are pretty off-colour from what I hear."

"Guess what, Annie Holly?" Katie says, interrupting, dear child. "Kids is habin' ice-ceam combs… Chokit ones." She is like a little bird perched on the bow of a sea-tossed ship. And word goes out: There is ice cream! Yes, only just now does it register that the child has ice cream, that pie à la mode is in the offing.

Suddenly, everyone feels the need to do away with the first course, although some speculate that perhaps the ice cream is only for the children, as the hot dogs had been. They become philosophical. Who needs ice cream in the midst of desserts that would cost five dollars or more in a restaurant? Six. Six dollars now in certain places like Toronto and Vancouver, where people will pay such crazy prices. This information is supplied by those who have flown to Toronto and Vancouver, and have, on principle, returned without having had dessert.

The mention of Toronto and Vancouver sets off a flurry of disclosures concerning recent trips to other destinations: Halifax, St. John's, Winnipeg... What gets everyone flying is all the dying: friends, former comrades in arms, relatives... To your chagrin, conversation hunkers down on Death like a flock of hungry vultures onto a massive carcass. You try your best to tune out, but details somehow filter through your resolve. Ignatius Delaney, who used to be a whiz at horseshoes, wasted away to ninety-eight pounds. When Mary Delaney-Kernan fell ill, her skin got so thin that, with just the slightest pressure, it split like the peel of a rotten apple. Poor Jack Delaney bloated up to nearly twice his original size when he got cancer — not from the cancer but from the drugs. It was a merciful thing he went so swiftly. *Swiftly.* That's the favoured way to go.

"What's dat noise, Annie Holly? Annie Holly...?"

"I don't know, love," you say to your niece, and like everyone else you strain to see who's creating the racket at the children's end of the table. Why, it's Chris. He's whacking an aluminium pie pan with the tongs used for the corn, and continues to do so until all the chatter is reduced to a hush. "Sorry to interrupt, folks," he says, "but I have an announcement to make. The rumour is true: there is indeed ice cream, thanks to my sister, Holly, who has come all the way from Montreal to join us today." He gestures in your direction and describes in an amusing manner your after-breakfast quest for tubs of ice cream — and the dry ice to pack it in. Perhaps you're overly sensitive, but he does seem to be implying that you inconvenienced him. He doesn't mention that what you'd wanted to get was gelato, not ice cream, but he was loath to go out of his way to get something he'd never even heard of, something that might be too unusual for sensible people. "Please have your plates ready, ladies and gentlemen," he says finally, which earns him enthusiastic applause, appreciation he gallantly redirects to you.

Well, this is more like it: Holly the heroine. A pain-in-the-neck heroine, but a heroine nonetheless. You graciously accept smiles of gratitude from far and near. And questions. How are things in Montreal these days? What will it take to make francophones happy? Will the separatists succeed in breaking the country apart? Where, exactly, did you get the dry ice?

"Dry ice," says Agnes. "Isn't that dangerous to have around kids? Didn't someone bring some once, years back?" She repeats this question to the old-timer next to her, raising her voice, and he gazes into the past in search of dry ice. "Could be," he says.

"Didn't some boy get badly burned?" she asks.

"Not here," says the man without hesitation. "No one ever got badly burned here."

"With dry ice," she reminds him.

"Oh, I never heard tell of anything like that." This accidental authority blossoms in the limelight, and proceeds to list the various catastrophes in bygone years: fingers caught in car doors, soakers, bloody noses and the like.

"You can get a third-degree burn if you so much as *touch* dry ice," says Agnes.

"Really?" Your mother looks at you as if to ask how you could have been so careless.

"I'm not blaming you for bringing it, Holly," Agnes says smiling. "People can't be expected to know everything."

"Come on, Katie." You extract yourself and your niece from the picnic table. "Let's go find a swing to fall off of. Let's go break our necks."

Katie-the-kangaroo sproing-sproings all over the place as soon as her feet hit the ground. She sings bye-bye to her grandmother, but Gramma's attention has been stolen by Roy, the writer of limericks.

"Helen," you hear him say as you and Katie turn to leave, "I was seated down the hike there and sayin' to myself, 'Who is that beautiful woman?' And wouldn't you know, it isn't Katharine Hepburn, but my old flame."

"Katharine Hepburn," cries Agnes. "That's the name I was trying to remember!"

You're sitting under a tree downstream from where the ducks patrol the shore. "So here you are," someone says, and you look up to see a little old lady. "Am I intruding?" your mother inquires hesitantly, and you shake your head no. "Where's Katie? You haven't lost her, I hope."

You tell her that Carrie and Ben came a moment ago and took Katie away to be part of some game or other. "It must have required a small, willing victim," you say, and she asks where they are now.

"They're playing, Ma; it's what kids do." You watch the tentative dance of dragonflies on the surface of the water, and feel the force of your mother's disapproval upon you, feel it slowly surrender.

"Gee, it's good to get the picnic cleared away," she says, artificially upbeat. "It was so nice to see some of the men pitching in."

She's forever implying that there's a new breed of male unknown to women of her generation, and you ought to be grateful. Greg had been one of them, in her eyes. You wonder, will he try to resume the relationship when he hears of the cancer's recurrence? When you think of men — the faceless men of the future — you think of all the breast reconstruction you'll have to undergo. You think of the pictures you've seen of botched jobs, that you'd rather be dead than risk such mutilation. Of course, death is no afternoon snooze. Is the worst thing about cancer the prospect of dying, or is it the humbling effect it has?

"So what's up with Uncle Neil?" you ask.

"That's why I came to find you, Holly. How would you like to take a drive and find his old place?" She dangles the car keys. "It can't be more than twenty miles."

"Couldn't you just sit here and tell me?"

"Why don't we wait until we get there, hmm?"

"I told the kids I'd watch them run their races."

Instead of conceding that you'd better not disappoint them, your mother says in a pleading voice, "You've always made out that the summer vacation with Neil was the best time of your life. Who knows if you'll ever be up this way again?"

Silence.

Laughter drifts from the picnic area, cheers rise from the ballpark, a squabble of some sort comes from the direction of the playground, a girl's hair-raising shriek: "She's throwing sand! Daddy, tell her to stop throwing sand!"

"…I only meant that since you generally don't come to these reunions, you're not likely… Anyway, I spoke with Chris and he says to be back no later than four." With this, she holds out the keys and you reluctantly take them.

It turns out that your mother has a map and written directions to your uncle's, drawn up by Chris on company stationery, not some scrap he scrounged to facilitate a whim. No, this side trip has been planned in advance. You can scarcely wait to learn what your mother is up to, but in the meantime, you enjoy the open road, the cloudless sky, the soft crunch of gravel, the dust billowing in your wake.

The scenery is more than scenery. Each prominent feature in the landscape seems to be a treasure on this treasure hunt: a gangly aspen growing inside the remnants of a silo; a barn whose sparse boards look like cross-hatching against the blue sky; broken windmills left to stand alone in barren fields; shabby clapboard churches in waist-high grass.

"There's the old one-room schoolhouse we're supposed to watch for," your mother announces by and by, her way of reminding you to turn at the next intersection, which you do. "That's got to be the rock pile Chris means," she says, pointing to the fruit of endless labour, a mountain of rocks in a field strewn with yet more rubble. Nearing your destination, you anticipate the lane that once led to your uncle's, sense it just around the next bend. "Here, Holly, turn here."

"I'm turning, for god's sakes."

"You might signal, dear. Then I'd know, wouldn't I? Oh, look!"

As the house comes into view you're tempted to make a crack about the apparent *Anne of Green Gables* influence, but you hold your tongue. Your mother is wildly fond of the Canadian classic about a spunky girl. Yes, indeed, conventional people find spunky fictional girls very appealing. Real ones are another matter.

"It's not boarded up," your mother says. "I was told it had been boarded up for the summer."

"What does it matter? There isn't anyone about." You park under a maple tree, turn off the ignition.

The house, when it had belonged to your uncle, was nothing like it is now. It was a simple wooden structure similar to the shed, only larger. The grounds, now as perfect as golf course greens, had consisted of wild grasses, daisies, black-eyed Susans, buttercups, Queen Anne's lace. The old pump, once the only source of water, is now the central ornament in a rock garden.

"Who'd have guessed it held such possibilities?" your mother says. "So tell me, the, uh, the summer you spent here, did something in particular happen that made you say you were going to write a novel one day?"

"Happen? Nothing happened." You scan the long-ago summer in search of an incident, some *one* thing that may have, after all, given impetus to the notion, but no. What you'd loved was freedom, the way days went by as they went by. No schedules. No having to measure up. No criticism. You fell in love with your uncle's lifestyle: living alone without much in the way of material possessions. Lots of books, though, all the great works of literature, books on every subject under the sun, especially art.

It occurs to you that were it not for that summer, you may never have ventured far from your birthplace. You'd have married a high-maintenance guy like your dad, most likely, and had a family. And with this thought, a question comes to mind: would you have developed cancer? Had it been in the cards, no matter what? You don't really believe in things being in the cards or not in the cards, but still, you wonder.

"Neil didn't ... *say* anything to you then?"

"Say anything about what?"

Your mother clears her throat, the wheels in her mind turning; you imagine them as little windmills. "Well," she says, "let's just suppose this really was your novel, Holly, and you had a character such as Neil to deal with. What kind of a history would you give him to explain the life he's chosen?"

You dismiss the story angle and tell her she frets far too much over her brother, that just because he's reclusive doesn't mean he's unhappy.

"And *why* do you suppose the sister frets so?" she asks, sticking with third-person narration. "Oh, dear... A bee!" She swipes at the air frantically.

"It's a wasp," you tell her, letting down the back windows, not solving the problem, in fact, accommodating other wasps seeking to find their way in. In a fit of exasperation you say, "Mom, why not just tell me what's on your mind?"

"Supposing his parents are actually his grandparents." Your mother looks off into the distance.

For a moment you are stunned, but you have a pretty good idea where the plot to this soap opera is going. "And let me guess, his sister is really his mother," you say matter-of-factly. You rummage in the glove compartment and find some paper to roll into a swatter, but, wouldn't you know, the wasps have settled on the back windshield quite out of reach. Your mother, meanwhile, is silent. "No kidding!" you cry. You are thrilled, now that you think of it, to learn Neil is your brother, but at the same time you wonder what difference it will make with him on the other side of the world.

And now, in the rear-view mirror, you catch sight of a car coming up the lane. "Look how she stares at us," your mother says as the car pulls up alongside. "She can't get many visitors."

The woman steps out and continues to stare. "Lost your way?" she inquires. A lanky Doberman follows at her heels, circles Chris's van, sniffing eagerly. It raises its head in recognition of a truck roaring up the drive. It wags its tail.

The woman peers in at the two of you, and you and your mother hastily provide overlapping explanations for your presence. You say: "This was my uncle's place and we were curious to see it again." Your mother says: "My son built this house. We dropped by to have a look." Is the look on your mother's face because she was surprised to find herself openly referring to Neil as her son, or is it because you referred to Neil as your uncle, having just learned otherwise?

A portly gentleman extracts himself from the cab of his pickup and slams the door. The frown he wears is similar to the one your father had. "This is my assistant, Holly," your father used to say to his customers. "She's the one who mixes up all my nuts and bolts." There was something about his gruff claim on you that moved you then, moves you still.

"Lyle," the woman says, "this woman and her aunt — *great* aunt it must be, yes — have come to see the place. They're Neil Delaney's people… remember, the chap who built the, uh… original structure?"

Your mother begs to differ. *"Mother,"* she says. "I am this dear girl's mother."

"Excuse me," says the woman. She peers directly into your eyes. "I seem to recall you saying before that Mr Delaney is your uncle… and this lady's son."

"It turns out he's my brother… or half-brother," you confess.

The woman levels a very chilling look at the two of you. "Really," she says. "Well, I can't imagine what you hoped to accomplish here, but I do trust you can find your way out." She indicates the direction you should take, nodding approvingly at her husband, who is stationed at the rear of the van recording the licence number.

Your head is absolutely spinning at the ludicrousness of this situation. You would like to say, "Look here, lady…" but where would you go from there? As you start the engine, the woman leans in again. "First thing you have to remember," she says sarcastically, "is to get your story straight." Bad enough she thinks you're casing the joint; she thinks you're incompetent.

"Thank you, thank you very much," your mother says, smiling bravely, giving a queenly wave as you pull away. "What in heaven's name was *that* all about?" she asks.

"Country people aren't what they used to be," you tell her, sparing her any blame. "For one thing, a lot of them are city people."

Your mother sighs wearily. "I've missed my afternoon nap. I'm done in."

You'd like nothing better than to take up the conversation you'd been engaged in prior to the interruption, but your mother is, after all, elderly, and it *has* been a tiring day. "Why not have a little rest?" you suggest. "We'll talk later. Put the seat back and stretch out. I'll wake you if I get lost."

As you drive, your mind commutes back and forth between past and present. The wasps, meanwhile, measure and remeasure the dimensions of the back window, their number diminishing as one by one they find their way out. By and by, you get the feeling that your mother is not asleep at all, but pretending to be in order to avoid you.

"This is quite a bomb you've dropped, you know," you say quietly, turning to watch her response.

Nothing.

So you drive on, trying to reconstruct your history. Your father, having married a woman with "a past," seems less stuffy now. Kindlier. If only he could've taken Neil in as his own.

You recall a photograph in the family album: Neil, a baby in a pram, his so-called big sister next to him seated on a porch step, holding a baby bottle in one hand, picking a scab on her knee with the other. She looks about twelve, but doing the math you arrive at sixteen. *When*, you wonder, had Neil learned the truth? You wonder, too, who his father might have been. Considering the men your mother currently attracts — Roy, Rev. Dick — you think you'd rather not know. Could it have been Agnes's father? Your mother has obviously been paying visits to the nursing home — visits she failed to report, as she does every other little thing. And she responded so defensively when Agnes mentioned that her father's mother's name had been Holly. Good heavens! Supposing you, too, were born out of wedlock, supposing you are Agnes's half-sister? After all, you don't physically resemble the father who had been your father. Is it possible?

Within your peripheral vision you catch sight of your mother's eyes peeping open a crack. "This is quite a bomb you've dropped," you say again — one of her old expressions. When you'd quit nursing school, left a so-called "perfectly good" job to go to Europe, took up with a man old enough to be your father, you had, supposedly, dropped bombs on her. "I know you're awake," you tell her.

The great Hepburn rouses herself, pats her hairdo, sighs. "You woke me with that bomb business," she says. "Little wonder I've hesitated to tell you things. You're really quite intolerant, you know, judgmental."

You know she's right. In your quest for what you imagine to be the truth or authenticity, you *are* often intolerant, judgmental. Your few friends regard you as a dear curmudgeon, but to most of your colleagues you're simply difficult, autocratic, a nitpicker. You were going to change, become more *laissez-faire*, but here you are, Wallis McCarthy's daughter, blood or no blood.

"Surely you're at least a little relieved that your family isn't as conventional as you imagined," your mother asks hopefully.

You argue that there's nothing unconventional about secrecy, and then in need of reassurance you broach the subject of your parentage by asking about Neil's: "Neil's father... do I know him?" But the timing is off. You've arrived back at the park, and your mother pretends not to have heard, points to a rail fence where the kids are perched.

"Little chickadees," she murmurs, causing you to be visited by that soft flutter of sadness, as you are from time to time, because it's too late for you to produce even one little chickadee.

Ben's the first to leap from the fence to the ground, then Carrie. Chris helps Katie.

Carrie opens the car door the moment you cut the engine and breathlessly tells you that you've won a prize. Such well-mannered kids: not a single whiny word from any of them about your failure to watch them run their races. Chris must have given them an explanation, instructed them not to complain. "I won a prize?" you ask. "How's that possible?"

"It's for coming the furthest distance!" Ben is triumphant on your behalf.

"How did you do in the races?" you ask them.

"I won mine," says Carrie. And you can tell right away that Ben did not win his. He turns away from the family and starts throwing stones, aiming them at a garbage receptacle.

"I winned too," says Katie.

"You did *not* win," Ben tells her.

"Katie ran the fastest," Carrie explains, "but she didn't wait for the man to say *go*. They had to start over four times because every time the man said *three*, Katie took off. It was really funny, Aunt Holly. I wish you could have been there."

"Dey gibbed the prize to a boy," Katie says without resentment.

"I'm glad you ran like blazes," you tell her. "Next year I'll come and watch you, I promise."

Yes, if you survive, you'll henceforth commit yourself to attending family reunions. Desperate times call for desperate deals.

Chris loads the picnic gear into the back of the van and asks, offhandedly, if you enjoyed your excursion. Then this brother or half-brother searches your eyes, and you search his. You tell him that it had been quite the trip.

"Please, can Aunt Holly sit with us in the back, Dad?" Carrie asks, and he has to think hard on it. He says "huddle time" and gathers the kids into a tight pack all around him. While this conference takes place, you tidy your mother's hair, reinserting the pins that have loosened during the course of the day.

When the huddle breaks up, Ben is the first to speak. "You can sit with us but we have to be good this time. We have to keep our socks on," he says earnestly. He himself has none to worry about, having lost one out the window en route to the reunion, and having had the other confiscated by his father.

You supervise the buckling up business. "Bye-bye, park," Katie sings. Grubby, yet incredibly lovely, she plays with your bracelets, puts them on the paws of her beloved stuffed bunny, Biscuit. Ben looks troubled and says, finally, that it wasn't fair that he had to run against boys a year older than he is.

Chris reminds him that there's no gallantry in making excuses. "It's more important to be a gentleman than a fast runner," he says.

You whisper to Ben that you're willing to bet that one day he'll not only be a gentleman but a fast gentleman, and Ben, sweet innocent, is buoyed by your confidence in him.

Katie wriggles against you and strains toward your ear. "Taste my toes to see if dey is tiger food," she says. She presses the toe of one shoe to the heel of the other, freeing a foot.

"Too bad Aunt Holly can't show us her tiger-striped toenails again," Carrie says. A bright idea flashes across her face. "Wait a minute," she says. "You're an adult, and Dad said *you kids* when he told us to keep our socks on."

"Show us, Aunt Holly," says Ben. "We forget what they look like."

"Keep your socks on back there," says the meany in the driver's seat, a command that's met with gales of laughter, laughter that fills your ears and courses through your veins, the miracle drug your doctor has prescribed for you.

Above the anarchy, you hear your mother murmuring to Chris that they need to talk when they get back to the house, but in the meantime he's not to say anything about Neil coming home.

Neil is coming home. Neil, your brother, is coming home. The timing is suspicious though, isn't it? All this truth and togetherness.

They must think you're not going to make it this time. What a family, really, when you think of it. What a tainted elixir.

But wait. Biscuit bunny is pretending to be bouncy bunny. "Are all the windows closed?" you demand of your nieces and nephew. Biscuit must not go missing as Ben's sock had.

Then a question from somewhere beyond the scrimmage line: "What's going on back there?"

"Nothing," comes a reassuring chorus, but it is not reassuring enough for Chris. He's pulling off the road and stopping the van. He's been given no choice, he says. He must think of everyone's safety.

"We kept our socks on," you say in your defence. Nevertheless, you're shifted to the front, the implication being you are somehow the rabble-rouser. It's so unfair because the person at the very heart of all the family discombobulation down through the years is the silver-haired woman about to be strategically placed in the back with the kids.

"Look at this," your mother whispers after only minutes of being on the job, and you turn to find three sleeping cherubs and the goddess of harmony.

Oh, the irony! Still, you know the image is one you'll call up again and again in the months ahead. You don't even mind that it's more Norman Rockwell than Rembrandt; you will hold it in your mind, hang on to it for dear, dear life.

Modern Women

If you want to *get* mail you have to *send* mail, my mother used to say. Today though, there was a letter in my box, albeit not to me but to a Ms Skye Bleue from U-CAN Film Inc. Skye Bleue has got to be the young woman with the purple hair who moved into the flat up on the third floor a few months ago. I've seen her — and her boyfriend, presumably — flying out of the building, coats flapping in the wind, no boots, no scarves.

You have to be young to live on the third floor, I can tell you. This act of kindness could be the death of me. I should have stopped in at my place before setting out, applied a bit of colour to my cheeks, subdued my hair. I wakened at an ungodly hour this morning, and rather than toss and turn I got up and made bread. Then I got doing other things. I can't recall just what, but I was on the move and now my hair is like a blizzard about my face. I wouldn't want to do this every day, climb Mount Everest.

Outside apartment 312, I pause to catch my breath before knocking on the door. Right in front of my nose is a notice of some sort. Actually, it's not a notice at all; it's a cartoon. A rat, surrounded by litter, sits in an easy chair reading the newspaper while another rat looks on disapprovingly. With a bit of effort I decipher the caption: "Clean it up? Clean it up? Crimmony, it's *supposed* to be a rat hole." Still, when the door opens I'm surprised to find myself confronted by the aftermath of what must have been a relentless search for the proverbial missing sock, or some such.

Nothing stays the same, my mother used to say.

"Pardon me, dear," I say to the young woman whose hair is no longer purple but black-black, whose expression is not animated but as blank as her complexion is white-white. I extend the letter, wonder could it be hers? She doesn't say yes, she doesn't say no. She opens the letter and squeals. She jumps up and down on her invisible pogo stick. I can hardly imagine springing about in such a fashion without a bladder leak, but that's youth for you. Anyway, I'm kissed on both cheeks, I'm pulled into the apartment, I'm invited for tea, which she just happens to have brewing. This was my best-case scenario, the fantasy that sustained me up those terrible stairs.

Skye shares the good news she's just received. She has been selected from hundreds of applicants to pitch her idea for a film. She has a great Great GREAT idea and now someone will listen, someone in a position to make her dream come true has actually agreed to give her twenty minutes. Twenty minutes, no guarantees. This information makes me feel extremely old, I don't know why. I have to ask myself, first of all, if I have ever in my lifetime jumped up and down with happiness. Yes, September 2, 1945, when it became official: the war was over. Not everyone involved was present or accounted for, but still I jumped up and down. I can think of only one thing that would make me that excited now, but it isn't something I can dwell on when someone is explaining to me her magnificent idea. Rambling generalities about alienation are hard to follow, but I try. Skye asks me what I think. The truth is, I think she's got some serious editing ahead of her, but I say it's wonderful that, at her age, her thoughts are occupied by something other than clothes and boys and parties and fun. I congratulate her for looking at life and trying to make sense of it. I regret that it sounds a bit condescending. But do I get a sour look? No, I get a sly smile. I am being moved up a notch in her esteem. She's thinking that for someone my age I'm pretty on the ball, which annoys me and at the same time — I have to admit — gives me satisfaction because I do realise there are certain members of my generation whose minds have withered or have been dulled by medication. I try not to feel smug about my good fortune lest it is taken from me.

Never mind that when I've just about finished my tea, it occurs to Skye that she has some crackers "somewhere." She opens a cupboard and moves things around. Barley, lentils, split peas — there seem to be holes in some of the packages. With a bare foot, she daintily sweeps the spilled grain and legumes under the cupboard to nestle along the baseboard with some other debris.

"I have some cinnamon buns at my place," I tell her.

"No kidding?" she says, looking famished. The girl is thin. No, the girl is skin and bones. Today's ideal. Why would a bright young woman eager to conquer the world choose to go out into it looking emaciated? I don't ask.

Think ahead, my mother used to say.

I would have preferred to put off demonstrating to my new-found friend how decrepit I am until some later date. Going down the stairs is easier than going up, but not faster.

"Take your time," Skye says, but still, I hate myself for having to move so slowly. She probably thinks I have bad legs. My legs are dandy; it's my eyes that are giving out. On the streets I can fake it. I move about in a rather sprightly fashion compared to some. Faking it on the stairs could be deadly. I have no depth perception. "I'm not in any hurry," she assures me, dear girl, her courtesy quite genuine. We can tell, you know, when people behind us are impatient, thinking unkind things about us. You're all so busy, I know. Your time is valuable. Still, you'd think that with your fifty, sixty years left you could find it in your hearts to allow us last-lappers to deal with our infirmities without your deep sighs of exasperation and those knowing looks you share with one another. And if that isn't enough, you cut our services, you throw all kinds of newfangled devices in our way. Sometimes when I think about the way some of you are my blood gets boiling so hard I could get dizzy and fall down the stairs. I've had to devise tricks to get my blood pressure down.

"I first noticed you when you had purple hair," I mention to improve my humour and to help pass the time because there's still another flight to go.

"Oh, that wasn't me," Skye says.

"You have a twin?" I ask, and she explains that it *hadn't* been her but it *had* been her. It had been a character she'd played in a friend's film. The character had had purple hair. She herself would never have purple hair. It is passé. But the film was set in the late nineties. The late nineties…? She must mean the late nineteen-nineties, five minutes ago. I begin to dread having to unlock my door with her looking on. It's a task I manage not too badly when no one is present, when I'm not trying to be an Olympic-calibre door-opener.

"Would you like me to…?" she asks after a few moments of pretending not to notice my difficulty, and I surrender the key to her because she means well, and because there are days when it takes a long, long time to get it just right, and who knows, maybe today would be that day.

My dachshund welcomes us. "His name is Oscar," I tell Skye, who is all over the dog murmuring endearments. She remembers now having seen me in the neighbourhood. She cannot be blamed for having not recognised me earlier. I dress for winter when I go out. I protect even my sinuses. I'm a pair of eyes walking down the street.

Oscar likes Skye more than he does his beef chunks and gravy. He isn't built for jumping up and down and spinning madly in circles as some dogs are but he manages to get his point across. He licks her toes, causing her to squeal with delight. He loves children, my Oscar does, and Skye is chirping like a six-year-old. This is his September 2nd, 1945. This is his twenty minutes of someone's attention. Make that two minutes.

Skye's attention is drawn from Oscar to the charm of my flat, the only one in the building that hasn't been renovated. I tell her that my parents had been the first tenants in the flat, that they leased it when the building was new. Confirmed renters, my parents, loved the urban lifestyle and freedom from the tyranny of home ownership, as I do. "Ohhh," she says. "Wow, I love the fifties look!"

"Some of it goes back before that." I indicate certain articles that I'd had in my earliest years of independence, and others that had belonged to my parents. There are rather a lot of paintings so I name only the best-known artists.

And now her eyes shift to the wall of photographs. "This is you?" she asks, and she compliments me on the beauty that once was mine. She asks me what I used to do, and I win more approval when I tell her I had a little gallery. I don't mention that its popularity petered out to nothing when the neighbourhood filled up with fast food outlets and discount stores, or that in order to open it in the first place I'd sold the leather goods business my parents had founded and maintained as their humble contribution to the world of commerce. Not that I ever regretted scrapping the leather goods for art. Not only did I feel liberated from the smell of animal hide, but I helped launch the careers of many young artists, and at the same time managed to make a fairly decent living.

"Wow," Skye says peering closely at one particular photograph in which my beau, my husband-to-be, and I are standing together arm in arm.

I haven't really looked at these pictures in some time. I'm stunned to see that I look a bit like Skye, and right away my heart starts pounding against the wall of my chest like it wants out. But it settles down again because I see there's no similarity at all in the features. It's just the bobbed hair, the straight-cut bangs that had me fooled there for a second. I notice now that we're not warmly dressed, my love and I. My coat is open from neck to ankle. I'm wearing pumps, not boots. My legs are bare. Harry wears no coat at all, just a cable-knit sweater and a jaunty cap, flaps folded up to expose the ears. We are looking cool. I remember the softness of Harry's trousers. I don't know why they don't make trousers like that any more. Perhaps they do. What would I know about the current fashions in men's apparel?

"You wouldn't still have the clothes you wore back then, by any chance?" Skye asks, and it pains me to tell her no. I pour a nice tall glass of milk for her to have with her buttered cinnamon bun and she takes a seat at the table and begins to eat.

"You made these yourself!" she exclaims, having spotted the pan on the counter, and I tell her I'd made bread and that the buns are only a bit of leftover dough rolled up with butter and brown sugar and cinnamon. I tell her that I'm not really the domestic type, that I make bread maybe once a year, that while it's not difficult it's a lot of messing around and it's easier to take the dog for a walk and come back with it under my arm. However entertaining I might think I am, I have to face the fact that I've lost my audience.

Skye is looking terribly pensive. She tells me she has a problem. Her boyfriend, Kyle, is not only her boyfriend but her collaborator and they are going through a crisis in their relationship. He has given her herpes. He claims he didn't know he had it, but, while possible, it turns out that the claim is probably not true. Skye has learned too late through the grapevine that his previous girlfriend had publicly accused him of "contaminating their love with the residue of his past exploits," which to Skye sure sounds like herpes. She says she's angry at herself for having given in to his pressure to have sex without a condom, and that she's angry at him too, of course, for having pressured her. She says she can hardly believe that the body she'd had for twenty-two years — healthy, disease-free — is irretrievable. She raises the glass of milk to her lips, tears streaming down her pale cheeks.

I refill her glass, which seems to help somewhat. I give her a tissue and she blows her nose — a vigorous blow, I must say. It's as though she's expelling her troubles, or trying to. She would like to split up with Kyle, she says wistfully, but she sort of needs him.

The frankness of this conversation is a testament to the power of images. Those pictures on the wall have convinced Skye that however

I may appear now, I was once a modern woman. I must admit I'm not feeling all that modern right now. I am, in fact, wondering where her mother is, wondering if her mother is judgmental or supportive. To reinforce the notion that I am indeed a woman of my time, I mention the diseases that had been the perils of my generation, syphilis, gonorrhoea. I assure her I'd had neither, keeping to myself the other thing, the pregnancy when I was seventeen. Having a child out of wedlock was about the worst thing that could happen to you back then.

Just keep your mouth shut if you know what's good for you, my mother used to say.

I tell Skye what every woman — regardless of the era — comes to know, that to put one's personal well-being into someone else's hands can prove disastrous. I'm not thinking of the pregnancy but the solution I'd been pressured into by my parents.

Skye says that at least it wasn't AIDS she'd contracted, that, actually, although a drag, herpes has lost a lot of the stigma once attached to it. "Almost everyone has it," she says, not very convincingly. What worries her most, she tells me, is that Kyle is less committed to art than she is, so has much less to lose if the project fails. If she splits from him now, well, he could sabotage this opportunity of a lifetime.

I offer her another cinnamon bun but she declines, has to watch her weight. She also has to go; it's almost noon, and she's meeting a friend for lunch and has tons to do first.

Oscar has been keeping one ear on our conversation and rouses himself now, his doggie heart full of anticipation. Since the unexpected has happened once today, perhaps it will happen again. Perhaps he will get an extra outing. "Sorry, it's not in the cards," I tell him, feeling tired suddenly, and his tail drops and his eyes turn away. Maybe I will, after all, bundle up and take him just to the end of the block and back.

"Gee," Skye says, "I guess I really laid it on you, eh? I didn't mean to." She actually has a little colour high in her cheeks now. Maybe it's the milk, but most likely it's just occurred to her that she's made a very personal disclosure to someone who, only an hour or so ago, was a total stranger. I tell her it was not an imposition, not at all, and that I know how to keep a confidence. I tell her, too, that it has been a real treat to spend a little time together, that I hope we'll get together again soon. She tries to smile and says sure. It feels to me like good-bye forever. An idea comes to mind.

"I may not have any clothes from way-back-when," I say, fetching from a corner cabinet a small wooden chest, "but I do have jewellery, and I'd like you to choose a piece to wear for luck when you make your pitch." Her eyes widen like those of a child in a candy shop advertisement as I open the lid to reveal the tangle of beads, bangles, earrings and curios of all sorts. "Go ahead, take your pick," I urge her. "Anything at all." I mean the offer as a loan, but I worry as her fingers take up and curl around a gem-encrusted brooch — an heirloom, my paternal grandmother's — that she has misunderstood. And I think *Why not*, why not let her have it?

"You're sure about this?" she asks, and I say I couldn't be more certain, which I know isn't the case at all. Out there, somewhere in the world, is my daughter — and perhaps granddaughters — to whom these things should go once I am gone. But Skye is here, now. Her hazel eyes are glistening with pleasure and appreciation. Again I'm kissed and held in her fleeting embrace.

"It will always be special," she assures me as we stand together in the open door. She touches the treasure she has pinned to her long black sweater. Such a fragile hand, like a piece of blue-veined porcelain. I'm thinking a bottle of vitamins might have made a better gift, but as I watch her ascend the stairs, listen to her take them by twos once she's beyond the first landing, I figure she must be hardier than she looks.

How could I have not thought to ask when exactly she's to have her twenty minutes, to mention that I'll be waiting to learn the outcome? Was it something that was understood? Perhaps I should have shared with her my secret. We might have forged a bond.

There were no documents, no record of the birth that I recall, but then I'd been sedated and was not in charge of the transaction. Even after all these years I dream of a slip of paper surfacing in my daughter's life, evidence of my identity that can be traced back to where I am, and I wait for a rap on the door, a letter in the mail. I am now exactly where I was then — I returned after Harry died to care for my father, who was old and alone — and being a modern woman of my time, my name, too, is unchanged.

Perhaps tomorrow I shall tackle the stairs again and explain to Skye about the brooch, the misunderstanding. She seemed so nice, but you never know, she might get nasty — like the paperboy when I realised it was a mistake to let my father's fountain pen out of my possession.

"You old people," he said, "you shouldn't give stuff away and expect to get it back."

The Long Way Home

Holding the steering wheel with both hands, Livvy peered over it, concentrating intensely on the road as it unfolded beyond the shiny blue hood of the car. The exaggerated caution was for her parents' benefit; the car was new and belonged to them.

Despite her efforts to appear totally in control, her mother, sitting in the front beside her, pressed down on an imaginary brake at every stop sign. Her father, at least, seemed relaxed. He sat in the back, smelling up the car with his spicy aftershave.

Livvy longed to roll down the window but knew it wouldn't get halfway before her mother would complain about the dust in her throat, the wind wrecking her set, or not being able to hear herself think.

"You know, Olivia, you really should sit on a cushion when you drive," her mother said. "You can hardly see over the steering wheel."

Livvy assured her she could see just fine, but her mother continued. "You look just like Oaffie. He sticks his nose up in the air like that when he smells another dog coming around."

"Thank you, Mother."

Tilting her head downward a bit, Livvy took a deep breath to prepare herself for the speech about being short that was surely on its way. She wished they'd gone straight home from church rather than taking this unnecessary detour. Her mother had talked her into it — said they should enjoy the autumn colours.

"You might as well face the fact that you're short."

Here we go, thought Livvy.

"It's not the end of the world. You could be crippled or blind or something. There are nice clothes for short people now, and you can wear as high a heel as you like. Think of poor Margaret standing up there in the choir, taller than most of the boys. Can you imagine being six feet tall?"

"Five ten," corrected Livvy.

"Is that what she tells people? Anyway, she has to wear flats all the time, which certainly does nothing for the leg. Having to sit on a cushion is nothing to be ashamed of... being short is nothing to be ashamed of. Some very famous people were short: Napoleon, Einstein ...I don't know of any women."

"Laura Secord," said Livvy dryly.

"Was Laura Secord really short? asked Mrs. Harris, looking at her daughter in wonder. "How do you know? Did you read that somewhere?"

"Oh yeah, it's recorded in all the history books," Livvy explained earnestly, increasing pressure on the gas pedal. "Laura Secord: five foot one, one hundred and ten pounds, thirty-six twenty-four thirty-six, led her purebred Jersey cow through the American lines to warn the British. I thought everyone knew that."

"I can tell when you're being sarcastic."

Her mother shook her head sadly. "It's bitterness, Olivia, and not a very attractive trait. I don't know where in heaven's name you get it — of course I don't know where you get your height either. There isn't a woman on my side of the family under five four."

"Why, that's a fact, isn't it?" said Mr. Harris, turning his attention away from the medley of fields: grass, corn stubble, and those just freshly plowed. "None on my side either that I can think of."

Mrs. Harris picked some lint from her skirt, then, rolling the window down just a crack, pinched it through to the outside. "There's your cousin Alice," she said.

"She's stout, Ellen, but she's not short," insisted Mr. Harris. "She may look short, but it's an optical illusion."

"There's no way she's five four." Turning to Livvy, Mrs. Harris added, "There's one thing to be thankful for, Olivia. You'd really have something to complain about if you were fat like Cousin Alice — though I think you've inherited her heavy foot. Must we fly down the road like this?"

Mr. Harris stretched himself out sideways and remarked how nice it was to just sit back and let someone else do the driving. Livvy felt grateful for the comment, which seemed to express some faith in her ability, so when they reached an intersection she asked if they'd like to go home by Woolich Road and stop by the quarry. Her father said he was game for anything, and her mother — still pressing on an imaginary brake, was agreeable on the condition that Livvy stop driving as though there were no tomorrow.

Livvy drove down Woolich Road, passing the familiar farms, noticing touches of recently painted trim, repaired fences, thinking how she really should come over some day and visit Mrs. Mason, her first piano teacher. She wondered how someone so old and wrinkled could stand being alive.

"Potatoes!" burst out Mr. Harris suddenly. He sat up and rested his arms along the back of the front seat between Livvy and her mother.

Mrs. Harris was skeptical. No one for miles around grew potatoes, and anyway, it was too late in the season. "Where?" she asked.

"No," he laughed, "I'll bet it was the lack of potatoes. Remember, Liv? I used to say, 'Eat your taters, Puddin-head,' and you never would. That must have been what did it, made you tiny. What d'you think, Livvy?"

"I say, why don't you talk about my nose for a while? It's been days now since either of you has mentioned my nose."

"What d'you mean?" he asked, leaning back, offended. He tried to think what it was he'd said that could have been taken the wrong way.

"She's being contemptuous again," explained Mrs. Harris to her husband. "She always has to take everything so personally."

Right. *I'm* the one at fault, as usual, mused Livvy. I wonder why she hasn't accused me of ruining the Sunday drive.

"The other day I just mentioned to Olivia," continued Livvy's mother, addressing her husband in a very controlled voice, "I said if she wanted to, she could have her nose fixed — made a little smaller. Only if it's what she wants. Why, lots of girls in her position would recognise a gift when it was offered and jump at the chance."

What position am I in? Am I in a position? Livvy blew at the bangs on her forehead. "It's hot in here," she said, and opened the vent on her side of the car.

"I just wanted to make her aware of an option open to her," Mrs. Harris went on. "There's absolutely no point in going through life with flaws if it isn't necessary." She gave a dry cough and gestured towards the open vent. "We can do without that arctic breeze, Olivia."

Livvy inhaled a deep breath of the fresh air and pushed the vent back in. "I like my nose," she said, surprising herself at how much she meant it; she had despised it for as long as she could remember. "If I had it fixed I'd look just like everyone else."

"That's ridiculous," argued her mother. "You can't look like *everyone*. You'd look more like me, I think. You got that nose from your dad." She reached over and brushed a strand of Livvy's bangs aside. "You'll ruin your eyes letting your hair hang in them like that. I don't think glasses would suit you either, and from what I hear, contact lenses are quite a nuisance.

Livvy looked at her father in the rear-view mirror. He was running his finger along his nose pensively, as though about to say something. Protest, Livvy figured. Deny being responsible for her nose. He started whistling the children's hymn from the morning's church service: "All Things Bright And Beautiful."

"Let's just drop the whole business," suggested Mrs. Harris with a deep sigh. "This over-sensitivity is ruining the drive. Just look at the sunshine. How could anyone be so touchy on such a gorgeous day?"

She straightened her skirt and settled more comfortably in the seat, as though starting over.

Livvy turned the possibility over in her mind that she was hyper-sensitive, touchy. She'd been just fine when they started out. Her father's whistling played on her nerves. Rather than say anything, she looked back at him, glaring, hoping that maybe he'd get the hint. That nose looks fine on him, she thought. It matches the rest of his face: big, square. But he's no movie star. Mother's just fixed him up, made him look as though he's not a 'dirt farmer' — made him match her in the same way she matches her renovated kitchen: clean, efficient, colour-coordinated. Livvy glanced at her mother, now the picture of serenity, gazing out the window, toying with the gold pendant that was usually down in her cleavage. Big tits, thought Livvy. Always saying, Olivia dear, you should wear blouses with tucks or gathers to fill yourself out a bit… don't slouch… don't be ashamed of your breasts. Livvy was not ashamed of her breasts, she only wished they were larger. I must have got my tits from my dad, she thought.

"You're speeding again, Olivia," said Mrs. Harris, then: "Would you look at that!" she exclaimed, her annoyance evaporating. "The Wilsons have finally got their circular drive put in. And paved yet. Seems ridiculous to have a driveway paved when even the roads aren't done, don't you think, Edward?"

"Oh well," said Mr. Harris, "that's George for you. He'll be happy now. He's been planning that thing ever since we put ours in five years ago."

Mrs. Harris shook her head incredulously. "Why has Ethel gone and put her shrubs in those awful tractor tires? It's so tacky. It's ruined everything really. Why spend a fortune on a driveway and then plop those …those *things* there?"

Livvy started to shake her head too, thinking sarcastically of her mother's criticism, Why, oh, why has she done it? God has made all things bright and beautiful and Ethel Wilson with her tacky taste is messing it up.

"Livvy. Olivia!" said her mother in exasperation. "I know I said to slow down, but this is ridiculous. Are you tired? Don't slouch. Good heavens, but you need a cushion!"

Livvy leaned back trying to look casually competent, thinking how she *was* competent. She'd had her licence for over a year and her driver-training instructor had never mentioned anything about a cushion.

"Is that Caroline out raking leaves?" asked Mr. Harris, sitting up and looking keenly in the direction of the young woman he knew full well to be Caroline. Caroline looked up when the car passed, but not in time to recognise them. "Honk the horn, Livvy! Livvy — you should have honked the horn."

"I think it's a shame that no one observes the Lord's day anymore," said Mrs. Harris.

"Some people find raking leaves relaxing," Mr. Harris said, sitting back again, flushed, annoyed that he hadn't been driving. "I don't think you could call it work." He thought about how it would have been if he'd been driving the car. He could see himself tooting at Caroline, stopping to remark at what a lovely day it was for raking leaves. His wife would have made some comment, he thought. Something that would have made him feel ridiculous. He started to feel ridiculous. Caroline was barely older than Livvy.

"That Caroline is a lovely girl, though," said Mrs. Harris. "A wonderful cook too." There was a note of condescension in her voice.

"Oh, for sure," said Mr. Harris, confessing, "I had a piece of her sponge cake at the strawberry social this year. That girl will have no trouble a'tall getting a husband." He felt better; it was all such a lot of silly nonsense that he could only wonder how he'd gotten caught up in it again.

"The men hang around her like flies," said Mrs. Harris, thinking how silly her husband had looked last June hanging around with the others, making such a fuss over an angel cake.

"I think Margaret is a much better cook," said Livvy. "The things she makes aren't all fluff. And she makes her own clothes too."

"She'd have to, I'd think, being as tall as she is." Mrs. Harris wound her watch and held it to her ear a second. "And since when have you been so thick with Margaret?" she asked. "I didn't know you were chummy with her."

"We're not *chummy*," said Livvy abruptly. The car swerved slightly and the wheels momentarily spun through a ridge of thick gravel. "I just think if you're going to hold someone up for admiration it ought to be someone nice, someone smart…"

Mrs. Harris gripped the dashboard as if to steady the car. "All right, all right, let's not get ourselves killed, okay? Perhaps your father ought to take over driving since you seem to be in a mood."

Is that what this is? wondered Livvy. Is it a mood when you feel like going a hundred miles an hour with the windows down, the radio blaring, and your parents screaming for mercy?

"Don't you worry your little head about Margaret," said Mr. Harris soothingly, staying settled in his seat, making no move to do as his wife suggested. "Her folks have a nice farm set-up there for a bright lad with an eye for more than just a beautiful girl. The good Lord has a way of compensating."

Why doesn't he just go back to whistling? Why doesn't he just shut up and whistle? Livvy wondered, then said, "Margaret isn't sticking around to marry someone who likes her dad's farm. She's going to university next year." Livvy wanted to say that *she* wasn't sticking around either, but she didn't have the nerve — and then, what if she *didn't* leave? After all, she wasn't an "A" student or outgoing like Margaret.

Mr. Harris said he hadn't heard of Margaret's plans.

"They change with the wind," explained his wife. "First she was going to be a scientist, a biologist, I think it was her mother said. Now it's a pediatrician. Margaret's always thought she was better than the rest of us."

Livvy clenched the wheel and said, "Margaret's not a bit conceited. If her parents boast of her accomplishments it's because they're proud of her, that's all." Then she drove on in silence, recalling comments her mother had made to various people boasting about their children: Olivia's all thumbs; Olivia's got two left feet; Olivia's tone deaf. And her father's standard response was: I'm sure Olivia could do well too, if only she'd try harder.

Mr. Harris felt at a loss for words now. He knew something was troubling Livvy but wondered if it wasn't some 'woman thing' that he couldn't do anything about anyway.

Mrs. Harris was thinking about how her husband had referred to Caroline as beautiful. She cleared her throat. "I wouldn't say Caroline is beautiful, Edward," she said.

Oh, oh… Livvy thought.

"She's too thin really," continued Mrs. Harris. "Her elbows and knees are awfully bony, her ankles too. There should be enough flesh to smooth over the frame, otherwise it's just not very feminine, is it?"

Poor Caroline, thought Livvy. Throw her in the quarry and she'd probably drown. Not enough fat to keep her magnificent teeth and lustrous blonde hair afloat.

Mr. Harris thought it best to change the subject. He drew his wife's attention to some burnt ruins off in the distance.

"The Miller place," Mrs. Harris cried. "I haven't seen it since the accident. Slow down, Olivia."

Livvy obeyed, bringing the car to a crawl. Now we're going to hear all about the very handsome Larry Miller, she thought, and how there was something very fishy about the case.

"You know, Edward, there was something really strange about that incident, if you ask me," said Mrs. Harris. "He was such a nice boy. I just cannot believe he'd intentionally kill his fiancée. I remember when he ran out of gas once over by our place and came to borrow some. *Tall* — he bumped his head in the doorway." Her voice softened. "Such pleasant manners … Oh, you couldn't ask for better manners."

"The shed he killed her in is gone," observed Mr. Harris. "Somebody probably took it apart for the wood. City people, likely, finishing their basement. The nerve some people have. Wonder if his folks are going to rebuild or stay in town now. Foundation looks okay. I could never figure out why he dragged her into the house and set fire to it. Why not just bury her — or burn the shed down?"

"I don't think he could have done it," said Mrs. Harris. She leaned her forehead against the window for a moment, peering out; her breath visible on the glass.

"Did he pay for the gas?" asked Mr. Harris of his wife. "When he stopped by — did he pay for it? Did he bring some back or what?"

"It was almost a year ago, Edward. How am I supposed to remember some little detail after all that time?"

Mr. Harris took a white, folded hankie from his breast pocket, shook it loose, then reached forward and wiped the window. "I always remember whether people pay for things or not," he said. "Miller did it all right, Ellen — killed her. There's no doubt of that."

"If he did it — and I'm not saying I think he did — it was probably because he was too smart. You know, sometimes when people are very intelligent something just sort of snaps. They say he was extremely clever."

Livvy stifled a laugh, thinking, clever Larry banged his head twice a day for five years getting on and off the school bus because he was so busy thinking deep, intelligent thoughts. But not thoughts about how to strangle his beautiful, half-naked girlfriend and drag her body across the yard to the house so he could fry her up like a chicken.

When the Miller place was behind them, Mrs. Harris turned to her daughter. "It's nice to see you smiling, Olivia," she said. "If you're feeling better, maybe when we get to the quarry we could get out for a minute or two; it's always so nice in the fall."

Livvy turned off Woolich Road onto the narrow laneway that led to the quarry. They were less than a mile from home — the quarry had been one of her favourite childhood places. "It *is* nice," she agreed. "But it could be so much nicer. They should tear out some of the wild bushes and lay down some sod. What the place needs is grass and some patio blocks. What the place needs," she said, smiling with mock earnestness at her mother, "is *total* landscaping."

Livvy's parents looked at one another. Mrs. Harris could tell that her husband was thinking it was *her* Livvy was making fun of, and she hated him for it. She turned and sat with her arms folded, looking straight ahead. The Sunday drive was being ruined by a smart-mouthed brat and there seemed to be nothing she could do about it. And weren't they speeding again? "Slow down!" she commanded.

Livvy tried to ease her foot from the pedal. It felt numb. She wondered what would happen if she were unable to control herself, if she were to actually press the accelerator to the floor. She imagined the car bouncing wildly, the trees and the road blurring in front of her. She blinked her eyes, trying to clear the image from her mind.

"Now, Liv," said Mr. Harris, patting Livvy on the shoulder. Their eyes met in the mirror and he thought she seemed about to cry. "Let me take over, Livvy; it isn't your day, is it?"

"I'm just fine," she said, looking back at the lane and shrugging his hand away. "Who couldn't be fine on such a glorious day?" She honked the horn. "That's a cheer for the beautiful day!" she declared.

"You're not funny in the least." Mrs. Harris's tone was calm. She was determined not to give her daughter any satisfaction by getting upset.

Something white running among the bushes ahead caught Mr. Harris's attention. "It's Oaffie," he said, pointing. "For a minute there, it looked a bit like Sheba."

"Sheba," repeated Mrs. Harris softly, remembering. There was no way Oaffie could look like Sheba. "Sheba was one in a million," she said. "A purebred. Oaffie's a mutt, for heaven's sake."

"Sheba was special all right," agreed Mr. Harris.

"She knew enough not to run all over the countryside. She didn't mess with skunks or mate with any old thing," said Mrs. Harris. "Never again do I get myself attached to an animal like Sheba. In a way, it's better just to have a dog like Oaffie."

"Oaffie's a good dog," said Mr. Harris. "He's a whiz at rounding up the cows."

"He's a wonderful dog." Tears sprang to Livvy's eyes, blurring her vision. "You gave Sheba liver and hamburger and let her into the house."

"What does that have to do with anything?" asked her mother. "What's the matter with you, anyway?"

"Slow down, Liv," urged her father. "The potholes along here can be wicked."

Livvy's hands gripped the wheel as she aimed the car down the middle of the lane. "Oaffie gets stale bread soggy with bacon fat," she said.

"Are you going to let her drive like this, Edward?" demanded Mrs. Harris.

Mr. Harris leaned over the back of the seat. "Liv, stop the car."

"Leave me alone," Livvy hissed. "Both of you just leave me alone!"

The car jolted as it hit a pothole. "For godsakes Edward, the quarry's not far..." cried Mrs. Harris, clutching at the dashboard, her face twisted urgently towards her husband.

Out of the bushes on the right hand side bounded a white mongrel. He raced alongside the car, tongue hanging, ears back, eager. In a burst of speed he started to cross over to the other side of the lane the way he often did when racing with the tractor. To Livvy he was but a small fuzzy image that moved within the blurry tunnel of trees, a white splotch that seemed to hang suspended for a second in front of the car before she heard her mother's scream, a deep resonant thud, and her foot, quite on its own, found the brake.

There was a moment when the noise of the engine roared in Livvy's head, distorting her mother's voice nattering about a cushion, about how she knew something like this would happen. Her father reached for the keys, turned off the ignition and got out of the car. With the silence came a vague realization of what had just happened. *"Oaffie,"* Livvy cried, quickly opening the door and following her father to the ditch where the dog was lying motionless.

She knelt next to Oaffie and watched as her father stooped and examined him — his hands moving with the quick efficiency of a man who'd handled animals all his life. "He's in pretty bad shape, Liv," he said. "His hind legs are both broken — no more chasing groundhogs. And there's bound to be internal injuries."

Livvy stroked Oaffie's forehead. "If we take him to the vet right away, Dad…"

"Don't go getting blood on that good wool skirt, Olivia," yelled her mother. She was out examining the bumper.

"How's the car?" asked Mr. Harris.

"Well, it'll need a wash, but it's otherwise all right," she said, running her hand over the surface. "Is … is he gone?"

"There's a heartbeat."

Livvy scratched Oaffie gently behind his ears. "I'm so sorry," she sobbed. "Wake up. Please, please…"

"It was an accident, Liv," said her father. "Now go on and wait with your mother." He went and opened the trunk of the car, removed his suit coat and rolled up his sleeves. Then he removed some tools from an old feed bag and left them in the trunk, taking the burlap back to where Oaffie was. "I said for you to run along, Livvy," he said sternly.

"What are you going to do?" she asked. "Are we taking him to the vet?" She could hear her own voice rising, shrill.

"No, Livvy — there's no point taking him all that way and paying good money for what I already know."

"You took Sheba when she was hit by the milk truck. You took her and she was already dead."

"We weren't absolutely sure. Anyway, it's not the same thing." He shooed Livvy aside and placed the sack on the ground next to Oaffie, easing the dog over onto it, his hands avoiding the knots of burrs that were now wet with blood. "He won't suffer this way, Liv. You don't want him to suffer, do you?"

"How are you going to murder him? Are you just going to throw him in the quarry? That's what you're going to do, isn't it? Isn't it!"

Mr. Harris picked up the dog, struggling to get a good hold. "I'm not going to *throw* him. I'll just put his head under for a minute. He won't feel a thing." He adjusted the sack to protect his clothes and headed down towards the water.

"I'll take care of Oaffie myself," cried Livvy, calling after her father. "I hate you," she screamed when he didn't stop. "I hate you both." She turned toward her mother, who was sitting in the car with the door open. "I want you to know I gave him hamburger. I gave him all kinds of things when you weren't around."

Mrs. Harris looked though her purse for a Kleenex, and when she found one she held it up, motioning for Livvy to come and get it.

We mustn't look a mess, thought Livvy at the sight of the tissue. Not even out here with no one around. "No!" she yelled, backing away from her mother. She turned and ran, stumbling through the brush along the ditch, tripping as her heels caught on clumps of earth and stones. She crossed over into a field at a place where the fence was down, and headed toward the hill that faced the quarry.

Mrs. Harris watched her daughter and thanked God that the teen years would soon be over. She thought that maybe it would do Livvy some good to run home — let off some steam. She turned to see her husband attending to things at the water's edge and wondered for minute about Larry Miller and what it was his girlfriend had done to provoke him so.

Mr. Harris knelt on a flat white rock that jutted out into the small lake. He held Oaffie over the water, the brown sack drawn over the dog's face so he didn't have to see death quite so vividly, and to protect himself in case the cold water should revive consciousness. When he lowered Oaffie's head into the water the small furry body convulsed, almost making him lose his balance. He felt a shiver flutter through the dog; bubbles gurgled up to the surface. He thought of Oaffie rounding up the cows, darting eagerly into the woods to search out the strays.

Livvy scrambled to the top of the hill. She had discarded her shoes; her feet were bleeding and her stockings were riddled with holes and runs; bits of weeds clung to her skirt and sweater. She stood panting, wiping her hair from her eyes, and looked down over the quarry where she could see her father huddled over the dog. For a moment she imagined she saw Oaffie snap to life; she pictured him tearing away from her father and racing back up the lane toward the car. She could almost hear her mother scream, see the horror on her face as she reached too late to close the door on Oaffie who lunged, teeth bared... But Oaffie did not rise, did not fight back.

Exhausted, Livvy sank to the ground. She breathed the crisp autumn air and slowly pulled the clinging weeds from her clothes.

Before her lay the quarry, the leaves on the trees dazzling in the sunlight; and the water, usually dark and cold looking, reflected the vibrancy. Even Oaffie, lying now on the ground, looked from a distance like one of the little white rocks, speckled with beautiful red leaves and radiating warmth.

HUMAN INTEREST

I rang the doorbell again, pressing the button really hard this time in case my neighbour was hard of hearing, and sure enough, after a few moments came a series of muffled sounds, then the tumbling of lock innards. The door opened a crack, and peering in, I saw eyes peering out: clear blue eyes, in front of which ran a safety chain.

"Hi," I said. "I'm your neighbour. Our back balconies face each other across the alley…?"

"You don't say." The old woman studied the length of me.

I wished I'd taken the time to change into a dress or slacks, instead of coming straight from the garden in my denim jumpsuit. I ran a hand through my unruly brown curls and apologised for my appearance. "I've brought you some vegetables," I told her.

The woman unlatched the chain and tentatively invited me in.

From the glare of afternoon sunlight I stepped into what seemed, at first, total darkness. Down a long narrow hallway a dim light flickered, and I spotted on a far wall a picture of the Pope. It seemed there was no escaping it, religion.

I told my neighbour I rented a garden plot from the city, and explained that though it was small, I'd ended up with more than I could possibly consume myself.

"I see," she said. "It was very nice of you to think of me."

She took the bag and peeked inside. Her facial expression said: *My Lord, what's a little bird like me to do with all this?* From a distance she'd looked to be about seventy. Now I realised she was considerably older. "What did you say your name was?" she asked.

"Oh, I'm sorry. It's Miriam. You must have seen me across the way...?"

"I've seen someone out there fussing over flower boxes — especially lately, but my eyes aren't what they used to be. You could be my neighbour or you could be anyone." Again the old woman looked me over. "It's my son who's the cautious one really, reminding me all the time not to let anyone in. He thinks I could be sweet-talked into buying stuff I don't need. Anyway, I suppose you're not selling anything." She introduced herself as Gertie Bond, no relation to *James* Bond, and said to just call her Gertie. She remarked on the heat. "Could you do with a glass of beer?" she asked hopefully.

Beer, not tea or coffee. I saw this as further evidence that she was the character I was hoping she'd turn out to be, because while I wasn't selling anything, I wasn't merely delivering vegetables. Dissatisfied with my job as a copywriter for a mail-order company, I was looking to find my way into freelance journalism via human-interest stories. Something that felt beyond mere hopefulness had drawn me to this woman who fed pigeons every day up on her balcony and was known throughout the neighbourhood, both affectionately and disparagingly, as the pigeon lady. They came in droves, the pigeons, some perching on her head and shoulders, feeding from her raised hands. I had meant to spend my entire vacation on this writing venture but put it off initially — insecurity, inertia, all my old bugaboos — and then Gertie had not been home the first two times I'd called — or hadn't answered the door, at any rate — so now, with only a few days left before returning to work, there was a sense of urgency.

"This way," Gertie said, and I followed her down the dreary hall, through a sparsely furnished living room where a black and white TV flickered soundlessly in a corner, then past the picture of His Holiness to the kitchen. The window was closed, the curtain drawn, presumably to keep out the heat. Pocketing a rosary that had been lying on the table she motioned for me to have a seat. "I'm not as religious as it might appear," she said. "You couldn't pay me to read the Bible. Stoning, eye-plucking, rivers of blood — this I don't need. It's worse than reading the news."

I had to smile, and when I did I sensed my mother, recently deceased, disapproving, shifting in her grave.

"You may think it silly," Gertie went on, lowering her voice to a whisper, "but whenever I'm really worried about something, I give the Pope a kiss — his picture. On the cheek, not the lips. It seems to help." She laughed a most charming little chuckle. "Not that he's a bad-looking man, mind you. Do you find? I think I'll just put these vegetables in the fridge. Gee, you must have quite a garden."

She got rid of my gift, took out a single beer and put it on the table, then went to the cupboard, stood on her tiptoes and extracted two small fruit juice glasses. "These ought to do the trick," she said sprightly. "*Miriam*," she said. "Now there's a good solid name. You don't see Miriams getting into trouble with the law or out on the streets calling their kids fucking this and fucking that. Sorry, but you know what I mean. I don't use the F-word myself ordinarily."

She filled the glasses, which still left plenty in the bottle for another round. "Now then, here's to us."

"To us," I said, raising my glass.

"So…" Gertie paused to sip the head from the beer. "What really brings you here?"

I would have preferred to get to know my possible subject matter before declaring her the subject matter, but Gertie was watching and waiting so I figured I'd just have to go with the notion that every human being had a story worth telling if you looked closely enough. I told Gertie I planned to write some articles about local people and that I was hoping for some input from her.

She seemed very pleased, if a bit doubtful. The loose flesh around her mouth drew up into a winsome bow smile. "Well, it sounds like fun…" she said, "but I don't know how I could be of help… I used to type, but that was years ago."

I assured her that I'd take responsibility for the typing, that her contribution would be to share some of her experiences.

"Oh, heavens!" she said. "Dear girl, do you think I'm old and wise? Is that it?"

"I wouldn't put it that way exactly," I told her, "but, I trust that during your long life you've had…"

She looked at me squarely. "You *do* think I'm old!"

I took a drink — what amounted to half the glass — and told her that age didn't matter, even though my own age — I was approaching forty — was beginning to matter.

"How old do you think I am?" she asked.

I said I regarded age as a positive thing, a measurement of experience.

"Just take a guess," she said.

A number, seventy-five, drifted into my mind. I was known among friends and colleagues for being, if not actually psychic, highly intuitive, but seventy-five seemed too young. I was about to guess seventy-nine — still very doubtful, but flattering and marginally believable, when Gertie confided she was — as I had intuited — seventy-five. Obviously Gertie had had a very hard life. "You don't look anywhere near that," I told her kindly.

"Why, thank you," she said, beaming.

Saying things that were at once truthful and yet dishonest was what my job as a copywriter was all about. It's what I hated most about it — not that I felt bad about letting Gertie feel complimented. My discomfort when tinkering with the truth at work was something else entirely and it set me apart from my colleagues, who found my naiveté and sensitivity amusing. They themselves "lived in the real world" and were proud of it. They believed in selling so completely that the thing being sold — invariably some useless trinket or ready-to-break household gadget from "The Orient" (Taiwan or China) — was totally irrelevant. Their motto was: for every product there is, somewhere, the perfect customer.

"So, you're a writer," Gertie said. "My son writes poetry, but I can't make head nor tail of it."

It seemed I could scarcely go to buy a litre of milk without hearing about someone's friend, nephew, or brother's wife being a writer. "Do you have any other children?" I inquired.

"No, there's just Michael. Let me show you one of his poems. I'd like to know what you think."

Gertie went into the living room, coaxed a reluctant drawer to open, and returned with an old Smiles 'n Chuckles box. "We're going to have to go through this one day, you and me. I'll tell you, this box has some stories in it," she said.

My heart fluttered at the prospect of stories.

"Here we are."

Gertie handed me a sheet of graph paper with some red dots randomly placed in thirty or forty squares. "No, no," she said when I turned the sheet over in search of poetry. "It's the dots you're supposed to read."

"Gee…" I said.

"What do you think… Are you up on these things?"

Gertie's question hit a vulnerable spot. My years in marketing had left me feeling out of touch with literary trends. Still, this "poem" had to be sheer lunacy. "It's quite interesting," I said. Having caught sight of some old photographs in the box, I wasted no time in handing the page back.

"I hope he's all right. You know…in the head," Gertie worried aloud. "Though, I suppose if they can get rid of the rhyme they can get rid of the words, right? It makes you wonder, what next, eh?"

"Well, they'll likely get rid of the dots," I told her, for my own amusement more than hers. "Is that you?" I asked, pointing to the photo of a blonde bombshell.

"Me? Dear me, no. That belonged to Earl, my husband. My *ex*. He was crazy about Betty Grable. I hung onto the photo in case it's valuable. I don't have much to leave Michael," she said.

Gertie's attention turned suddenly to the clock. "My goodness!" she exclaimed. "It's five past three already!" So naturally I asked if I'd dropped in at a bad time. "Oh, I guess it's nothing," she said, not very convincingly. "I don't mind if I miss *All My Children*, but I have been sort of anxious to see what will become of my favourite character on *As the World Turns*. Would you be interested…?"

I thought, God, I'd sooner perish, and quietly demurred. I suggested we get together again the following day, and while we debated what time would be best, I watched Gertie's dainty, crinkled hands tidy the precious contents of the chocolates box and replace the lid.

"I hope you don't feel you're being given the bum's rush," Gertie said, accompanying me to the door, and I assured her I didn't; but I was disappointed, and glad to get a firm appointment for the next morning at ten o'clock.

As I mounted the stairs to my neighbour's flat the following day I had a feeling I was being watched. My visit to Gertie's could have aroused the curiosity of almost anyone in the neighbourhood, but glancing up at a window I saw that it was Gertie herself watching my progress, and before I had a chance to ring the bell, the door swung open and there she stood, breathless, smiling. She was wearing large rhinestone earrings. Her blue eyes sparkled. "Here we go again," she cried, stepping aside. "Come in, come in." She'd dipped happily into the rouge and been far too generous with *eau de* something, something too sweet, floral.

She led me down the dark but now familiar hall to the comfort of the kitchen. It was going to be another hot day, but maybe not as humid as it had been the day before. The window was open and a pigeon sat on the ledge, plump and contented-looking, its eyes blinking open and closed, dreamily. The Smiles 'n Chuckles box was on the table. I sat in the same chrome chair as I had the day before, opposite Gertie.

"Don't mind Ralph," Gertie told me, and I assured her I didn't. How could there be a story of a pigeon lady without pigeons, I reasoned to myself while in my heart of hearts I did sort of mind Ralph and his friends, the health hazard they posed and their disregard for clean laundry.

"I was up till all hours last night trying to think of something about me that would be of interest to anyone," Gertie said. "I'm not exactly Grandma Moses."

"And I'm not a talent scout," I assured her. She seemed relieved but still doubtful.

"Problem was, I got off to a bad start — I married too hastily; married a man for his looks, if you want to know the truth. And I was only eighteen."

This was something I could relate to. I met my husband, Brent, ex-husband now — a handsome med school reject — at the yacht club where I'd been working as a waitress. Brent tended the boats of his parents' friends, a job his father had set up for him. During our so-called courtship — a very haphazard affair during which I never knew where I stood — I considered him to be lazy, irresponsible, and spoiled beyond belief. But he'd given me a picture of himself in which he looked tender, melancholy, vulnerable. The photo version of him — the version I fell in love with — gazed upon me beseechingly from my dresser each night after he'd dropped me off and sped away.

"It's too bad I threw out all the pictures I had of Earl. You could've seen for yourself how handsome he was," Gertie said. "He was wild about the track, but the only horse he ever picked that he didn't lose his shirt on was me. *Work* horse, that is." She encouraged me to laugh along with her, so I did, even though the joke was hitting far too close to home. "Maybe you should forget about me and write about pigeons," Gertie suggested. "Don't laugh, I'm serious. They're like humans, eh? There are bossy ones, timid ones, sneaky ones, and cock-of-the-walk types. And see that speckled one on the balcony? She's a flirt. And then there's Ralph, dependable, steadfast, and true."

Dependable, steadfast, and true. *Mooch*, more like, I thought. "I'm sure you can outdo this bird," I said in no uncertain terms.

Gertie looked hopeful. "Perhaps we could embellish things a bit...?"

"There'll be none of that." I explained that I was on a quest for truth and this set Gertie reaching for the Smiles 'n Chuckles box. She opened it and found a small clipping, brown and brittle-looking.

"Listen to this," she said, pausing to don eyeglasses drawn from a pocket. Smudged eyeglasses. Very smudged, but she didn't seem to notice.

There was a young lady named Ruth,
Who had a great passion for truth.
She said she would die
Before she would lie,
And she died in the prime of her youth.

Gertie chuckled as she pawed through the pile of photos and clippings. "I went through this box last night looking for ideas. There are lots of good jokes. I don't know why we don't see good jokes around anymore... they're all about sex or technology nowadays. Here's one." She paused and looked to see if I was paying attention before reading:

"Goodness sakes, Mrs O'Hara, how do you tell them
twins of yours apart?"
"Aw, 'tis easy — I sticks me finger in Dennis's mouth,
and if he bites, then I know it's Mikey."

Gertie slapped the table. "Is that rich or what?" Her fit of delight startled Ralph, who flopped to attention and scrambled dazedly off the sill and into the air.

Good riddance, I thought.

"He'll be back. We're best friends, he and I," Gertie said, peering from the window as though experiencing the notion that he might *not* return. "Sorry, Ralphie," she called after him. Then turning her attention back to the box, she said, "There are lots more jokes. Oh, here's a good one. Listen to this."

So I listened and wondered how many more jokes I might have to endure. I felt impatient to get to the heart of Gertie's life story, but I had to smile at her delivery of the punch line, her voice wavering yet still convincingly that of a petulant little girl whose part she had taken on. "Did I mention I had a granddaughter, Miriam?" she asked when she'd finished.

"No... Michael has a daughter?" To think the dotty guy was someone's dad!

"Let's see..." Gertie rummaged through the Smiles 'n Chuckles box. "I've got a picture I keep handy. Yes, here we are."

I took the photo. The image was so out of focus it was hard to comment. "What's her name?" I asked.

"Lara. I only saw her the once — didn't know she existed until she was seven. I'm told she's been placed in a good foster home."

It was such a pathetic photograph. Nothing to see really: an empty merry-go-round, a ghostly child in the foreground gazing into the distance, feet pointed inward.

"She's ten now," Gertie said, and she went on to explain that Lara's mother was with the Hari Krishna for a time, and that Michael had gone to Legal Aid to try to get custody. "I don't know what happened," she said. "I hate to think it, but I wonder sometimes if maybe Michael is into drugs. I told the social workers I could take care of Lara myself, and I would have too, but they felt she'd be better off with a young family. They said that they worried about Michael's access to the child if she were with me."

"I guess you talked to Michael about this."

"I did, Miriam. I hated to risk upsetting him, but I did, for Lara's sake, and at first he claimed that it was all a bureaucratic misunderstanding. Then he said it was a personal grudge the social workers had against him — that he didn't buy into their value system, is how he put it. He was very upset that I'd gone behind his back."

I told her what I figured she needed to hear, that never mind what authorities had against Michael, she still had a right to see her grandchild.

I imagined, for a moment, intervening on Gertie's behalf, lining up legal counsel for her if necessary, putting up a real fight. I imagined documenting the process, of turning out an article on the rights of grandparents — but it was too demanding a project to undertake until after I'd established myself, after I'd quit my copy-writing job. So I was relieved when Gertie said she wouldn't want Lara's life disrupted.

Seeming to read my mind, Gertie added, "Anyway, Michael would find out. He has radar." She traced my gaze — I'd caught sight of another photo in the box, one of a strikingly attractive man in uniform. "That's Buzz," she said fondly.

I helped myself to the photograph. The only Buzz I knew of was Buzz Aldrin, the moon walker. This was not the astronaut. "Buzz ... who's he?" I inquired.

"Who's *he*?" Gertie cried, then she explained that Buzz Beurling had been the greatest Canadian flying ace of World War II. "And our own boy from Verdun," she said. "Oh, you must have heard of him! George was his real name. That picture was taken the day of the big do for him at the Verdun Auditorium."

I reminded Gertie that I wasn't born until the late fifties. I turned *Beurling* over in my mind and recalled there was a street by that name down near the aqueduct. A very short, unspectacular street. Buzz Beurling. Perhaps resurrecting a local hero and doing a commemorative piece for Remembrance Day was the way to get my wobbly ball rolling. Perhaps Gertie's role had been, all along, to lead me to the real material. There was certainly something about the man in the photo that made me want to know more, and yet, at the same time, made me feel I knew him already. "Is he still living?" I asked.

"Oh, no, he's long gone. Would you like some lemonade?"

"Sure," I said, but as she rose to get it, the doorbell rang.

"Dear me, who could that be? Oh, goodness, I plumb forgot. It must be Michael," she said. "He stops in every month to accompany me to the bank with my pension cheque. He worries I might get mugged."

Momentarily, I heard Michael's voice down the hall: "So who are you expecting? You never doll yourself up on my account. What's going on?"

Gertie told him that there was someone he had to meet, a writer who was going to do a story on her. The degree of excitement in her voice alarmed me. Where had the reluctance gone? I hoped it wouldn't be too tricky letting her down.

When I turned to greet Michael it was like confronting my dread of him personified. Soiled clothing hung on his skeletal frame; his teeth were stained and rotting. He looked almost as old as his mother. I said hello and tried to smile, said I should probably be going and that I'd drop in another time when it was more convenient.

Gertie wrung her hands and apologised, explained again that in all the excitement she simply forgot about going to the bank. "You'll stay for some lemonade at least," she asked, only to get a dirty look from Michael, and a reminder from him that I'd said I had to go, which was not exactly what I'd said, but I agreed. "I'll expect you at the same time tomorrow then?" Gertie inquired anxiously, accompanying me back down the hall.

"She's writing *what* exactly? And who the hell is she?" Michael demanded from the other side of the closing door.

I pitied Gertie. How sad to have such a creepy son. Still, I hurried home in relatively fine spirits, convinced that I'd found in Buzz the perfect subject matter for a first story.

The following day, a Saturday, I climbed the stairs again to call on Gertie. My feet were heavy, my head still dull and achy after a restless night. I'd gone to sleep thinking of Buzz Beurling, picturing him flying low over my building, tipping his wings. When he appeared in my dreams however, he wasn't doing aerobatics, he was on the street, begging.

My memory of the dream that Saturday morning was fuzzy. As I climbed the stairs to Gertie's and approached the landing, I recalled that I'd smiled at him in the dream, flirting, and he'd followed me, and that, yes, there'd been a stairway involved — the stairs to Gertie's, in fact! I shook the rain from my umbrella, trying to retrieve other details of the dream, but was interrupted by Gertie's sudden appearance.

"Come in, dear girl."

Gertie's tone was welcoming but her smile was subdued as if in accordance with the change in weather. "Gosh, I felt so bad about you leaving early again yesterday." She paused while doing up the locks. "I wanted to phone last night to apologise again, but I don't think you ever mentioned your last name."

"Oh," I said. "Perhaps I didn't. It's Bricker."

"Bricker, eh? Now how shall I remember that? I know. I'll just think of the story of the three little pigs, the third little pig who built his house of bricks and outsmarted the wolf. Now," she said, leading me into a bedroom rather than down the hall as usual, "I was wondering if I could get your opinion on something." She opened a closet door and removed a huge fur coat. "This was Earl's," she said. "It was stored in a garment bag up until yesterday, so it's almost like new."

"Earl was a big man," I told her, saying nothing about the state of the coat. I hoped that when I got old I wouldn't lose my objectivity.

"Earl *is* a big man," Gertie corrected. "He lives over on Gordon Avenue with a dame silly enough to drive him places. I'm sure he drives her crazy. Anyway, it was me who bought him this mink farm here."

I moved in for a closer look. "This is mink?" I asked, examining a sleeve. I was no expert on fur, but still, I doubted mink could get so ratty.

"This," Gertie said without apology, "is beaver or racoon or dearknowswhat … it cost me a zillion dollars! Now," she said, shifting under the weight of the thing, "the question is, what do you think I could get for it these days?" Her face was so hopeful, expectant, that I hated to say. She told me that Earl had worn the coat only a winter or two; then, exposing the lining she said, "I wonder if it's silk, do you think?"

A woman's nylon stocking dangled from an inside pocket. "It was supposed to bring him luck at the track," she said, stuffing it back into the pocket hastily. "Those were the days," she sighed. "Anyway, about this coat, I was told when I bought it that it was an investment, as good as money in the bank. It's gotta be warm. Just feel how heavy it is, Miriam."

I took the coat, lest it topple her, and hung it back in the closet. I told her that perhaps someone in the theatre might be interested, or a collector of fads in fashion. As for the amount they might pay, I couldn't begin to guess. I told her she probably shouldn't get her hopes up.

Gertie moved along to a bureau and opened the top drawer. She unwrapped a hanky to reveal a tangle of tarnished pendants, bracelets, brooches and buttons. "Some of these might look pretty decent polished," she said with certainty that seemed mustered up. "There's that Betty Grable photograph too. Maybe a second-hand store…?"

It was all too hopeless for words, but I had to say something, so I agreed that second-hand stores might be an option. Though doubtful, I mentioned the antique shops on St. Jacques Street, suggested she call first. I did wonder about her apparent need to raise money, but didn't ask about it. The truth was, if I hadn't already more or less abandoned her as my story subject, I might have asked.

Gertie stood motionless and silent a moment, then folded the hanky tenderly around her treasures and tucked them back under a flanelette nightie. "Those are good ideas," she said. "And would I find the numbers in the Yellow Pages, do you suppose?"

I said I imagined so, and Gertie thanked me warmly. "It's so great to have you nearby," she said. "I hated to have to bother you but…" She closed the drawer and squeezed my arm with such gratitude that I was a bit ashamed that I hadn't put some effort into being helpful. No doubt sensing my desire to escape the situation, she said we'd just try to forget all about it now. "Where did we leave off yesterday?" she asked. "Are you okay? You look a little worse for wear."

"I've felt better," I conceded. I told her I'd been up a good part of the night wondering about Buzz Beurling. As we made our way to the kitchen I told her I'd like to have my hooks into a story by the time I returned to work.

"Oh, you're considering Buzz, are you? That's a relief," she said, patting her hair. She removed one of her clip-on earrings, massaged the lobe and put the chunky rhinestone bauble in her sweater pocket. "I was a wreck worrying that there wasn't anything to say about me. You're a smart girl to pick up on Buzz."

"I'm not letting go of *you*, Gertie," I hastened to assure her. I did hate to think of her as being so disposable, but supposed that maybe that was the way journalists had to be. "There'll be two stories. Perhaps two intertwined," I explained, improvising out loud, annoyed with myself for my soft-hearted, soft-headed approach to the very serious job of writing. The thing was, Gertie was seeming to be less and less the feisty spirit I'd imagined. Although, when I saw her fumbling in a pocket, retrieving the earring and clipping it back on her ear, I had to admit there was something endearing about her that in the proper context could very well capture the public's imagination. "Perhaps you could begin by telling me what you remember about Buzz," I suggested as we took our customary places. "Did you know him before the war?"

"I knew him, yes, though I knew one of his sisters better," Gertie said. "His people were from a strict Evangelical sect, real Bible-thumpers."

Bible-thumpers. That would explain why I felt a vague sense of kinship. Buzz would have grown up with the same bedtime stories I had: Jesus walking on a storm-tossed sea; David decapitating Goliath; Samson slaying a thousand men with the jawbone of an ass. Miracles and mayhem colourfully illustrated. "But you were at that welcoming ceremony, right?" I asked.

"Oh, sure."

I could see Gertie mentally scrambling for something exquisite to tell me. "I never saw such a crowd. And noisy! Poor George looked as though he ought to have been home in bed."

Taking up his picture, I studied again the face of the handsome young man. It was true, he looked weary, haunted. "Did you go alone?" I asked.

"I went with a friend from work." Gertie smoothed a white lock from her temple, exposing a dark blue vein. "Rumour was that at such affairs pretty girls were selected by the newspaper reporters to stand next to Buzz. And, though it sounds boastful, I was young and, well, our boss told us that we ought to go, and to make sure, if we were chosen, to mention the company name to the press." She chuckled ruefully, then admitted that there'd been no getting anywhere near Buzz, who was flanked by a bunch of dignitaries. Her friend had taken a camera and a cadet was kind enough to muscle through the crowd to snap a close-up for them, the photo I held in my hand. "Do you suppose, Miriam, that it might be valuable now, that picture?"

"Golly, I don't know. It could use some restoration work."

I handed back the snapshot and watched as Gertie examined its imperfections and lost hope. "Such a long time ago... Like another lifetime," she said. She suggested that I check the library because there'd been plenty written. "You know," she said, "I was just fond of Buzz because he was from here, because instead of making trouble out there in the streets as so many did, he somehow learned to fly — this was during the Depression, don't forget — and then he went into a dangerous situation and did his best."

"You put that very well," I told her. "I just may use that."

"Really?" Gertie beamed. "It just came out the way I felt it. I never did believe what people said, that Buzz Beurling was a cold-blooded killer. Not for a minute."

"People *said* that?"

"Some did." Gertie nodded sadly. "Not folks around here," she said, "because we knew George from before the war, knew him as a nice mannerly lad — not a good student, because his mind was forever on airplanes, but no troublemaker either." She reasoned that perhaps somewhere along the line he rubbed some people the wrong way, and explained that Buzz had been turned down by the Canadian Air Force initially, despite all his flying time, because he hadn't been to university, that it didn't seem right that he had to get himself to England in order to serve with the RAF. "Or at least that's what Earl always said," she added. "Earl said it was no wonder Buzz had a chip on his shoulder when his own country... Shall we have some tea, Miriam?"

I said okay, that tea would be nice. I wanted to pursue the issue of Buzz's fall from grace, but I figured, why browbeat an old woman when well-documented material must be available elsewhere.

"Here, why don't you keep this for the time being?" Gertie said, handing me the photo. "You can drop in anytime to return it, no rush. You're always welcome here."

The next day, the last day before returning to work, I went to the library to embark on some serious research. War, I found, was a very popular subject. So many books, and the name Beurling not difficult to come by. There was even a book by the hero — co-authored by a journalist — accounts of his skirmishes primarily. The dialogue reminded me of my elementary school days, the noon-hour war games boys played. Still, it was not without pride that I read — in various biographical accounts — that a lad from Verdun had been just what the nation needed to break the tedium, the bleakness of war: a handsome youth of humble origins; a high school dropout who proved himself to be not just a great marksman, but a genius when it came to calculating the speed and angle of the enemy's aircraft in relation to his own; an individual, rather than a man among men, who declined promotions and all the trappings of high rank. He was, initially, a publisher's dream: the public clamoured for stories of his exploits. He was the prime minister's dream, and the recruiting officers' dream: his daring persona sold Victory bonds and inspired young men to enlist. *The Falcon of Malta,* they called him in the media.

Then somehow the dream unravelled. He was forced to accept a commission — the military couldn't very well have its officers being upstaged by a sergeant-pilot. Some complained that he'd grown arrogant. Thanks to the media, the public grew to believe it was the killing itself, not just the thrill of flying and the challenges of staying alive, that motivated the youth. When the war was over and the restless, out-of-work hero signed up to fight for the new state of Israel, it seemed all the proof anyone needed that Buzz had a thirst for blood. And when his plane mysteriously went down in flames on a test flight before he saw any action, Canadians didn't mourn his death, nor was the government's investigation into the cause of the mishap very thorough. The war was over, and people were eager to turn the page, they'd lost interest. It made me wonder if they'd ever really cared about the man, or if they'd only been caught up in the heroics.

The following day I returned to work, and as I ate my sandwich at my desk and stared out the sealed and grimy window, I spotted a lone pigeon beyond the busy boulevard. It circled some fast food joints, then settled on the roof of a seedy topless bar, quite unfazed by the spastic pink gyrations of the neon stripper. Then it made its way over the stream of traffic and came to light atop the company's sign, where it shat a gob and commenced to preen. Aware, suddenly, that I too was being watched, I turned to find Barry, my supervisor, in the doorway to my cubicle. I hoped it was registering in his little brain what a dedicated worker I was, staying behind at noon to meet the deadline. Working extra hours was what I felt I needed to do to compensate for my very negative office karma. Important documents — faxes, correspondence from wholesalers and manufacturers — evaporated in my possession; the photocopy machine that clipped along merrily for others, would, while I was at the helm, suddenly spring an inky leak, or paper would mysteriously wad up inside. I was no longer allowed to touch the coffee-maker without supervision.

Barry had some updates, he said. The butterfly wall ornaments were not porcelain as stated on the "new items" list. (*Porcelain-like chinaware,* went through my mind as a quick-fix.) He told me that numerous poly-glass pedestal dishes had been returned — the pedestal being not so high in real life as it had appeared to be in the illustration. I was to write an explanation for the mix-up that would accompany the yet-to-be-determined substitute being sent to the disgruntled customers. He said that any old blarney would do and I was to *please* not be so apologetic; after all, I hadn't severed anyone's leg.

Barry had no sooner departed when the phone rang. It was the lawyer, Tom, regarding the sweepstakes copy I'd faxed him that morning. Past lawsuits made it necessary for promotional material to be verified.

"What's this nonsense about 'Each item purchased means another chance to win'?" he asked. "The law requires that no purchase be necessary."

I told him where to look on the cover copy for the statement to that effect.

"Okay," he said. "It *is* here. God, you really should issue free magnifying glasses to your customers."

Part of my mind stayed with the lawyer, doing its job, the rest of it considered the Gertie article. …Yes, I'd given up on Buzz.

While I really had wanted to help Buzz sort of fly again, apply some lustre to his memory, I had to ask myself, Would the present generation care? Besides, he was dead, whereas Gertie was not. So… *Homing in on the Pigeon Lady,* thought the would-be writer of human interest stories, as the lawyer confessed that, personally, he didn't give a damn what type size the company used, that he had little sympathy for those foolish enough to respond to such come-ons. "Ultimately, people get exactly what they deserve," he said, seemingly trying to impress me with his philosophical ruthlessness. "How's your writing going?" he added, his tone becoming warm and personal. "Didn't you say you were going to branch off into freelance work?"

"Oh, right, I told you about that, did I?" I really wished I hadn't told people. It made me feel under pressure to produce; but then, that had been the idea. "It's coming along," I told him. "I'm writing about a neighbour whose closest friends are pigeons."

Silence.

"Tom?" I said. "…You still there?"

"I was just wondering… *Pigeon ladies,* they're a bit old hat, don't you think?"

I had intended to call Gertie during the week, just to say hello and to mention my renewed interest in our collaboration, but somehow it got to be Saturday, so I went over at the usual hour. Standing on the landing, I anticipated the warm welcome I was bound to get. Tom had been right about the pigeon-lady angle being old hat, but that didn't matter because I'd decided to pursue the issue of a grandmother's visiting rights. I had no idea how we'd begin, but oddly, the doubt was no longer overwhelming. Gertie and I were, at very least, going to enjoy one another's company while we learned the ropes of exercising one's rights and getting a message out. I rang the doorbell once, twice, three times…

A woman wearing a red bandana a couple of balconies over was sweeping cobwebs from the iron railing. I called to her, "Do you happen to know if Mrs Bond has gone out?"

The woman set the broom against her door and leaned on the rail. "Gone out? No, I wouldn't say she's gone out. She's passed on. Monday it was. Fell down them steps."

"My God, no," I said, but the woman assured me yes, *yes,* and it was then I recalled the dream I'd had, the dream in which I'd assisted the wounded hero up Gertie's stairs. I was going to feed him in the dream, him and Gertie. I was going to serve up vegetables from my garden in grand style, and the occasion was going to be featured in the food section of the *Gazette.* However, in climbing the stairs Buzz grew heavy and I let go. And now Gertie had stumbled and tumbled to the street just as he had. …*No,* I thought, it couldn't be.

The woman wearing the bandana shook her head in wonder. "Carrying a big fur coat, if you can imagine, in this heat. They say she fractured her skull. Tripped, maybe, or maybe her heart gave out. Eighty-seven, coulda been anything."

"She was only seventy-five," I told her.

The woman laughed wryly and returned to her sweeping, creating a cloud of dust. "Eighty-eight next month," she said.

I felt foolish, but even more than that, annoyed. Annoyed that the woman so openly enjoyed having the scoop on the latest neighbourhood incident. I hated the thought of enhancing her role as an authority, but I had to ask, "Do you know where they took her?"

"Well, she died Monday, so she'd hafta be buried by now, wouldn't she?" The woman kept sweeping, kept talking in a way that suggested there was really no end to all she knew. "That son of hers had her flat cleaned out the next day," she said. "Not *clean*-clean. *Empty*-clean. I didn't know her except to say hello, but there's something awful sad about the way she went. God only knows what she was doing with that coat. Her son said her mind was going. ...Where'd you know her from?"

I told the woman that I was a friend, but, in the telling, felt undeserving. "I'm a neighbour," I said. "A friend," I added after all, remembering Gertie's invitation to drop in any time.

"I thought I seen you before, well... Anyway, poor thing, she's gone to a better place."

"Her mind was fine, more than fine," I said, just to set the record straight.

Following Gertie's death, I abandoned any notion of writing — other than the ads for bric-a-brac, writing that was easy, safe. But then recently I came across the photo of Buzz, whose image conjured up a sense of unfinished business — and fond memories of Gertie, of course, and Ralph too, oddly enough, because for the longest while after Gertie died, until I moved to make a fresh start, each time I looked from my kitchen window across to Gertie's vacated flat I'd see Ralph hunkered down along the eaves. No one was providing food anymore, and yet there he was, week after week, month after month, dependable, steadfast and true.

LIFELINE

It's the first day of class, and Anna Marie is looking for room H512. About ten minutes ago she happened upon H506, H507, and H508, but when she rounded a corner, fully expecting the numbers to continue in sequence, she was confronted with H500. She tells herself not to worry, that if she can only find room H512 she'll be able to handle the course, no problem. This thrilling, terrifying bravado comes from the satisfaction of having passed the qualifying courses she took this summer, of having been accepted as a mature student into the university Fine Arts program. However lost she may be at the moment, she is, officially, a Studio Art major.

A Studio Art major. The title turns itself over and over in her mind like a compliment or good deed remembered. Her previous status, dropout, had put her in some pretty good company back home in Newfoundland, but here in Montreal her past failures cast a foreboding shadow every time she errs. It's as though an invisible hand is poised above her, ready to grab her by the scruff of the neck and fling her back to high school to complete the two grades she missed.

In her continuing search for room H512 Anna Marie comes upon a set of large heavy doors that are, by now, familiar to her. She peers through the little windows and sees again the corridor she can only surmise is off-limits … unless it is *not* off-limits at all.

She opens the door, slips through, and glides past a row of lockers to find a classroom. It is H509! She lunges down the hall past more lockers, past rooms H510, H511. At H512 she pauses, she peeks inside the room just as the professor turns his attention from the board. "You're late," he says matter-of-factly. "You've missed introductions. Perhaps you could state your name and we'll continue…?"

The thing is, Anna Marie had actually arrived at the university with tons of time to kill, but had sought directions to the room from people who, although very nice, couldn't have known any more than she had that she was in the wrong building. Feeling she really ought to mention this to the teacher, she gives her name plus her explanation, but it comes out of her in a rush and is hopelessly tangled in apology.

"No real harm done, Ann," the professor interjects just as Anna Marie's tongue finally gains some co-operation from her brain. If he hadn't even grasped her name there's little chance he'd understood the rest of what she'd tried to say.

Anna Marie can only hope that creative writing, an option course, will prove less intimidating than botany had. She'd thought that her talent for identifying and drawing wildflowers would make the study of botany a breeze. A glance at the text in the university bookstore had sent her scurrying to change courses. Botany, heavens, she might as well have signed up for math.

She casts her eyes around the room. There are about twenty students, exuding an air of indifference, seated around a table. The teacher, a thin, dark-haired man — younger than her other profs, perhaps in his mid-thirties — indicates to her one of the two remaining places, the chair next to his. "I promise not to bite," he says.

Anna Marie feels the colour in her cheeks deepen. She prefers to sit well out of range of a teacher's full attention, but what can she do but oblige him? In such a fluster, wouldn't you know it, her foot catches the chair leg, and her backpack — loaded with art supplies — swings around from her shoulder to her abdomen and startles her back into the seat clumsily.

The teacher's eyes rest on Anna Marie amusedly, causing her to break out in a sweat. She plucks at her blouse to loosen it from her body, blows up into her bangs, then hastens to appear composed.

"Last one in closes the door," he tells her.

His smile is steady, cunning, like those of men she's seen at carnivals who offer an almost impossible chance at darts. Play a quarter, lose a quarter.

She tiptoes to the door, closes it silently, returns to her chair and opens a notebook to write down the name on the board, presumably the teacher's. She's aware that students are watching her, that some are deliberately not watching her. *Ray Hanson*, she prints with neatness she swears to herself she'll sustain beyond the first day.

Ray Hanson hands her a copy of the course outline that had been distributed prior to her arrival, and while he goes over it with the class Anna Marie tries to concentrate. Her heart is slow to wind down. It always is.

"That's *forty*, not thirty, not twenty," Professor Hanson says, referring to the minimum page requirement for written work. "Last year someone actually came to me at the end of the year with twenty-six crummy pages. And I mean crummy."

Everyone laughs softly as though each produces work of a high calibre. A pallid fellow in a torn tank top shares his hope that the course will provide him with the motivation he needs to complete his novel, and Ray Hanson says he wants novels submitted chapter by chapter. He does *not* wish to face a dozen novels at the end of term. Anna Marie has never written anything longer than eight pages — for an art history course she'd taken during the summer. It had taken positively forever because she kept typing *teh* for *the*, *si* for *is*, and *nad* instead of *and*. She contemplates the agony of re-entering the long, long line-up for another course change. Should she or shouldn't she?

"Any questions?" asks Ray Hanson.

The students gaze at one another idly. Some put the course outlines in a pocket or backpack to move things in the direction of dismissal.

"What about you, Ann? You look as though you might have a question."

Anna Marie shakes her head *no*. Attempts in other classes to ask questions only proved that there's a knack involved. Some students' questions serve to clarify; hers leave everyone perplexed, herself included.

"No questions?" says Ray Hanson doubtfully. "Okay, let's see then… Ah yes…" and he proceeds to give a reading assignment, a story Anna Marie figures has to be famous or something since she's the only one who has to write down the particulars. Before she's finished, quite, the professor hands her a sheet of paper to pass around and instructs everyone to find his or her name on the list, check it off, *then*, he tells them, they are free to go.

"Read the story carefully," he urges them. "Be ready to participate when you come next time. Participation will count as part of your grade."

Anna Marie had passed the page along as soon as he'd said it was to be circulated, so she has to wait for it to come back. She finds *Dempsey, Anna Marie* and makes a tiny tick.

"Anna Marie," says the professor, looking over her shoulder. "So which is it to be, Ann or Anna Marie?"

Alone with the professor, blood surges to Anna Marie's cheeks. Not wanting him to feel he'd been wrong earlier, she tells him that it doesn't matter which name he uses.

"It's up to you," he says good-naturedly, as though giving her a wide choice of names, not just her own and a piece of it both too familiar and too remote to find appealing.

"Anna Marie, I guess," she says.

"You *guess*? You mean you don't know?" he teases, standing with his briefcase in hand but in no apparent hurry to leave.

"*Ann*, then," she tells him, reluctantly.

"Well then, see you Thursday, Ann."

The professor lingers a moment longer, then leaves her to join the horde of students in the corridor who move fluidly, lyrically — like water over rocks.

Anna Marie feels weary and forlorn just thinking about the prospect of heading back to her studio apartment. It had seemed so cute and cosy when she'd found it last spring, but it will be an oven now. Its only window faces out onto St. Catherine Street, and whenever she opens it, the blast of traffic noise strikes her with such a blow it reminds her of news bulletins, the simplicity and finality of the words, *died instantly*. What she wouldn't do to be at home and stand down by the bay, feel the breeze on her face, even just for five minutes.

Not that she regrets leaving behind her former life of minding the Ryan kids, of having to pick macaroni out of the carpet or scrape muck from the bottoms of sneakers, or search for the whereabouts of the forever-grubby and inadequately stuffed Katie-Kitty or the wheels for a Lego hotrod or moon-machine. She's able, at last, to occupy herself with her much-loved drawing and painting. She hopes writing won't take up too much of her time.

The way to set things right with Professor Hanson would be to get to the next class on time and to be really prepared. Having reminded herself of this fact repeatedly, Anna Marie actually arrives ten minutes early, having read the assigned story three times. It's a long story about a married man having an affair and Anna Marie can't help but feel mildly disapproving. Her own father had carried on with women, but had always done so under mysterious circumstances that made blaming him difficult — although Anna Marie's mother had had no such difficulty. Her mother, unlike Anna Marie, has never been toyed with by spirits of any kind, so hadn't any patience for Anna Marie's father, who'd been the target of fairies all his life and drowned at sea during a storm when Anna Marie was just thirteen. On deck one moment — without a lifeline, securing everything but hisself — gone the next, was what Anna Marie and her mother were told. Maybe the fairies took him once and for all, some joked in the weeks that followed, perhaps reconciling themselves to the fact that the money they'd lent Paddy Dempsey was money they'd never lay eyes on again. They couldn't have known that fairies are hang-ashores, perhaps to be seen in streams, small lakes and such, or on the docks, but not on the sea, for they are not at all fond of salt water.

On canvas and in Anna Marie's imagination, her father isn't merely bones lying in a barren sea bed, but a person in the flesh, sometimes out and about, and other times resting in an underwater cave amid domestic clutter — broken pottery, a wrought-iron bed frame, and dilapidated table and chairs — enjoying a tranquil existence far removed from the eternal hell Anna Marie's mother had, when he was alive, always said he was destined for.

Actually, the wife in the story reminds Anna Marie of her mother. The fictional woman is more attractive, of course, because Anna Marie's mother has a tightly stuffed look about her, and her idea of making an effort is a swipe of lipstick now and then. But both women seem mellow or detached. In her mother's case, that calm frame of mind lasts only up to a point and then there are fireworks. When Anna Marie really stops to think of the story, she sees that everyone is a bit distant. She's surprised, as she sits through this second day of class, to hear the other students express enthusiasm. Ray — they've been invited to call the teacher Ray now — marvels with them over instances of foreshadowing and all it signifies, allusion, candour… It makes Anna Marie wish her mother's wish, that with a snap of her fingers she'd be home for tea. And it's a wish that almost comes true because Ray's voice becomes so faint and far away, and Anna Marie's mother sits plunk in Anna Marie's mind squishing out point of view and students' interpretations of various bits of thematic material.

"What about *tone?*" Ray wonders in the distance, and Anna Marie can't think for the kettle's hum and the muted voice of the TV commentator. Her mother is knitting as usual; the aluminium needles sliding rhythmically. In her lap is a skein of lovely heather-coloured wool. "'Tis a bawlin' shame this sweater isn't for you," she says, "what with your chestnut hair and those green eyes you got from my side."

Everything good about Anna Marie comes from the Lowry side of the family. Her subdued disposition comes from Granny Lowry, supposedly. Her talent for drawing comes from Paps Lowry, the grandfather who died at thirty-nine of nothing more than the flu and left behind a leather valise full of sketches — mostly of his dogs, Bud and Joe, and his horse Winnie. Anna Marie's willingness to pitch in and help out could have come from any of the Lowrys. All the negatives — her inability to keep track of time, her fondness for sleeping in, losing things, forgetting things she's been told several times, even a liking for fried bologna or Limburger cheese on saltines — are hallmarks of being a Dempsey, after all. And no wonder she can't knit for beans when her father had barely been able to string his own fiddle.

Anyway, Anna Marie has no great desire to knit because there could never be anything special about her knitting. What makes her mother's sweaters so valuable to Mrs Bentley — a buyer from Toronto and the lady responsible for Anna Marie attending this particular university where she'll not only study art but broaden her horizons — is something called *consistent irregularities*. Anna Marie's mother, unlike most knitters, makes no attempt at machine-like precision. Her knitting, with all its consistent irregularities, has been described by Mrs Bentley as being alive, of having a raw, coastal character evocative of the enduring spirit of the people of the Atlantic Region. Just thinking of Mrs Bentley's words makes Anna Marie's heart swell with pride in her mother's work — work that had always been regarded by friends and neighbours as being of haphazard quality, inferior even to Mrs Abernathy's, whose knitted things always smelled of goat.

"And what are *your* thoughts on this one, Ann?" Ray asks from another region of Canada entirely, and all Anna Marie can pull out of the sudden blank is consistent irregularities, which she prevents herself from saying. Choosing to sit at a far corner of the table today has not made her as invisible as she'd hoped.

"Well," she says finally, a fragment of the story suddenly flitting to mind, "I guess the part I found interesting was when the man and the woman — not the wife but the one he was preoccupied with — were in the car in the rain."

"Ahh-ha," says Ray, and Anna Marie could almost kill herself for having fallen into some sort of trap. But then Ray adds, "Yes indeed, Ann has put her finger on the very heart of the story, hasn't she?"

I have? she thinks, then while Ray explains to the class how everything in the story leads either to or from the six paragraphs she'd indicated, she recalls her own similar experience several years back. Similar in that it took place in a car on a rainy evening.

It was a Friday, she'd finished sitting the Ryan kids and gone to meet Jimmy Lafferty at George's Garage where he worked. He was, supposedly, going to take her out on a proper date for once. It had been her idea to meet him at George's. Her mother disapproved of the way he pulled up outside the house and revved his motorcycle to announce his arrival — never presenting himself at the door. He was, in her opinion, a ne'er-do-well in the courtship department, and she never made any bones about it. Anna Marie hadn't minded Jimmy's offhand ways and loved the feel of his heart, caged and throbbing beneath her hands as she clung to him on his motorcycle, the wind tearing at her clothes like a hungry animal. Still, she'd learned from the mistake her mother made when she was young, a mistake that made her mother forever beneath Aunt Flo, who was known far and wide as "a real lady."

When Anna Marie got to George's Garage, she found that Jimmy hadn't shown up that day. Neither she nor George had a clue that Jimmy had rammed into the back end of a car, that he'd been taken all the way to St. John's for treatment and was lying in the hospital more or less unclaimed, so they both felt taken for granted. Anna Marie asked for the key to the washroom and got out of her pantyhose, then set off for home, carrying her pinchy shoes — and the news, should she see Jimmy, that he needn't bother ever going to George's again, that the wages owed him would be put towards fixing all the things he'd buggered up.

Anna Marie had not gone far when it began to rain. Her dress became clingy, especially around the knees, so she hoisted it up to mid-thigh. She kept on the lookout for broken glass, and thistles that grew up through the the gravel, still her mind drifted. Far below the turbulent surface of the frigid Atlantic her father smoked the final inch of a cigarette and played a sad tune on his fiddle, enticing her, by and by, into a slow dance, her toes treading softly on an imagined blue bed of crushed abalone shells.

In her fanciful state she was only vaguely aware of the few cars that passed, so was startled to hear her name. "Anna Marie, is that *you* out in the rain?"

It turned out to be Mr Ryan. He'd had to lean way over to roll down the window. "Get in, for gosh sakes," he said, nudging the door.

Through the steamy back window Anna Marie saw what looked like a month's worth of groceries and a jumbo pack of disposable diapers for little Brad. Huggies, she read as she entered the warmth. She dropped a shoe while grappling with the door handle and had to grope under the car to find it.

While Mr Ryan drove, Anna Marie fidgeted, trying to inch her dress down from her thighs.

"Never mind," Mr Ryan told her, meaning, she guessed, that she shouldn't worry about getting the seat wet. He said to her, "I thought, 'That poor woman caught in the rain,' then I realised it was *you*, Anna Marie."

He shifted his eyes from the road when he mentioned this and seemed to take in all of her just by glancing in her direction — her bare legs, the water trickling from her bangs down her face, and the dress completely soaked and plastered to her. "It's a good thing I came upon you when I did," he said, increasing the speed of the wipers.

A wind had come up and it tugged at the front end of the station wagon as though urging them to follow the will of the invisible force that was as present as the fragrance of fresh bread and parsley. Mr Ryan tried rolling down his window but rain hissed in on him so he put it back up. "I guess you'll be thinking of marrying some nice chap one of these days," he said after a while, but Anna Marie felt down on the idea at that moment so she told him she didn't think so. The likelihood of finding someone as exciting as Jimmy yet dependable enough to be a good father seemed extremely remote. Mr Ryan was great with his kids, always saying good-bye or hello with tickles or wrestling or kisses, and depositing candies in their grabby little hands the way a daddy bird passes out worms, a candy short sometimes and really sorry, you could tell.

Mr Ryan had asked if she was warm enough, and she said pretty nearly. He increased the heat and turned on the radio, and they drove the rest of the way pretending to listen to an interview with an old woman who was some kind of crackerjack. "You'll want to wrap yourself in a blanket and have some hot lemon or something," he said when he dropped Anna Marie off at home. He reached as if to touch her, then withdrew his hand. "See you Monday morning," he said. And she'd thanked him profusely, grateful not only for the ride but for his resistance to the sudden unaccountable presence of temptation.

In the following years that Anna Marie worked for the Ryans, both she and Mr Ryan had to sort of kick the memory of the rain and the wind and that closed car out of the way before getting on with household demands. The memory would return — there was simply no getting rid of it — in fact his wife sometimes happened upon it, and even though she was too busy to take notice, it sent poor Mr Ryan into a panic. "Darling," he'd say, "we'll be late… Sweetheart, your coat… I have the keys, dear. I'll be out warming up the car, do hurry… Stop fussing, love, and just leave that for Anna Marie."

His behaviour was satisfying to Anna Marie in a hard-to-fathom way and so she was not altogether sorry a spell had been cast upon them. The fairy responsible must have hitched a ride too that rainy night. Perhaps it slipped into the car when she'd stooped to pick up the shoe she'd dropped.

The shrill scrape of chalk, the sound of it crunching and a piece rolling around on the floor draws Anna Marie to the here and now. Ray stands at the board, writing. There are dates and names, and alarmingly, her own name is written next to October 2nd. With his back still to the class, Ray asks, "Does this meet with your approval, Ann?"

Everyone looks at Anna Marie. "I suppose," she answers. She has no idea just how far behind she's fallen and it's almost more than she can bear. She tells herself that she's impossible, that this is exactly what happens when you take your mind off the teacher even for a moment.

Anna Marie eventually deciphers the significance of October 2nd, and by the time the day arrives she has managed to write her first story, complete with lots of description, real-life characters speaking actual dialogue, and she's made photocopies so it can be critiqued in class. It's ten pages, minus a couple of paragraphs, so she still has thirty to go. Thirty and a half if Ray chooses to be picky about it. The story is one her father used to tell about the terrible day he got married — a pack of lies, according to Anna Marie's mother, but Anna Marie is inclined to keep an open mind. Her mother's self-described "wedding facts" and her father's "infuriatingly whimsical account" — infuriating to her mother, that is — served as a kind of finale to their frightful rows. As Anna Marie watched them straighten the furniture and sweep up the debris, she tried to draw comfort, too, from the one detail they agreed on: things had been bad from day one.

Everyone in class seems to like the story except a guy who worries that it perpetuates certain myths about Newfoundlanders, something he finds vaguely offensive in this day and age. He reminds everyone that it's the eighties now, an age of communication, and Newfoundlanders are as enlightened as anyone. He backs down, however, when a girl he's been flirting with for over a month says that she herself is a Newfoundlander, having lived in St. John's until the age of two, and having a great-aunt who still lives there. "You shouldn't be so anal," she says, and he tells her that, come to think of it, the story reminds him of the work of Flann O'Brien.

Anna Marie has never heard of Flann O'Brien, but the name is Irish, so she imagines her father being especially pleased. It never took much for him to be especially pleased with her, which had annoyed her mother, who imagined the two of them in cahoots, and indeed they sometimes had been.

Come, my little misdemeanour, he'd say to Anna Marie when she was a child and wakeful at night, taking her from her cot into the living room. His night-time preparations for fairy visitations were generally made well in advance of his own retiring — the chairs placed in a circle and a provision of bread left visible, fairies being greatly appeased by bread. Sit here on my lap and have a nip, he'd say to Anna Marie. Just don't be tellin' your ma or she'll have my hide. Now, shall we do the one about Paddy and Anna Marie?

And Anna Marie would crawl onto his lap and she and her father would quietly recite their very own variation of "Wynken, Blynken, and Nod":

Paddy and Anna Marie one night sailed off in an empty bottle.
Sailed on an ocean of crystal light, with the bottle full throttle.
Where are you going, and what do you wish? the moon asked inquisitively.
We've come to gaze at the angel fish that live in the beautiful sea.
Tweedle-dee-dum and tweedle-dee-dee cried Paddy and Anna Marie.

Anna Marie had once heard the minister explaining to her mother that the trouble with Paddy Dempsey was that he worked too hard at maintaining his Irish. The conversation had taken place by the front gate where sunflowers — planted by Anna Marie's father despite her mother's prediction that they'd never grow — stood as tall as people and inclined their heads toward the walk as though they hadn't heard all there was to hear many times over. Anna Marie's mother had the church newsletter in hand, rolled up as though ready to bash flies. Paddy Dempsey works at *nothing,* she replied.

The minister had changed the subject by asking Anna Marie what grade she was in, and for a moment, she couldn't even remember. Adults had always asked about school, the subject of conversation she hated most. For more than a year after Anna Marie had dropped out, she enjoyed an almost unbelievable sense of relief. But while there'd been less anxiety working for the Ryans than trying to learn about integers and polynomials, that stifling listlessness she'd so often felt as a student returned, stretching out the days, making her deaf to the Ryan kids most of the time. Now that Anna Marie is in university and doing reasonably well, it looks as though Mrs Bentley, the woman who buys her mother's sweaters, might have been right when she said that getting a higher education can be a wonderful experience and can open doors to a whole new life.

Ray heaps praise upon Anna Marie's story. He says it is lively and charming. The fellow who has a novel-in-progress at home, however, asks if Anna Marie's story is, in fact, a story, or if it is an anecdote. He and Ray each seem to occupy a space apart from the rest of the class. Ray folds his arms and says that the story's anecdotal style is, in fact, very much in keeping with an ancient storytelling tradition that features interesting people at odds with one another in an environment that, possessing a quality of otherworldliness, is somehow more suitable for a subject as age-old as the incompatibility of the sexes. He suggests that the fellow, whose name is Rob, think of it as a tale rather than a story, and Anna Marie worries that Rob is sorry he asked.

Anna Marie feels her story is not as complex as Ray seems to want to make it. There'd been only her parents and a dog in it — a dog that may have been a fairy pretending to be a dog just to lead her father astray. It had been terribly difficult to write the dog's part, to make her father's abduction believable and yet at the same time convey the possibility that her mother had been right in her claim that there'd been no dog and no fairy, but just a man who showed up late for his wedding and added insult to injury by leaving his pregnant bride on their so-called honeymoon in order to pursue other delights.

Ursula, a woman wearing a fluorescent orange T-shirt emblazoned with the word EQUITY, says she finds the story moving, mildly ironic — not *funny*, as someone else had said. "Irony has been used to defuse pain," she explains.

Ray says "interesting," and looks at his watch. He asks everyone if they're familiar with the work of Isaac Bashevis Singer, which sets heads to nodding. He says that a certain quality in Anna Marie's story is reminiscent of this famous author as well.

Anna Marie is pleased to the point of embarrassment, but she's also left wondering about Ursula's comment because while she was writing the story there were times she could hardly see for tears, just as it had been when she'd done a painting of the same subject, a painting Mrs Bentley had described as poetic, exuberant yet haunting, folkloric in the tradition of Marc Chagall.

As the term progresses, Anna Marie begins to regard her writing course as a holiday from criticism. Her drawing and painting teachers had been enthusiastic at first, saying she possessed a high degree of technical competence and that her sense of observation was almost flawless, but as the weeks pass they seem to grow more and more disenchanted.

"You could get rid of some of this extraneous detail," her drawing teacher said only the other day, her finger indicating the intricate pattern Anna Marie had faithfully reproduced from the fabric surrounding the model. "Better to suggest rather than to be so literal."

Well, in fact, the only reason Anna Marie had gone into such detail was that she'd finished her first drawing of the model before some of the students had even decided what angle to take. She felt she'd better spend more time on the second one so as not to outdo the others, many of whom can't draw for beans. It amazes her that the teacher seems not to notice this fact. For instance, one day a fellow whose easel was next to Anna Marie's had drawn what looked like the outline of a seal on a rock instead of a naked woman draped in cloth on a chair. He explained to Anna Marie that his approach was conceptual. Admitting he was very bored because he'd really only wanted to study colour relationships, he named a university somewhere in the United States that would have been better for a colourist such as himself.

Anna Marie wanted to think about this and then say something that would prove she'd thought about it, but her brain threw up a brick wall, so she shared her own grievance, telling him that she was accustomed to drawing from nature or from her imagination and found it difficult limiting herself to whatever was put in front of her. She could have listed a dozen reasons for feeling every bit as disenchanted as he claimed to feel, but the teacher's sudden presence silenced her. The teacher nodded to the fellow and, to Anna Marie's astonishment, said, "Interesting, very interesting. It could be pushed further, I think."

What Anna Marie likes best about the writing class is that she's able to figure out what's expected. If she reads the stories that are to be critiqued and has some comment ready for when Ray says, "What's your take on this, Ann?" or "Thoughts anyone? *No* one? Ann?" she really doesn't have to worry that much. She does wish he wouldn't pick her name so often. It's as though he's been alerted to her inclination to daydream and advised to keep after her. And there's that unsettling smile he has sometimes that suggests he finds something in her to be amused about, something she has no control over. But still, by the end of October she finally feels brave enough to ask a question that's been plaguing her. Not in front of everyone, that would be far too nerve-wracking. Rather, she waits till the class is over, then she packs up her things slowly, and when the last person leaves she admits to Ray that she hadn't really understood what Ursula had meant when she referred, a while back, to second-person point of view.

"Ursula?" Ray says, puzzled. "Is Ursula the one on my left behind all that hair?"

Anna Marie says no, Ursula has short neat hair, so Ray asks if Ursula is the heavy woman with the thick glasses.

Anna Marie says no again, that Ursula looks to be about average weight and has never worn glasses in class that she can recall. She says that Ursula is the one who seems to know a lot and wrote a story about growing up in a ghetto in Chicago.

"The black woman," he exclaims, "Christ, why didn't you just say so? Yes, well, Ursula, very militant, wouldn't you say?" He looks at his watch and asks Anna Marie if she has time for coffee. He suggests they go over the whole point-of-view question in a more comfortable atmosphere.

Anna Marie can't think of how to say *no* because she does, in fact, have some time, so she says all right and finds herself on the way to a café, Ray chatting en route about a trip he'd taken a couple of years ago. "We rented a car in St. John's," he says, "and we drove from east to west, up the coast to St. Anthony. All in all, a most charming place, Newfoundland. Terrific people. Most accommodating, even to cranky people who'd have been better off travelling separately." Not until he's stirring the cream into his coffee, though, does Ray mention that the *we* he had used repeatedly referred to himself and his wife, not the disagreeable acquaintance Anna Marie had imagined. Ray and his wife, it turns out, have been married for eleven years.

"Marriage," he explains, "is an evolving thing." He sips his coffee, which reminds Anna Marie to sip hers. "You think things are more-or-less fine," he says, setting down his cup with extreme care, "and then a kind of chasm opens up between you and your spouse." He wonders aloud if Anna Marie understands.

Thanks to her parents Anna Marie does know quite a lot about chasms. "Sort of like in that first story we studied, the one by the famous writer that you said illuminated so many truths?"

"Indeed, indeed," he tells her. "You're a delight, you know," he adds, beaming such approval Anna Marie doesn't know where to look. He takes a lingering sip, then asks if she has a boyfriend. "You must," he says, and Anna Marie is so surprised by the question she can't answer right away.

"Sorry, you're right. It's none of my business," he admits hastily, "I was just curious."

Anna Marie tells him it's okay to ask, and tells him she doesn't have a boyfriend as such. "No one serious," she adds, feeling sort of sad for

Aidan, Kevin, and Cal — fellows she's dated and likes because they're not like a lot of the others. Cal has given up on her and has become engaged, and her leaving has further diminished Aidan's and Kevin's hopes, or so she senses from their letters. As for Jimmy, she wouldn't dream of mentioning him to Ray because her feelings for Jimmy are just too complicated. She says, instead, that she's too busy with classes and homework and keeping in touch with her mother and friends, and painting. She explains to Ray that she always has a painting in the works and everything else takes a back seat. She hastens to add that writing is important too, though not her major.

Oh, how she loves the word *major*. It is what she does. It is what she is.

Ray begins to tell Anna Marie that he would love to see her art sometime... but, fortunately for Anna Marie, the waitress interrupts to ask if they'd like their coffee warmed.

Coffee makes Anna Marie nervous, so she says she'd better not have more. She reminds Ray about the point-of-view thing, assures him she knows what first person is, and third, but second...?

"You put the reader into the character's skin," he tells her, as if to clarify. "You use the word *you* instead of *I* or a character's name, or he or she..."

"I see," she says, and perhaps he can tell she doesn't see at all because he looks into space the way he does in class when trying to think of examples. "You get home and open your briefcase," he begins haltingly, "remove the assignments and search through the stack for hers. In the margin she has written that the fifth paragraph is optional, if there's too much detail to just forget it. And so you begin to read, starting with the fifth, optional paragraph which is, even with all its flaws, a small revelation."

Anna Marie, in recognising her own self as a kind of character in his example, feels too startled to fully grasp the actual explanation, and now what was this he was saying about *flaws*? She is flooded with new worry and has to remind herself that overall he seems to have a positive feeling about the work she produces and her contribution to the class. She tells herself she'd better be careful not to tarnish his favourable impression. "I guess I better go," she says.

"Already?" Clearly disappointed, he asks which direction she's headed, then interrupts her complicated response to say that, no matter, he hopes she'll join him again soon.

Anna Marie attempts to gather herself together — her jacket, her handbag, her books all conspiring against her. She tells herself that the lesson here is to *not* stay behind to ask questions. Not long ago she would have blamed fairies for the unexpected invitation for coffee, but after these few months at university Anna Marie is becoming more and more uncomfortable with the fact that the only person she knows who believes in fairies is old Mrs Abernathy, whose closest companions are goats. Mrs Abernathy is what you might call an Orthodox believer. She never wears green, and whenever her neighbours gather for tea she talks endlessly of her misadventures with fairies without ever once saying the word *fairy* for fear of provoking "the little dickens" or the "little you-know-whos." Her daughter will interrupt and tell her she's crazy, but Mrs Abernathy pays no mind to scoffers and professes to know what she knows. Anna Marie envies people who are, by nature, complete non-believers, but feels that becoming one is not easy. When she was little her father used to tell her that if she dared to say, or even *think*, 'I don't believe in fairies,' somewhere a wee fairy would fall down dead. Anna Marie's mother said he stole the notion from Peter Pan and doctored it to suit his own fancy. But still...

Trying to sort out and put to rest her conversation with Ray, Anna Marie recalls that he'd referred to Ursula as *militant*. Of all the people in class, Anna Marie likes Ursula the best. She likes her stories too — everyone does, except maybe Ray who always has a stash of "quibbles" or "caveats." Ursula reminds Anna Marie of Jane, back home, a friend since childhood. Lots of times when Anna Marie has pointed out a beautiful vista to Jane, Jane has appreciated it for a split second then said something like, Yeah, well, enjoy it, kiddo, 'cause the power line's gonna run right through the centre of this nice little scene. Or, That's all gonna be logged and gone five years from now. Or, Those fishin' boats'll be in a museum before we're little old ladies 'cause there won't be any more fish, you watch. Ursula and Jane have a way of making people take a second look at things, but does that make them militant? Anna Marie doesn't think so. Another thing she likes about Jane and Ursula is that they put in a kind word when others don't, Ursula finding something nice to say about the worst stories, and Jane referring to Anna Marie's departed father as a colourful soul whose hand must have been a marvel. Jane is into palmistry. Examining Anna Marie's hand and tracing her life line, she foretold schooling far from home. A branch that runs from the life line toward the Luna mount is a sign of travel, and another branch leading toward Jupiter mount indicates higher learning and perhaps improved skills.

Anna Marie can't help wishing now that the drawing teacher had seen her with Ray in the café, overheard him saying what a delight she is. She replays the scenario in her mind exactly the way it had been, only with the drawing teacher at the next table, then over and over again, embellishing the fantasy until it seems completely real except that it's just too perfect.

November comes and goes in a blur. With Christmas approaching, Ray, before dismissing the class, suggests an end-of-semester party, then he reminds everyone of the forty-page course requirement, quite effectively killing the seasonal mood he'd only just kindled. "I won't name any names," he says, "but there are several people nowhere near where they ought to be at this time of year."

Everyone has to know he means Veda, for one, whose dark eyes are blackened with heavy liner and whose one-and-only three-page story had been a feverish study of betrayal and revenge — or at least that was what Ursula called it when she tried to defend it from a barrage of criticism, most of it Ray's. Anna Marie had had no clue what the story was about, and wasn't even sure if the character was alive or dead at the end.

"This is, after all, a writing class," Ray goes on, "not simply a social club or a substitute for therapy."

He gives a surprise assignment, a five-page analysis of a John Cheever story to be handed in first thing in January, no excuses. "It will count as creative work, so feel free to be creative," he tells them. "But within reason, please. I'd rather be impressed than astounded."

Everyone is swamped with papers and projects. They tell Ray this and claim to need a bit of a break over Christmas. "This is not in keeping with your course outline," Rob states solemnly, and Ursula agrees. Anna Marie is tempted to nod as others are doing, but doesn't quite. She can't risk annoying Ray, who is sticking to his guns on the issue. Who knows where she really stands now in his estimation?

After the success of her first story she had started to imagine herself getting a B or maybe B+, which for an option course would really astound her mother. But the second story she'd handed out had not been as well received by the class. The problem as Anna Marie saw it was that everyone seemed to think the story was about exploitation when it was actually her mother's success story. Mrs Bentley had seen her mother's knitted work at a bazaar — mitts, scarves, and sweaters made from any old yarn that people had given her — tracked her down and offered her hand-dyed, hand-spun wool, a dream to handle, from Newfoundland artisans mostly, but from Maine too, and as far away as Scotland and Denmark — with the promise of all the work she could manage at fifty dollars per sweater. It had seemed like a miracle. But Ursula had said it was criminal that a craftsperson should get fifty dollars for work that takes days to make and probably sells for three or four hundred.

Anna Marie had explained that Mrs Bentley provided the wool, and her mother would have been knitting and watching TV anyway. Knitting tatty stuff for maybe a little something, or knitting heavenly stuff for a guaranteed fifty dollars. Which was better? Not only that, but Mrs Bentley needed money in a way Anna Marie's mother did not. Flying here and there, renting cars, while Anna Marie's mother was content to stay put. But Anna Marie hadn't expressed it in such a straightforward way. She was willing to take a bit of the blame, but deep in her heart she felt these people didn't know very much about knitting and it seemed a little unfair that she could end up with a lower grade on account of that.

On the plus side, sort of, Ray had said she'd attained a sense of closure not evident in her first attempt. Closure was obviously good, but she'd thought he'd been wild about the first story, so to hear it referred to as an *attempt*... well, she had to acknowledge the possibility that to be dreaming of B's might be just more Dempsey pie in the sky.

"Is there something I can do for you, Ann?" Ray says, and Anna Marie is greatly startled to discover that she's in the very situation she'd been so careful to avoid: the classroom is empty save for herself and Ray. But how uncanny that an occasion to ask for permission to rewrite the second story should present itself almost instantly. Now, how to phrase the request...?

Sometimes if you just beat about the bush, what you're wanting to say emerges almost like magic, so Anna Marie wonders aloud if she were to rewrite her story — did he remember the second story? — if she were to rewrite it would it cancel out the first version? If it turned out shorter, what then? Would she get credit for having written a longer one initially? She reminds him that she is up to twenty-three pages now.

"Ann, Ann, Ann," Ray sighs. "Are you stewing over page requirements? And here I thought you were going to tell me you'd like to come for coffee with me. How are you for time?" he asks, sounding hopeful and tired.

Anna Marie feels she has sabotaged herself but says she has just a little time before having to be somewhere. The *somewhere* is nowhere in particular. She hopes he isn't able to tell.

On the way to the café, Ray gives her an inventory of his workload, which doesn't sound as bad as her own, but she tries to be sympathetic. Seeing herself walking with him as though she were someone across the street, she realises that, in fact, it is *really* something to be the one going for coffee with the professor. She feels she should maybe try not to think of it as such a problem. In her better frame of mind, Anna Marie remembers to order mint tea instead of just going along with what Ray's having.

"I guess you'll be going home for Christmas," Ray says to her while smiling in a familiar way at the waitress who's come with a cloth to wipe their table.

"Bad day?" the waitress asks. The name pinned to her snug checkered uniform is *Sheila*. She averts her eyes from Ray's steady gaze and redirects her welcoming smile to include Anna Marie.

"It's picking up," Ray answers, covertly admiring Sheila's bottom that jiggles while she scrubs at something sticky.

Anna Marie has forgotten Ray's question but sees now that he's expecting an answer. His eyebrows are raised in expectation. The last she can remember prior to the waitress's appearance is the inspired moment in which she'd made a request for tea.

"Christmas…?" Ray says.

"Oh, right, Christmas."

Anna Marie tells Ray that she probably won't be going home because it's a long and expensive trip. Actually, her mother had offered to pay the fare but Anna Marie has learned it's better to take care of her own expenses with her savings, otherwise she feels sort of beholden and worries even more about not living up to expectations. Another reason for not going home is that she'd likely be tempted to stay there, but she doesn't mention this to Ray.

As the beverages are placed before them, Ray says, "You know, I have an idea. Why don't you come have Christmas dinner with me… with my wife and me, hmm?"

Anna Marie tries to smile and blows on her tea. She sips the tea cautiously. "I guess I could hardly do that," she says. Her pity for herself luckily catches sight of Mrs Hanson: "Your wife shouldn't be expected to take in your students. And you mustn't worry," she adds quickly and truthfully, "I really don't mind being on my own."

Ray says he doubts his wife will allow Anna Marie to be on her own at Christmas. "After the hospitality we enjoyed in Newfoundland, it's unthinkable," he states firmly. Frowning, he drinks his coffee as if only now really tasting it. Then he explains that his wife grew up in a rural community and has never fit into the university scene, and the death of their dog recently has been devastating. "I think your company might cheer her up," he tells Anna Marie, "inspire her to produce the kind of Christmas meal she used to come up with." He chuckles in a way that suggests he's pleased with himself. "You see," he says, "it's not a generous offer. I'm being selfish."

Anna Marie is quite at a loss. It just isn't fair that he has latched onto her own excuse — his wife — and made it into *his* argument.

"Do you know Mrs Bentley?" she asks, because it would be so like Mrs Bentley to contact the university and ask someone to take her under their wing.

"Mrs *Bentley,*" Ray says. "*Should* I know her?"

"In that second story I wrote, she was Mrs Kindley."

"Oh, Mrs *Kindley*, the shark from Toronto! How could I possibly know her?"

Anna Marie doesn't like that her mother's friend has been referred to as a shark, but she tries not to show it. She tells Ray to never mind.

"I'll tell you what," he says. "Let's leave it up to my wife. I promise to just mention my idea to her as a possibility. Deal?"

Anna Marie ventures that of course there's still a chance she'll be going home.

"What? And ruin my Christmas?" Ray teases.

She tries to smile as he is doing, but at this moment she feels she could almost walk to Newfoundland. She clings to the hope that she will, yet, get to enjoy the roast turkey special at Murray's diner, as she had at Thanksgiving. She tells Ray that she has to be going but that first she'd like him to answer the question she'd asked, the one about rewriting the second story.

Ray stands and reaches for her coat to help her into it. He tells her to please stop worrying about her stories, to put her energy into new ones, to continue exploring, something she promises to try to do.

Anna Marie turns story possibilities over in her mind as she trudges along St. Catherine Street toward the bowl of chicken soup she's looking forward to having. With the sad hollow sound of snow underfoot, a slow dance, barely perceptible, stirs within her. The problem is, ever since she left her island home her father's fiddle has been silent.

As Anna Marie sets out for Ray's on Christmas day — a trek that involves catching a bus to the metro, a metro ride, then a walk of about ten blocks — her mind keeps returning to the end-of-semester party when she'd been issued a warning about Ray. Ursula had not been as blunt about Ray as Jane had been about Jimmy Lafferty. In fact, she hadn't even mentioned Ray by name — that's how skilful she is with words. Prior to Ray's late arrival she casually orchestrated a discussion with Rob and a few others about all kinds of university issues, and you just *knew* who she was talking about when she mentioned teachers on the make. Anna Marie had to wonder if Ursula had observed her leaving the university with Ray and leapt to the wrong conclusion — an understandable mistake to make because how was she to know he felt he owed all Newfoundlanders a debt of gratitude? Remembering the way Ray's eyes had lingered on the waitress's bottom, Anna Marie figures that anyway it may be true that he's no saint as a husband, though he seems to really care about his wife's overall happiness.

I don't know, Ursula, Rob had said, you have to admit that some female students make themselves pretty easy pickins for the profs. In fact, sometimes they're the ones on the make and the poor schmucks just … well … *cave.*

Ursula, sounding militant after all, argued that it was a teacher's responsibility to be aware of the psychology at play, to set boundaries and stay within them, otherwise it contaminated the learning environment. She said she was sick to death of men in positions of power who *caved* and made excuses, that things had to change.

You're so intense, Rob told her, but you're right of course, as usual. He tossed a paper streamer at her to remind her it was party time.

One thing Anna Marie is pretty sure of: the waitress at the café needn't worry. Ray Hanson with his woebegone ways is no Jimmy Lafferty — Jimmy Lafferty prior to his accident, that is. Even Jane had underestimated him — not his boldness, but his appeal.

Back when Anna Marie had given in to Jimmy, she'd been numb from the boredom of school and had found his restlessness and indifference to consequences very intriguing. On their second date that wasn't really a date but just a motorcycle ride out to a remote lookout, he'd breathed heavily into their kiss and said, Look, if you got any idea of backing off like last time you gotta say so now. Otherwise, I'm liable to go crazy, you know?

His black curls were damp with sweat, and the heat of his body carried the sweet smell of wild strawberries buried somewhere in the tangle of lush, sun-baked grass where they lay. The hum of the bees, the intensity of the sun, and the turbulence of Jimmy's kisses made Anna Marie feel light-headed and powerless. Earlier that day she'd seen him passing by her place, flying really, and leaning into the curve, and it had come to her in a flash, the meaning of the expression *Hell bent*. It's either what you want or it ain't, he whispered, the softness of his breath tickling deep in her ear. He stretched down the neck of her cotton top, and slowly worked his mouth ever closer to her nipples like a blind puppy nuzzling, seeking milk from its mother. Do you want to, yes or no? Tell me, Anna Marie. And Anna Marie had caved.

As Anna Marie continues on her way toward the Hansons' and her Christmas dinner she tries to shake off the general feeling of disappointment, but it's no use. Getting a higher education is not nearly as much fun as Mrs Bentley had said it would be. In her last painting class the instructor had stood next to her and, with Christmas closing in on them and the course half over, offered a load of advice. He told Anna Marie she ought to broaden her brush strokes and confine herself to fully saturated colours which would flatten the surface and make *shape* her subject matter and thus save the painting from being just another fishing-village landscape.

This greatly distressed Anna Marie because the landscape did not represent her usual painting any more than the nude drawings or still lifes had. She'd done what everyone in class had been told to do: she'd painted her place of origin in a way that was non-specific, ambiguous. She had understood the teacher to mean, in her own case, something emblematic of villages in Newfoundland rather than the actual one she grew up in. She called it *Somewhere North of Heart's Content*. Other students painted wombs, circles within circles, and strange murky places that grew muddier and muddier as the class progressed. Their titles were short and puzzling to Anna Marie: *Issue; Bent; Untitled 1*. She'd felt so confused and discouraged by the teacher's comments that after he'd moved on to someone else she took her broadest brush, loaded it with vermilion, and slashed through the picturesque sun-drenched town. Crimson rain dripped slowly from the crystalline sky to the higgledy-piggledy row of boats and their once-glimmering reflections.

Returning to Anna Marie's side moments later, the teacher considered the vandalism and stated, "Well, it's honest emotion but not very constructively expressed, is it?" Shifting his weight to his other foot and tilting his head so it almost rested on his shoulder, he added, "To gain a new perspective, sometimes all that's needed is to turn the canvas around." He took the liberty of demonstrating and the two of them stood pondering the almost apocalyptic image: blood-red tentacles wavering hungrily upward in the foreground against a chaotic backdrop. Anna Marie felt faint.

"Hmm," the teacher had said, "... it will be interesting to see where you take it from here. You might consider keeping your title in mind as you work. It's not half bad."

Mentally, Anna Marie had searched the ocean depths to find comfort with her father, but there were no welcoming arms, only red tentacles, a tangle of nets, and ominous dark shadows circling, circling.

But now Anna Marie becomes aware of being in Ray Hanson's neighbourhood, so she has to start paying attention to where she's going or risk taking a wrong turn. She removes Ray's instructions from her pocket and stares at the criss-crossing lines and little squares that signify various landmarks. According to Ray's map there ought to be an old bank nearby, but since there isn't one she continues walking in the direction of the arrows. Up ahead, she sees a fellow sitting on a duffle bag holding a makeshift sign. Even though he's wearing a heavy coat now, she can see it's the same fellow that had been sitting on a duffle bag holding a sign near the university in October. Back then, the sign said something like: Fredericton by Thanksgiving. Home to family and a new job. Grateful for anything you can spare.

At the time, Anna Marie was feeling poor herself, having spent a fortune on art supplies, but she gave him two dollars because he was obviously very down on his luck and there was his family to consider, and employment which he sorely needed. To think, it's the end of December now and he still hasn't raised enough to get to Fredericton. He missed Thanksgiving, and the job must've gone to someone else.

As she approaches him she sees the sign is a different one altogether. It says: Homeward bound, Windsor by Xmas. No amount of $$ is too small a gift. Bless you and happy holidays.

Anna Marie is confused, too confused to respond when the fellow says, "Hi, gorgeous." Windsor, she knows, is nowhere near Fredericton. It's somewhere on the other side of Toronto, she can remember seeing pictures of it, smoke billowing out of numerous tall stacks into the air. So his mother must have moved, unless...

And now she is visited by a memory, one of herself as a child out with her father for "a lark," a few hours during which they walked hand in hand, her father whistling as though he hadn't a care in the world, approaching one person after another, gabbing about the weather, the sad state of the fisheries, politicians and "higher ups," all conversations ending with, Just a tide-me-over is all we need, and then when his pocket was bulging with change he'd drop Anna Marie off at home, or fairly close to it, and disappear, sometimes for a day or two.

Anna Marie hurries past the man. His eyes bore right though her, seem to penetrate her heart. She supposes she could go back and give him fifty cents or a dollar. Perhaps he really is going to Windsor. But no, she's not completely convinced he's going anywhere, and she has to be careful with her money if it is to get her through university. As it is, she may have to get a job before she's through, as some students have done already. How will she keep up with all her courses when she can barely manage as it is? She certainly won't be able to go out after work, as some do, stay up until all hours, and skip classes. She would fail for sure. When she was taking her qualifying courses in the summer, she asked a fellow in her art history class — a fellow she'd seen working in the university cafeteria — how he managed, and his answer made her feel hopelessly ill-equipped. He said you had to assess your profs early on. He didn't say how to go about this, but he did say with conviction that about fifty percent of courses could be easily blown off because of the bullshit factor — his exact words. He also said that presentation counted almost as much as content so he never handed in a paper without first clipping it into a cover. Like this, he said, exhibiting the paper he'd handed in a day late and just got back. He flashed the grade on the inside page, an A that had been underlined with a visible degree of enthusiasm. This A is for *Absolute* bullshit, he whispered as he winked at Anna Marie. The exchange had made her desperate to hear a voice from home, so when she got back to her apartment she called Jane, who, after listening to her account, told her, "Maybe he's a genius and is too dumb to know it, or one of those guys always beating his chest. Either way, forget about it. According to the lines on your hand, you are where you ought to be at this time of your life, so you might as well relax and try to enjoy yourself. Besides, nothing special is happening here."

At the next intersection, Anna Marie catches sight of her reflection in a window and stops a moment to feel pleased with herself for being in a place people back home could scarcely imagine. As she regards her reflection more closely, her smile disappears behind a cloud of soft warm breath — much the way fog accumulates and obliterates rock. Wiping away the haze, she sees through herself to tellers' wickets that look as though they're from the olden days. This, then, has to be the bank she was sort of looking for. Happily, she locates herself on the map and scrunches the paper back in her pocket.

If she were not on this corner, but on one back home, she'd maybe call on Jane or go visit Jimmy, who lives with his mother now that she's left the man she'd left Jimmy's father for. Mrs Lafferty says she owes it to Jimmy to take care of him since she'd lent him the money for the motorcycle — borrowed it in order to lend it she makes sure people know, so they can see just how cruel life can be, as though Jimmy isn't proof enough.

Hopefully it would be one of Jimmy's good days. Then they'd turn off the TV and he'd watch Anna Marie flip through her sketchbooks. He'd make those little sounds of approval he makes, like *hmmmm…* but cut in half and abrupt at the end. *Hmn/.* Long before she left for Montreal, Anna Marie had started putting titles to her pictures in order to tempt him into asking a question, since his mother said he could talk if he wanted to, that there was no medical reason he couldn't. His favourite sketch, one Anna Marie had worried he might not like, is one of him flying through a star-strewn sky on the back of a winged creature. The creature has the thick mane of a lion, the sleek legs and heavily muscled haunches of a stallion, a face not sinister exactly, but wearing a gleefully wicked expression as Jimmy grips the mane with one hand and thrashes a flank with the other. Far below, pools of people gaze heavenward. The caption reads: *And some folks thought 'twas a dream they'd dreamed.*

Suppose Jimmy was having a bad day and didn't want to see her? Well, she'd say hello and give him a kiss if he'd let her get that close, then she'd go home and cry because in some ways Jimmy is still Jimmy. His eyes still draw you in, his black curls still tumble down over his forehead. Another reason for crying is, it had turned out the collision wasn't even his fault. The tourists travelling in front of him had stopped their car suddenly, thinking at the last minute that they'd gone through the intersection they'd been looking for. Which is probably why Mrs Lafferty has taken to being so saintly, on account of there being insurance money, though Anna Marie doesn't want to believe that there isn't anybody loving Jimmy, and that all he has in the world is one blasted TV program after another and the tedium of watching the clock to see how close the next meal is. Anna Marie figures he's really missing her by now, is no longer angry at her for leaving.

She remembers to check the time. Peeling back her mitt she finds she has exactly seven minutes to walk two, or perhaps three more blocks to Ray's. It would be just like her to be lollygagging and end up getting there late. *Led astray*, her father had called it, because he could, supposedly, see who was responsible. The best thing to do for protection is to have a pocket turned inside out, but that's like announcing to the world you believe in fairies, so Anna Marie would never do it, because she doesn't anymore, not really — although she tries not to actually think *I don't believe in fairies*. She prefers to just shoo them out of her thoughts. She has stopped keeping a piece of bread in her pocket and for this she is proud of herself, but it's a secret pride, not one that could possibly alert the attention of... well, anyway, she's making progress.

Arriving at the Hansons' front door with still one minute to go, Anna Marie pauses to catch her breath before ringing the bell. It is Ray who answers. He stands there in his boots, his coat in hand. "Ah, here you are," he says cheerily. "Merry Christmas. I was just about to leave to see if I could find you — figured you might have come out of the metro and turned right instead of left. But you made it... come in, come in."

He reaches behind Anna Marie to close the outer door she'd left open. "This door has to be lifted and pushed at the same time," he says, as though she'd be using it frequently. He offers to take her things. "It *was* two o'clock I was to be here, wasn't it?" she asks, because he seems sort of hurried. She hands him her coat and scarf.

"Well, I thought I said one, that dinner might not be until twoish, but it really doesn't matter now that you're here."

Anna Marie's cheeks are positively burning up with the shame that her stupid brain has been snatching at words in a random way again.

Ray says, "The cold weather agrees with you. You look lovely." He brushes his lips lightly against her cheek. "Did I say Merry Christmas?" His voice is lilting, hardly recognisable. Still recovering from the personal compliment expressed so warmly, she looks over Ray's shoulder and is alarmed to discover Mrs Hanson. Has she been there all along? What a relief when she smiles and steps forward to offer Anna Marie her hand.

"You must be Ann," she says. "I'm Sue. It's so nice you could come."

She is a large-boned, tall woman, seemingly older than Ray, or maybe it's just that she's formally dressed, except for the apron. Ray is wearing a sweat shirt and the rumpled cords he usually wears to class.

"I was just telling Ann how lovely she looks," Ray says. "Isn't she looking festive and pretty?" As though any wife ought to be put on the spot like that. Still, the openness is reassuring in an odd sort of way, and Anna Marie knows that what he says is fairly true. She's wearing her special-occasion skirt and pullover, and her shamrock pendant her dad gave her when she turned twelve.

"I expect that lovely complexion comes from growing up in ocean air," Mrs Hanson says. She turns to Ray. "Please don't just stand there. See what Ann would like to drink while I put the finishing touches on dinner."

Anna Marie thinks to offer her assistance in the kitchen and both Ray and Mrs Hanson laugh softly at the ridiculous suggestion.

"We'll just stay out of the way," Ray says, indicating a seat on the sofa which is long and sleek and beige. Just about everything in the living room is white, off white, or beige, or a combination of these colours. Anna Marie supposes the Christmas tree must be in a den or family room. She asks about it, both to make conversation and because she'd like to see it, never dreaming it would turn out they don't have one.

"We got tired of flogging traditions that simply have no meaning for us," Ray says. "We write letters to friends, mail gifts to the youngsters in the family, but beyond that, well, we just have a nice dinner and feel content not to be part of the rat race. Let me guess," he says, "White wine… or wait… a spritzer perhaps?"

Anna Marie doesn't know what a spritzer is, but perhaps it's better than wine, which she's not as fond of as most people seem to be because it seems almost sour. Beer is okay when it isn't bitter, but the truth is she prefers plain old ginger ale. Even when she'd done some drinking as a child with her father, it was really just to please him. It was rye he liked, awful stuff you wouldn't want more than a sip of unless you had a terrible chill to be rid of, which she never admitted to having. It loosens the bones, her father would say, showing her how loose his bones were getting.

Anna Marie says *spritzer* to Ray. She decides that if it isn't tolerable she'll just sip it till it gets to below the halfway point, which she considers a decent attempt. She remembers she brought a gift and rummages in her bag. Such a load of rubbish she totes around. Shoes that could use some polish, a sketchbook, pencils, conté, and a note pad for reminders that she almost always forgets to use, makeup she rarely wears, gum that's gone hard, and tons of Kleenex, used and fresh. For a few horrible moments Anna Marie is sure she's left the chocolates at her apartment. She can see them laughing at her from where she'd set them, right on the table next to the door where she'd be bound to remember them.

"Are you looking for slippers?" Ray asks. "I can get you some."

"I brought shoes," Anna Marie says, heaving them out onto the floor so she can see what she's doing. "Thank goodness!" she says, flushing deeper. "Here, I brought some… it's not much…"

"How nice," Ray says, exchanging a spritzer for the chocolates. "You needn't have, but it's very thoughtful."

Anna Marie wishes she'd bought the bigger box. This one looks tinier at the Hansons' than it had at the store. It's about five inches by five inches, and to think the Hansons are going to give her a great big meal! She must be crazy to have come with such a meagre offering, though it had cost more than you'd think to look at it. She sips the spritzer, sets it on the coffee table and both she and Ray watch her feet find their way into her shoes. She can't identify any of the spicy smells that are coming from the kitchen and feels sort of lonesome for sage and cloves and grease-spattering goose. She wonders if maybe there isn't a whiff of fish in the air, under the spice and something scorched.

Ray goes to the bookcase and takes a thin book from a shelf. "I have something here you may get a kick out of seeing," he says. He hands the book to Anna Marie, taking a gulp from his glass at the same time.

The painting that illustrates the book is non-figurative. Anna Marie can't help but smile with the satisfaction of knowing. Oh, and now she notices that the book is by Ray. *The Distance Between Points of Interest, and other stories by Ray Hanson.* "Wow," she says, which makes Ray laugh in a voice full of pleasure. She turns the book over and there he is in a not-very-good photograph. He's leaning against a car in a way that looks more awkward than casual and he's squinting into the sun. Her eyes scan the words printed beneath the photo:

Parker Lambe, a portrait painter with flagging aspirations, the main character in Hanson's linked stories, takes a trip to Newfoundland with his wife in an attempt to rejuvenate the senses and restore intimacy in their floundering marriage. Sweeping landscapes and lyric prose make for an impressive first collection.

Ray Hanson grew up in various small Canadian towns. He and his wife presently live in Montreal with their dog, Cheever.

Cheever, that must be the dog that died. The name seems familiar to Anna Marie, sort of. Should she ask what breed the dog had been? How old? Why it died?

"Would you care to borrow it?" Ray asks, and she says sure, if he doesn't mind. She's never read a book written by someone she knows, and has never read a book about a portrait painter either.

"I look forward to hearing your comments," Ray says, filling Anna Marie with dread. Reading his book will be like an assignment now, and it comes to her that *Cheever* is the writer of that story she has to pick apart and make sense of before classes resume. No, not pick apart. *Deconstruct.*

Mrs Hanson interrupts Ray's satisfaction and Anna Marie's misery to say that dinner is ready. "Perhaps you could pour the wine," she says to Ray, who murmurs that he'd be delighted. Anna Marie can only wonder what's for dinner. She has determined it isn't chicken or turkey or goose or ham. And she hasn't heard anything that sounded like the mashing of potatoes.

When she's led into the dining room she thinks of her mother, how surprised she'd be to see that there are no curtains on the windows, only a paper blind rolled to the very top. The walls are completely white, and aside from one painting they're bare. Not like at home, where Anna Marie's drawings, family photos, and all sorts of ornaments bought at craft fairs or won as door prizes give folks plenty to look at and comment on when they visit. And even more amazing: the table is almost as bare as the walls. Anna Marie has been in homes where a bed sheet or curtain had to suffice, but *no* tablecloth on Christmas Day?

Mrs Hanson indicates where Anna Marie should sit — at the setting on the far side of the long table. She and her husband take their places at either end. "We'll begin with some prosciutto ham and melon," she announces somewhat grandly. Perhaps she doesn't realise that there's no bread. No bread or pickles or cheese — basic things back home, especially on Christmas. "We don't say grace, Ann," she goes on, "but if you wish, we could have a silent moment."

"That's okay," Anna Marie assures her, meaning she doesn't generally pray either. If she were to pray it would be the prayer her family used to say when there was only cabbage and potatoes. *Such as it is, Lord, we're grateful knowing it could be worse. Amen.*

Ray says, "No flowers? What happened to the ones I bought?"

Mrs Hanson tinkers with the melon and the ham, arranging a bit of each on her fork while explaining that she'd put the flowers in the back entry as there was no room in the fridge, that they must have found it too cold. She frowns at Ray, whose nose has determined something amiss and crinkles in an exaggerated way. "So I scorched some oil, Ray. So I killed your flowers," she says.

"It's just that it's not at all like you to scorch something," Ray tells her.

"It turns out I'm human after all." Mrs Hanson smiles at Anna Marie as though maybe looking for a word of support, but Anna Marie learned long ago how to remain quietly in the middle when disappearing entirely is out of the question. She thinks to herself that Mrs Hanson doesn't really look like the country woman Ray had said she was, unless it's the type you see in magazines that have stone houses with spacious gardens. Mrs Hanson has dark hair with a white streak that makes her look daring and like someone you shouldn't argue with.

"Where did you get the prosciutto?" Ray asks. He nudges a dry bit he'd cut off toward the edge of his plate. "I've had better," he states matter-of-factly.

Mrs Hanson scowls at the dry bit and turns again to Anna Marie. "How do you find living on the mainland, Ann?"

"Actually," Ray interjects, "she's gone island-hopping in a way. Montreal's an island too, remember?"

Mrs Hanson does not shift her gaze from Anna Marie's face, so Anna Marie tries to focus on the question. "Oh, quite exciting," she says. It's what she'd told Mrs Bentley when she called to ask Anna Marie how she found her studies. "This is very nice, Mrs Hanson," Anna Marie says of the ham and melon, aware as soon as she says it that she's contradicting Ray. The thing is, she's hungry enough not to be finicky. She'd had only a light breakfast, not wanting to spoil her appetite.

Mrs Hanson leans in Anna Marie's direction and urges her to call her Sue. To Ray she says, "Next is artichoke soup."

"My favourite," Ray says. "I don't get it as often as I used to."

While waiting for the soup and listening to Ray talk about how wonderful Montreal is with its ethnic mix and the food specialities that abound, Anna Marie realises that the painting with the solitary job of sprucing up the room is identical to the one on the cover of Ray's book.

"This work was done by a friend of ours," Ray says. "I'd be curious to know what another artist thinks of it."

It is not something Anna Marie would paint herself, as it is only a wash of orange over burnt sienna and grey, but it's all right. After wrestling with her thoughts for most of a minute, she says she guesses it reminds her of fire rising out of a bog on a misty day, like waking up, sort of.

Ray chuckles and says to his wife, "What did I tell you?" And Anna Marie can only wonder what he has told his wife.

As the various dinner courses are accomplished, Ray ponders the food and seems as disappointed as Anna Marie, but for different reasons. He asks if there is too much garlic in the soup, if his wife had forgotten her intention to cut down on the basil in the herbed lemon pilaf, and weren't the almonds supposed to be blanched. As for the *Turbot Véronique*, he says she is brave indeed to serve fish to a Newfoundlander.

Mrs Hanson wonders aloud if a Newfoundlander exists who is not bone-weary of being associated with fish, and Ray imagines that his reference to fish is no worse than hers to the "ocean air" supposedly responsible for Ann's lovely complexion.

Anna Marie pretends to be mesmerised by the painting and hence deaf to their exchange. She hears Ray note that his wife seems to be eating even less than a bird, and hears Mrs Hanson's mysterious response: "Have you forgotten? I'll be eating again very shortly."

"So you will," Ray says, and he turns to Anna Marie and tells her that his wife has a friend nearby with whom she is going to share this exact same dinner. Anna Marie assumes he's talking about a shut-in so says that it's a shame to be sick over the holidays, which causes an especially uncomfortable lapse in conversation.

Finally, Mrs Hanson murmurs that no one is ill. She looks at her watch the way Ray always does, and announces dessert. *Crème caramel.*

Mrs Hanson shares her secret for *crème caramel*, the addition of cardamom pods while scalding the milk, then a bit of instant coffee. So it is not entirely true, she says, that instant coffee is a travesty. It has its place. "The cardamom pods are removed of course," she adds, and Anna Marie nods knowingly.

Anna Marie eats the dessert slowly because it is just dreamy. It has been a very weird meal, an experience not at all like when you know right off what everything is. Grapes, for goodness sake! That's what the mysterious round globs on the fish must've been, or at least that is her best guess. Even the dessert, which looks like no more than custard with sauce, she finds herself trying to imagine cardamom pods, if they're like peas or what.

Mrs Hanson says she's running late so they'll have to excuse her. Anna Marie, feeling responsible for her being late, is quick to say, "Oh, sure, Mrs Hanson."

Mrs Hanson indicates to Ray that if he and Anna Marie wish to have coffee he'll have to make it himself, to which he replies that he feels he can handle it.

Anna Marie dabs her mouth with her napkin and says, "Mrs Hanson, that was an unbelievable meal. Thanks so much." Her words seem as inadequate as the chocolates had seemed. "I'm afraid you went to a lot of trouble," she adds. But Mrs Hanson dismisses the notion, focusing instead on the fact that Anna Marie has not called her Sue. She is not, she stresses, Mrs Hanson. Her name is, and always has been, Sue Wesley.

"Am I really so formidable?" Sue Wesley demands of Anna Marie with a strained and almost desperate smile, and Anna Marie wants to say, "Oh no, Sue," but she just can't. So she says, "I've got such an awful memory."

Mrs Hanson seems to no longer care and vigorously works a handle on the sill so that the window yawns open at the top. "You'll have to remember to close this, Ray. The one in the kitchen too," she says.

"I hope you'll let me do the dishes," Anna Marie tells her.

"That's terribly kind, but please don't. I'll attend to my kitchen later."

Mrs Hanson is so brisk clearing the dishes that Anna Marie hardly dares to reach out and scrape the last of the caramel from her dish. She allows the spoon to linger in her mouth for only a second, then under Ray's amused gaze, she slides the dish and cutlery towards the quick hands of her hostess.

"Someone liked her dessert," Mrs Hanson says with a pleased but harried look.

Ray doesn't help clear the table. He makes Anna Marie another spritzer, which is no more than wine and soda water. Anna Marie can feel the effects of the first one, little soda bubbles gathering on her brain the same way they collect and cling to the inside of the glass. When Ray suggests they retire to the living room, she gets up and follows. She feels almost in a trance and worries about how long she should stay. Perhaps she's expected to leave after her spritzer. She takes a good long sip. Meanwhile, Ray gets to talking about his book again, but it's hard to keep track of what he's saying with the uneasy feeling that Mrs Hanson is preparing to leave. Now Anna Marie hears Ray ask, "What kind of music do you like?" so she tries to think of something specific. Finally she says that she likes pretty nearly any kind, causing him to ask if there is any kind of music she doesn't like. She says not really, hoping he doesn't pick something classical because sometimes it starts off okay but then becomes too urgent, laborious, or solemn for her taste.

Ray troubles himself to find something in particular then sinks down into what has to be his chair, considering the way it conforms to him. A moment later, voices in perfect harmony begin to sing about love, how it is just like a wheel, *"If you bend it, you can't mend it…"* the voices sigh, and Ray grows so sulky Anna Marie doesn't know if he's about to cry or get mad or what.

Mrs Hanson appears in the doorway and says, "Can you save that until I'm out of the house, and in the meantime find something a little cheerier? I'm sure Ann could do with something a bit more uplifting." She looks to Anna Marie, daring her to deny it, and Anna Marie feels moved to take another sip of her drink.

Ray stays put. He asks Anna Marie to tell him what it was like to grow up on the Rock, a term for Newfoundland that always makes her a bit homesick. Before she has a chance to even consider the question Mrs Hanson passes through the living room loaded down with bags of containers, bottles and whatnot, and announces that she is off.

"It was so nice to have met you, Ann," she says to Anna Marie, not setting down the packages. Anna Marie is about to stand but Mrs Hanson says not to. Ray offers, from the comfort of his chair, to help his wife with her things, but she says for him to please just take care of his guest because she can hardly imagine what Ann must think of them.

Anna Marie opens her mouth to deny thinking anything at all, but words fail her.

"The bickering earlier," Mrs Hanson begins. "That was not in the spirit of Christmas at all, was it?"

Thankfully she doesn't wait for Anna Marie to respond. At the fumbling sounds of the door being closed Ray gets up, peers out the window briefly, then pours himself another drink. "I'll just top this off while I'm up," he says, pouring more wine into Anna Marie's glass.

"No thanks," she cries, but it's too late.

"Whoops," he laughs. "Well, we might as well..." he says. "You're far from home and I'm far from far. Does that make sense to you?"

"Not really," Anna Marie says, and she can't help but giggle. Ray raises his glass so she raises hers and takes a sip about equal to his.

Ray doesn't return to his chair. He sits down next to Anna Marie on the sofa. "I can't tell you how glad I am that you came," he says softly.

"I thought I'd have to cook us an omelette or something when Sue's plans changed, but she came through for me. I owe her big time, she tells me." He laughs miserably. "She's a great cook, though, when she puts her heart into it. She was a bit off her game today."

Anna Marie isn't thinking about the food anymore. She's wondering, Where exactly did Mrs Hanson go? Why not invite the friend to the house? Unless the person is maybe some kind of boyfriend? Ray had confided over coffee that he and his wife weren't as close as he might like, but he seemed to be chalking it up to the fact that marriages have their ups and downs. He certainly hadn't said anything to suggest that his wife was actually keeping company with someone else. In fact, he seemed to think his wife's loneliness could be remedied by Anna Marie's friendship.

Suddenly Ursula and Jane appear in Anna Marie's imagination clear as day and give her a look that says *wise up*.

"You *did* like dinner, didn't you?" Ray asks earnestly. "I just assumed that being so creative you're not one to be all hung up on tradition. You *can* say, you know. I'd like for us to be close enough to be honest with one another."

"That was just about the most wonderful dessert I've ever eaten," Anna Marie says, forgetting for a moment her mother's Figgy Duff. She closes her eyes, recalling Mrs Hanson's custard. She is determined to remember the ingredient that had so transformed it. *Carmondon* or something. Then sensing Ray leaning closer, feeling his breath on her face — warm, yet as startling as a splash of cold water — she draws away.

Ray whispers, "When you licked that spoon you stepped right off the pages of a Nabokov story, you know…?" He has mentioned Nabokov in class any number of times but there have been too many references to writers for this comment, now, to hold any meaning. He leans into the space Anna Marie has just created and presses his lips to hers. His tongue, hard and quick, penetrates her mouth but she instantly blocks it with her own, causing him to withdraw his. He gazes at her, and she sees on his face a certain look. It is a cagey look. It is, in fact, the one he'd had that first day of class when he watched her go through all the trouble of getting settled, only to ask her to close the door.

"Would you excuse me a moment?" he asks, rising, using the coffee table to steady himself.

Anna Marie had been sort of thinking about asking where the washroom was; now she doesn't bother to watch which direction Ray is headed. Her hand reaches out for her bag at the end of the sofa and brings it to her lap. She considers her options. If she were to leave, how could she ever face Ray again? If she were to stay, how could she make it so he'd back off and yet not feel rejected and maybe put out?

As she ponders her situation the most amazing thing happens. The front door opens. Not a few inches, but wide enough for someone to have entered. And there's a sprightly, tinkling sound exactly like her father's description of fairy music. Could her imagination and the wine be playing tricks? But no, the door really is wide open and the airy, melodic tinkling is distinct. You could scarcely get a clearer message, so she steps out of her shoes and stuffs them in her bag. She gives not a thought to Ray's book, hurries into her boots, helps herself to her coat, and once she is on the safe side of the threshold, lifts and pulls the door closed behind her. It is with this movement that she recalls Mrs Hanson opening the window in the dining room. She considers the possibility of a cross-draft, of chimes somewhere — in the kitchen maybe — and, feeling a wave of embarrassment, finds the possibility very likely, but never mind. She takes a deep breath and begins to retrace the steps she'd taken not two hours earlier.

Every bend in the road from Anna Marie's to Jimmy Lafferty's garners knee-high snowdrifts. Anna Marie, her eyes half closed against the icy wind, her sketchbook tucked under an arm and pressed to her chest, steps gingerly into the indentations left by whoever'd ventured earlier. She could have stayed in bed until much later, then extended breakfast till after the snow plow had passed, but she had been keen to get out of the house early. Her mother has been heartsick and hard to bear, going on and on about wasted opportunity, *wasted* being a word Anna Marie hasn't heard in years, at least not in a tone that has conjured up images of her father empty-handed on pay day. Worried that Jane's reaction might be similar to her mother's, Anna Marie has put off phoning to say she's home for good. She has let Mrs Lafferty think she's on Christmas break, and sooner or later will have to confess that she's no longer a Studio Art major.

No longer a Studio Art major.

Well, at least she's been spared having to pore over Ray's book… and the Cheever story, not that she has minded poring over stories these last few months. The agony was having to prove that she had, having to organise thoughts that were restless, ever-changing, having to choose just the right words.

Sometimes, between drifts, Anna Marie turns and walks backwards, opening her eyes to appreciate the blue sky high above the Arctic system that had put the TV weatherman in such a bluster. He told viewers not to despair, that more moderate temperatures are on the way. If you don't have to go out, don't, he said, as Anna Marie was bundling up, and she'd told him, Just try to stop me, Harv. Yes, she's taken up where she left off last spring: she's back to being familiar with the weatherman.

She hasn't told her mother the whole story of why she left school. Not a word about Ray for fear of the grilling it would provoke. And of course not a word about the timely way the door had opened, inviting her escape. Instead, she said she needed to be where painting felt as natural as breathing rather than like an exercise, and when that reason failed to have the desired effect, she went on to name all those who'd been away and returned disillusioned, and put it to her: How could so many people be hopeless cases?

But now Anna Marie has to prepare herself for Jimmy's grim circumstance. She hums a few bars of "Yellow Submarine" and sings, "So he sailed up to the sun, 'til he found a sea of green…"

Even though the snow is deep, she tries to march, and when she tires she stops to drink in the landscape, blocking off certain images that please her, framing them in her mind: silvery-grey fences tilting this way and that, like sure-handed strokes of lead on a pure white page; distant buildings in a rainbow of muted colours strung across the horizon like faraway laundry frozen stiff. "Papa," she murmurs, dredging her father up to accompany her, his green plaid scarf wrapped round his neck, his lucky cap that failed him jaunty as ever, his melton coat wide open, billowing like he's set to sail.

"It's good you're home where you belong, girl," he says, and she wants so much to believe it's true. "Remember what I always told you," he goes on, "your imagination can take you anywhere. It's the ultimate getaway."

Warm tears cut a path down Anna Marie's frozen cheeks. She wonders for the millionth time if her father had been swept overboard as the fishermen maintained, or if he'd taken off with their assistance and was at this moment basking in a warmer climate, charming people, ticking them off, living the life of a rogue and a runabout as her mother has long ago decided is the case. But no, it's worse than death and she cannot bear to believe it.

She stops to rearrange her sketchbook, takes it from the crook of her arm, raises it high in front of her, uses it as a shield against the bitter wind.

GIRLS IN THE SUNLIGHT

You leave your office earlier than you generally do and happen upon several of your mother's employees talking in the stairwell two flights down. Their hushed voices drift upwards. Someone asks, "So what's the son like? *Nigel*, I believe his name was."

The speaker has got to be the guy your mother just hired. She'd taken him around following his interview, introduced him to staff. His name is Tim or Tom.

You stand perfectly still, hear the snickering at the mention of your name, then listen to a conversation similar to those you've heard snippets of any number of times, those that come back to you at night when you're trying to sleep. You're faulted now for being aloof, uncaring, chummier with the deadbeats that end up at WeCollect than with colleagues. Then, Jen in accounting, or maybe Sue the receptionist, credits you for at least not being on the make.

"I wouldn't give him any points there."

This voice belongs to Perry, the fellow your mother seems to be taking under her wing, grooming for a new position, some kind of personal assistant.

"His wife is young, a real looker," Perry goes on. "You'll meet her at the Christmas party." He describes Maureen as a bit vague but sweet. Doe-eyed, he says. Milky skin. Nice long legs.

Perry, at office parties, spends most of the time chatting up Maureen while you serve as bartender, not that you mind serving as bartender; it's preferable to standing around making polite small talk with people who later use your words as fodder for their amusement.

"It's hard to imagine," someone else says, "but rumour has it Nigel's a great shortstop in a pretty good league."

"You've got to be kidding," says Maureen's schmoozer. "Nigel Kingsley's an athlete?"

"I'm serious."

You hold your breath, listen keenly, hoping for more.

"The first baseman is engaged to my sister, and he says that while Nigel may be getting on and is nothing special at bat, he's amazing in double-play situations."

Who *is* this speaking?

You review the possibilities. It would help to know who has a sister and who doesn't. Just as you lean toward the railing to sneak a peek down, the door to the outside opens and the voices spill out into the parking lot, everyone wishing everyone else a great holiday weekend. You descend the stairs feeling light-footed, happy almost. You had no idea you had a reputation for being a great shortstop.

It's early Labour Day morning. You're asleep and in the throes of a heady dream when you become vaguely aware of an insistent warbling sound, aware too that the sound is the real world beckoning. The woman straddling you in your dream does not respond to what you hear, but continues to grip your wrists and ride you, and you're almost there…almost…

Maureen nudges you, really jabs an elbow into your side. "Would you, for Christsake, answer the frigging phone! Or turn it off before it wakes up the boys."

Who the…? You thrust off the phantom lover, pick up the receiver, but can't quite muster hello. "Yeah," you say.

It's your mother and she's actually crying.

"What's up?" You try to recall if you've ever before heard your mother cry. "Mom, what is it?"

You feel the fog slowly lift, and something else too, excitement or panic, and a sudden urge to pee. "Are you okay? Should I be calling 911?"

"No, you shouldn't," she sobs angrily. "If I'd wanted an ambulance I'd have called for one, wouldn't I?"

"In that case, I need a minute. I'll be right with you, I promise." You hand the phone to Maureen, who's propped up on a pillow.

"What...what is it?" she asks.

"Take care of Ma a minute, will you?"

She gives you a funny look, a look that says *You've got to be kidding. Your mother needs care?*

As you make your way to the bathroom you realise the woman in your dream was not a stranger after all, but Louise, the woman before Maureen — the only other woman...ten years your senior, as driven sexually as ever, at least in your dream.

You relieve your bladder, flush the toilet, curse the noisy plumbing, and return to the bedroom to find Jason standing there.

"Are you guys up?" Jason asks.

"What does it look like?" You figure your son ought to know by now that once you're up, you're up.

Now Tyler appears in the doorway and says goody, everyone is up.

You tell them to go have some cereal, then take the phone from Maureen, who whispers, "It's about Betty. She was in a car accident last night and died an hour ago."

"God, no kidding," you say, blown away by the news. Betty was your mother's favourite person on the planet.

"No kidding," Maureen assures you. "Betty's bought the farm."

She removes the extra pillow supporting her, snuggles into the bedding and closes her eyes. "Out," she says to the boys, who haven't budged. They want to know who Betty was. "Out," she repeats, and they ask again, "Whooo, who died?"

"You know who Betty is. *Was,* "Maureen tells them. "She was your cousin, the angel of mercy. Now, out."

Jason says, "Oh, her."

"I'll be along soon," you call after your sons. There's something in the way they turn to leave that catches at your heart. They look like two little replicas of yourself as a child. Loneliness envelops them.

"For god's sakes, talk to your mother."

Maureen doesn't like your mother, but lately, she scarcely misses an opportunity to imply that you're failing in the most fundamental ways. Her don't-give-a-damn attitude about Betty's death really rankles. Betty was, at very least, way too young to die.

"Ma?… Gee…"

What else can you say…? As always, talking to your mother feels like walking a fine, invisible line. "I'm sorry to hear about Betty. I know you were…very fond of her."

"Fond of her?"

Your mother tells you she's *fond* of any number of things — mangoes, chocolate — that Betty was her godchild. As she struggles to accurately describe her feelings, you remember with more than a little resentment that Betty has always served as a ready example of what you and your sister could become if you'd only make the effort. Betty never forgot a birthday or cancelled an outing, and was, in your mother's words, "a real trouper," whipping up sandwiches or pastries or salads for fifty people with little notice, allowing herself to be dragged off to all kinds of events, all this to satisfy your mother's conviction that civic-mindedness is a business tool not to be overlooked.

You run a finger through the dust on the night table and consider the likelihood that Betty's husband will gradually extricate himself from the family now, from his association with WeCollect. You won't blame him at all.

"Are you there?" your mother asks, and you assure her *yes*, yes of course. You see your cousin lying dead, remember the way she used to lay a clammy hand on your arm and say something nice about you, the gesture, you suspected, less about her affection for you than her own deep need for approval, approval you'd withheld, something you regret now. But at least you'd been courteous to Betty, unlike Stephanie, whose jealousy and dislike were palpable.

You remember now that you have a ball game later this morning, wonder if Betty's death means you'll have to opt out, wonder what opting out would prove, really, so you decide that, unless your mother has some plan up her sleeve, you'll go to the game. You have a reputation to keep up.

"You haven't even asked how she died," your mother says, always thinking the worst of you.

"How *did* she die?" you ask, then you listen to the account: Betty had been on her way home after a late night visit to the palliative care unit, and the driver of a passing truck veered into her or she veered into him. At any rate, she lost control.

Your mother pauses to blow her nose. "It's eerie, really," she says. "Betty'd been so upset about what happened to Diana, and then this happens, so similar, really."

"You've lost me. Diana who?"

"Princess Di, who the hell else?"

"What about her?"

"Don't tell me you haven't heard!"

Your mother's tone is more than incredulous. A thrill runs through it. You hear her rein it in. "It's terribly unfortunate," she sighs. "She died in a car accident early yesterday morning. The entire world has been talking of little else. Where in heaven's name have you been?"

You explain that you and Maureen and the kids were up at the lake closing up the cabin, that Maureen had had enough roughing it for the season.

Actually, Maureen had wanted to keep the cabin open until after the first snowfall as a getaway for you and the boys. The idea had had a certain appeal, but this attempt of hers to get out of family time had made you uneasy, so you told her you'd had enough too.

"The Princess Di thing, how did that come about?" you ask, and your mother tells you about Diana's late-night dinner at the Paris Ritz with Dodi al-Fayed, the Mercedes speeding through the streets, the photographers in pursuit, the mysterious crash in the tunnel. When she runs out of steam, you say, "Well, I'll be damned. I can only imagine what the tabloids will be making of this."

"What's up?" Maureen asks sleepily. She digs her toes into your side. "What's this about Di?"

You ask your mother to hold on a sec and, cupping your hand over the mouthpiece, tell Maureen that if she's awake enough to care about Di she should consider making the boys' breakfast. By now she ought to know that you hate it when the kids are left to forage. It reminds you of when you were a kid. Your father was never around and your mother's idea of parenting was to issue orders from her home-office doorway. With Maureen staring at you icily, you get back to your mother, apologise for keeping her waiting, tell her you really need to go and see to the boys.

It's true that you're trying to escape her grief, but also, Maureen hasn't budged and the boys really could use some supervision. You mention again that you're sorry about Betty, tell your mother to take all the time she needs, that you'll see to things at work. "For the next little while," you add, lest she worry you're overstepping your position.

"Okay, Nigel, I'll let you go since you're itching to."

But she doesn't let you go before mentioning that as soon as she has the details about visitation and funeral plans she'll let you know. "I want you and Stephanie to make yourselves fully available," she says, sounding crisp and businesslike, very much like her old self.

"What about Maureen?"

"What about her?"

"Well, you know, being a part of things?"

"*And* Maureen then. I didn't say *not* Maureen. Now remember to call Russ soon, to offer your condolences."

You tell her that you don't always have to be prompted, that you'll call this afternoon.

"Call this morning," she says, and then, as though as an afterthought, "In case Russ is still talking nonsense about the accident being a possible suicide, I can assure you it was no such thing." She goes on to say that she spoke to Betty two days ago and they'd had the usual upbeat chat. "I know my goddaughter," she says, "and she has always been a real credit to the family and would never do anything that might tarnish our reputation."

You try to think of a comeback to this, but can't. You know that if you wanted to kill yourself you'd feel obliged to make it look like an accident. Your mother is still going on about suicide, how cowardly etc., but she's winding down. "Not a word to anyone, you hear? I want that notion laid to rest," she says.

You start to assure her, but realise she's gone and you're talking to yourself.

"What did you mean by *What about Maureen*?" Maureen asks, and you're happy to explain that you want her to feel included in funeral plans, not excluded like when your father died. You watch for your thoughtfulness to register, but it doesn't seem to. "I liked your dad," she says. "But this is Betty, so go ahead and exclude me all you want. What about Di?"

"Di, Di, Di." You can't help feeling annoyed with Maureen's preoccupation with Diana. There was a time when you felt sorry for the princess, the starry-eyed girl who'd blundered out of one dysfunctional family into another one — and even before that, when she and Charles first dated, when she was working at a nursery school and the photo of her holding a toddler was circulated throughout the world. How sweet and innocent she looked despite her skirt being almost transparent on account of the backlighting. But then as time went on you decided she was not sweet and innocent at all. She was a complicated character and really quite a crafty manipulator, blabbing about her husband to the media, fishing for sympathy, setting a horrible example for the young women who admired her. You aren't glad she's dead, but you aren't heartbroken either. You open a bureau drawer and rummage for socks without holes. There's no underwear either. You think of Diana, the odd feeling of empowerment the knowledge of her death has given you.

"You have clean underwear but it's still in the dryer." Maureen stretches, yawns, complains about being dog-tired, then hauls herself out of bed, raises the blind and begins tidying the pillows and sheets, asks again what your mom had been saying about Di and the tabloids, she asks if Di's suing or what. She levels a look at you, her eyes probing, then cruel. "I know that smirk. You're taking me for some kind of ride. God, what an asshole."

She's standing next to the window with the morning sun behind her, her shapely silhouette discernible through the gown. You're tempted to approach her, manoeuvre her back to bed, but no, the boys might come up, and besides, maybe your mind would drift to Betty and the accident, and Maureen is sick of your excuses when you can't finish what you start, is already convinced she just doesn't turn you on anymore, which is not the case. Besides, she's just called you an asshole, not exactly a come-on, and Lester said it was paramount to pay attention to the signals.

During the process of drawing up a payment schedule for Lester, who'd been overly optimistic about a business venture, you managed to learn quite a lot about how to avoid marital discord. Lester, now in a solid twenty-year marriage, had been married before. He said that much of the time he wasn't present in his first marriage. He was *there*, but not present. You figure that maybe you've been guilty of that too, not really listening, and not really being there for Maureen.

"So Stef's back?" Maureen asks.

You tell her that *yes*, your sister is back from vacation. You pull on yesterday's socks. "She's back, but in mourning," you say.

"Yeah, right."

Maureen assumes, as you knew she would, that you're being sarcastic, because if there's one thing for sure, it's that Stephanie will *not* mourn Betty. Maureen tells you that she knows it isn't nice to speak ill of the dead, but … Then she goes on to say that it was sort of ghoulish the way Betty volunteered to help strangers die, and considering she had a family to take care of, one had to wonder if she was trying to win some kind of medal or what.

You remember something nice Betty said to you once. She said you had a real way with kids. After that, you'd tried to muster up a little interest in other people's children too, not just your own. Yes, Betty had been okay. It was hardly her fault your mother had tuned in to her insecurities and milked them for all they were worth, making her a tool and a weapon. You ask Maureen if, say, Betty had helped AIDS patients or land mine victims, would she have admired her then?

Maureen doesn't reply. She holds up the end of the bedspread. "Would you *please* lend a hand with this?"

"Oh sure, sorry."

"Every damned day you say you're sorry," Maureen grumbles, "so how sorry can you be?"

You wonder if this is true. Anyway, you know you *are* sorry, sorry your mind darts all over the place in a futile attempt to avoid dwelling on issues at work, not just the problems with staff and your mother, but on the misery of the job itself, putting the screws to people whose lives are already in tatters. You only stay because you're too gutless to leave, and because if your mother ever steps aside you can make changes — make the business more about financial counselling than just a money grab, the kind of company your sons might like to join one day.

"Stef really is in mourning," you say to Maureen. "But you're right. Not for Betty. Turns out that while we were away, Princess Di … Oh, how should I put it? … Bought the farm." You repeat the story your mother told you about Diana's accident, your tone matter-of-fact, but your heart is pounding.

"You're making this up," Maureen says, but the way she sinks down onto the bed suggests she knows it's true.

You place your hand on her shoulder as if to comfort her, then, feeling deliciously wicked, leave the room. As you descend the stairs, you see yourself fleeing and know you ought to go back, that this behaviour is no way to build the loving relationship Lester held out as completely attainable. You expect to hear Maureen's footsteps behind you, her cries for further details, but this doesn't happen. You stop, consider going back to her, but then change your mind when you hear her talking on the phone — to Stephanie, or one of her other friends, pop culture addicts, all of them.

Joining the boys in the kitchen, you find yourself in the middle of a volley of Cheerios. Instead of lecturing your sons on having respect for food, as you feel inclined to do initially, you scoop up some cereal from the floor and get in on the game, taking careful aim, ducking away from the line of fire. This is the scene Maureen encounters when she enters the kitchen in search of coffee. Her eyes are puffy, her face blotchy from crying. She screeches, "How can you goof around at a time like this?"

You're flooded with a sense of shame, feel your dead cousin there in the room, a witness to your horseplay.

The boys, too, become instantly sombre. Maureen tells them about Princess Diana, that William and Harry's mother has died, that Wills and Harry are never going to see her again, not *ever*.

She gathers Jason and Tyler into the folds of her dressing gown and bestows tearful kisses on their foreheads. It's an appalling spectacle. "What about Betty's kids?" you want to know, stepping in to loosen Maureen's grip on the boys, pulling them aside. "Treena and Paula are never going to see their mother again either, and they could actually benefit from our sympathy."

Maureen glares at you malevolently, then turns away to make the coffee, tells you she hopes you aren't planning to run off to your silly ball game and leave her saddled with the kids.

"I think Betty wouldn't want me to let my teammates down," you say, realising it's probably even true. "Why don't you and the boys come too? ... Get your mind off things."

"I'd rather have my share of the holiday alone," Maureen tells you angrily, prompting Jason to slip his hand into yours.

"I'll come, Dad," he says.

Tyler is still deeply attached to Maureen and attuned to her moods. He remains by his mother's side, looking pensive. "Do I have to go?" he asks, breaking into a whimper.

Maureen tells him yes, then caves in to the tears and says she supposes not.

The game is just getting under way when you arrive with Jason at the ballpark. You blame the Princess of Wales and her untimely demise for being late, mention the stupid argument with Maureen.

You nod to the first baseman, someone you've always dismissed as immature, clownish. Now, having learned this fellow regards you as a great shortstop, it seems he's more significant than anyone else on the team. In fact, as the game progresses it feels more and more that you're performing as much for the first baseman as you are for Jason, who sits quietly in the bleachers, away from the other youngsters, seemingly paying no attention at all. You feel off your game, distracted by Betty's death. It's so hard to fathom really, that she'll never again be in the stands cheering you on — not that she came regularly, but, unlike Maureen, she never let a season pass without putting in a few appearances.

"How come you stopped playing?" Jason asks when the game is over, and you concede it was a short game, assure him there were nine innings. It had been amazingly fast-paced. Three up, three down, three up, three down. Seldom a hit that didn't go foul, and only one run.

"Did you really lose, Dad?"

"Why do you have to ask? Weren't you watching, Jason? I thought baseball was your favourite sport."

You hand him the glove — Jason loves to carry your glove.

"Baseball *is* my favourite, but my stomach hurts."

"Are you hungry, maybe?"

"Maybe… I don't know. I wish you won, Dad."

You explain that sometimes the team that plays the best doesn't win. You say this because it's true, and also for the benefit of the pitcher, nearby. Other players chime in in agreement, playing down the loss.

The pitcher says nothing about the game at all, says he'd had a disagreement with his wife too, about Diana. "What I'd like to know," he says angrily, "is what kind of mother is out tooling around Paris in the middle of the night with the world's most notorious playboy?"

Had everyone just been going through the motions of the game, biding their time until they could talk about Di's accident, the events that led up to it, all its ramifications, their wives' mysterious grief? It quickly becomes apparent that that's probably the case. Perhaps if you hadn't mentioned Diana when you arrived it would have been a better game.

You use Jason's stomachache as a reason for rushing off, verify the date of the next game, take your son's hand and, heading for the car, hear someone say, not to you but to someone else, Well, if you ask me, the way she died was the logical conclusion to the life she lived.

This makes sense to you, not that you'd repeat it to Maureen. She'd accuse you of saying Di got what she asked for, and that isn't the same thing at all… Or is it?

What bugs you most about Diana is not Diana herself but that Maureen has identified with her, has tried to draw parallels between her life and that of a princess. Maureen, who grew up in a row house in the semi-industrial part of town near the ballpark, has actually referred to Diana as a *soul mate* and made a list of all they had in common: both she and Diana had married an older man who carried a torch for another woman; had two boys; had husbands who often dismissed them as crazy.

You have to admit, you have sort of carried a torch for Louise, but it wasn't like you ever held Louise up as an example or anything, or even mentioned her at all. Maureen had heard about Louise from Stephanie, then asked you about her, grilled you actually, then complained that your response came too quickly and your description — self-confident, unaffected, funny, wise — was excessively flattering.

One of the things you had liked about Louise was that she'd always urged you to regard the agency as an employment option, not an obligation. Not that you believed her entirely because she made getting out of the family business sound so much simpler than you knew it would be. But it had been sort of therapeutic just to hear that maybe you could go back to school and get into some other line of work.

Still, you knew your relationship with Louise hadn't been what Lester would call a "give and take" relationship between equals. She gave advice but didn't need any herself. She had a full life: a marriage, a career, and you on the side. For a time you hadn't minded the situation. It meant having little in the way of responsibility outside your job. But it got to feeling creepy, and besides, you dreamed of having a wife and family. Why had you tagged along for sixteen years, until she finally met the man who rendered you, and her husband, fully expendable? Why did she still show up in your dreams?

You try to recall the dream you were having this morning when your mother called, how it began, what it was about.

It took place up at the lake, that much you recall. It was night in the dream. The boys were in bed, and Maureen wasn't there.

But what was the actual substance of the dream?

You remember leaving the cabin and going down to the lake for an evening dip — something you often do. You remember the stillness, the moonlight, the water lapping against the wharf, the smell of a campfire somewhere, all this recorded by your brain in real life and played back ... so amazing really, the vividness of the dream. Your brain had recorded your fears too, such silly fears for a middle-aged man. But when you go for an evening dip, your imagination gets the better of you and you have to push back the notion that someone is about to grab your legs and pull you under. Sometimes you imagine sinister characters hiding in the woods, watching your movements. In the dream you experienced these familiar concerns, but there was a new worry: the boys were alone, and you too were alone and separated from them.

No, it wasn't a pleasant dream at all. There'd been something ominous about the sex with Louise, too, which took place on the shore as you were returning to the cabin. Louise had been there suddenly. You turned your back to her, but she followed you, overtaking you. You surrendered to the power she had over you, but not out of any real desire, rather to test your ability to satisfy her.

Driving home from the game, you decide you'll surprise Maureen and pick up some take-out food — save her the trouble of making lunch. It's unlikely she'll have started preparations yet, since you're almost an hour earlier than usual.

"What'll I get, Jason, pizza or chicken?"

"I don't care. Pizza, I guess."

You wonder if Tyler has been sent elsewhere to find amusement. It seems to you that Maureen, who plays the martyr as a stay-at-home mom, makes a career of sloughing off the kids. You don't understand how she can spend so much time reading magazines and watching TV talk shows, garbage, in your estimation, but you try not to think of it that way now, try instead to think of her entertainment choices as simply different than yours, and for that you can thank Lester.

The best of luck, son, Lester said when you escorted him to the door, the word *son* moving you almost to tears, but you resisted the impulse to bestow a bear hug on the man. I want to thank you for making the terms of this financial mess of mine doable, Lester went on. I was worried I'd get some hard-nosed chiseller like that boss of yours who quizzed me on my first visit.

No problem, you said, pumping his hand, knowing the terms *would* be a problem — for you, not him — when your mother, the hard-nosed chiseller, found out. You thanked Lester, too, there in the doorway, which caused several people in the outer office to turn and look, to see what the outpouring of gratitude was about.

"Goody, pizza," Tyler says when you and Jason step through the door.

"Dad lost," Jason announces grimly, so you tell your sons you'd rather lose a close game than win a cakewalk, something you know isn't true.

"Where's Mommy?" you ask, taking the pizza to the kitchen.

"Having a bath," Tyler says. He stands in front of the TV, the sound turned down to a mere whisper. On the screen are mounds of flowers at the palace gate, close-ups of cards with hand-drawn hearts, tender outpourings of undying love.

You reach behind him and turn the TV off. "She left you down here alone?"

"Gary was here but he had to go home."

"Mom's going to kill you," Jason says, unaware that his own comment is far more damning.

"So, who's Gary?"

You feel like you do when a ball's coming at you low, hard, and fast, the kind of wild ball that's likely to hit the dirt and veer off in godknowswhat direction. You get four dinner plates from the cupboard. "Do you have a new friend, Tyler, or ... has Mommy got a new friend?"

"He isn't new. He's Mr Norris," Tyler says meekly. His thumb goes into his mouth and he crosses one leg over the other.

"Remember what I told you about sucking your thumb?" Your voice is hostile, unreasonable, almost unrecognisable as your own. "You don't want your teeth to stick out, do you?"

Tyler puts both hands behind his back, shifts his weight from foot to foot. "You know what, Dad?"

"What?"

"Mr Norris said he was really sorry about Diana, that she was special."

"Special, eh?" You slam a cupboard door and tell Tyler to stop jiggling, that if he has to go to the bathroom, he'd better get going, watch him bolt from the room and disappear down the hall. You yell after him, "I've had enough of your pissing, you hear?" Then softly, apologetically, "Hurry back, Ty, there's a piece of pizza waiting for you, Champ," because it isn't the boys' fault that they know more than you do about whatever it is that's been going on.

Gary Norris, of all people. When you phoned to arrange driver training for Maureen, Norris assured you that you were doing the right thing by opting for a professional, that nothing could be more dangerous to a marriage than one spouse attempting to teach the other to drive. To think, the sneaky goddamned weasel has actually been creeping around behind your back, has actually been in your house.

Jason takes his place at the table and sits up very straight. "Are you worried, Dad?" he asks.

"Worried?" Your voice exudes contempt, but as you lift a slice of pizza from the box onto your son's plate your hand trembles and betrays you. "I'm not happy right now, okay? But don't worry. This is not about you boys. It's just about Mommy and me."

You think about Betty, what it must have been like for her behind the wheel, even if the accident was no accident: a merciless outcome barrelling toward her, the life she'd previously known beyond retrieval. No, you think, *no*, this can't be happening.

"Don't cry, Daddy," Jason says sobbing, picking at the cheese.

In the silence of the kitchen, you listen to the water gurgle from the upstairs tub down the drain, tumble with abandon through the pipes — down and down, away and away — contemplate how news of your troubled marriage will be received by your mother, people at work.

You imagine Maureen stepping onto the bath mat and reaching for the towel. The mother of your boys. Your wife. The same girl-woman who'd been walking outside the ballpark eight years ago when the ball you'd slugged made it over the fence for your one and only home run. Looking for this? she'd said, retrieving and holding up the ball when you went looking for it to keep as a souvenir. You told her it was the bottom of the ninth, that your team had been losing but the score was now tied. Things were looking very promising, you said, meaning more than the game. When you asked if she'd stay and go for coffee later, she turned, looked back over her shoulder to the row house where she still lived with her parents, and said, Um ... I guess, her face breaking into a shy smile, the memory of which still stirs affection and longing for the girl you'd imagined Maureen to be that day, the girl who never was, really, yet whose body is there in the room above you, vivid in your mind: lush, sweet-smelling — like fresh-cut grass on a warm summer day.

HOW TO COOK A GROUSE

When you were growing up, you dreamed of seaside holidays, park safaris, rented cabins in the woods, places your friends went to on vacation. But your parents weren't like your friends' parents; yours preferred to put their hard-earned money into the house rather than into hyped-up amusements. Your parents professed a belief in the simple pleasures in life.

At the top of the list of simple pleasures was going for drives, *touring,* your parents called these family outings that occurred without fanfare two or three times a year. "Never mind where we're going, you'll see when we get there," your father would say, words that came to mean it wasn't going to be any place special. He did all the driving, while your mother, in the passenger seat next to him, retrieved things from the glove compartment whenever necessary — his maps, sunglasses, antacid tablets — and after what seemed like an eternity she dispensed sandwiches, crackers or cookies, juice from concentrate, always made with that extra bit of water.

Settled in the back seat, you and Freddy played card games or worked on puzzles, exchanged riddles and such, but in your memory now it's Barbie and GI Joe you relied on most to help pass the time. This was especially true in the winter, or if the weather was chilly or wet, because then your father would simply drive to any town or city within an hour or two, and there he'd seek out broad quiet streets in upscale neighbourhoods so he and your mother — and you and your brother, supposedly — could soak up the splendour.

While your parents gaped at the houses and speculated on the lives within, you dressed Barbie for the beach, disco dancing, dinner dates. Freddy and GI Joe fought off assailants, thwarted their diabolical plans to take you hostage. You didn't try to follow your parents' conversations, nonetheless you couldn't help but absorb certain information: a truly fine home had to be stately not sprawling; there was a certain elegance to leaded glass windows; portals said a lot about the people within, whether they were welcoming, reserved, or stand-offish. "Oh look, a rotunda," your mother would say every now and then — she was wild about rotundas — and you'd sit up and take notice, claim to like them too. Your brother was never one to suck up. He hated rotundas and portals, and ordered GI Joe to search out and destroy leaded glass windows. The sounds he made with his mouth, sounds of heavy artillery and destruction, were muted, of course. "Don't you just hate coming here?" he'd say in a whisper, and you, always worried your parents might be tuned in to your response, claimed you didn't mind. You stayed focussed on dressing Barbie, mixing and matching, helping her dodge bullets whenever Freddy and GI Joe became vexed by your compliant attitude.

Not that all outings were as miserable as this, no. In the summer, or on fine spring or autumn days, your father would take to country roads. On these trips Barbie and GI Joe spent most of the time looking skyward through the back window while you and Freddy counted or simply observed the grazing cattle and horses, or searched the landscape for whatever your parents were scouting for — rocks deemed to be the right shape and size to pry out of the ground, a certain kind of bush or sapling to haul back to your humble suburban property. Your parents had no qualms whatever about removing these things from the waysides. They felt they'd paid for them through their taxes, so even Freddy, when he was younger, co-operated. As he got older though, he refused to take part anymore, to be gawked at by passers-by. He began to rebel against everything, became a delinquent, a shame and a heartbreak for your parents.

You, on the other hand, never rebelled, not as a youngster, not as a teen, not as an adult. You've tried to make up for your brother, to do your parents proud, and for the last week you've been doing them proud in Scotland. You and your husband, Argyle, are touring, real touring, mostly in the Southern Uplands. Right now you're at his Aunt Beitris McInnis's summer house — the McInnises being Argyle's mother's side of the family. You're in a drawing room painted robin's egg blue, your brother's favourite colour — the colour of his lucky marble when the two of you were kids. You don't know why, but you find yourself thinking about Freddy on this trip, more than you have in years. A young man begging on a street in Glasgow had looked just like him, and now here's a bronze sculpture on Beitris's mantel, a lad with a petulant stance, a dead ringer for Freddy.

Above the mantel, you realise, is the painting Argyle's mother had mentioned prior to the trip, the one she had expected to inherit along with a share in this cottage, a portrait of Alastair McInnis, your husband's stodgy-looking great-great-grandfather, and his plump, elaborately coiffed wife.

There's not a single photograph in the room. No curios of any sort. There are orchids, slews of them by the windows, and several other sculptures besides the one that reminds you of your brother. There are chunky crystal highball glasses too, emptied by Argyle's aunt and Angus McCabe, her invited guest, not you and Argyle. On the last leg of your trip you've dropped in unannounced, more or less. That is, Argyle called just one village away to say he was in the neighbourhood.

"Thalia's boy," Beitris said upon hearing his voice. "Come, I guess, since you're … *where*?"

Argyle related this to you as you'd made your way up the stone walk to his aunt's front door. He also mentioned the guest, so you arrived feeling like a party-crasher. "For god's sake, don't apologise," he said as he reached for the brass knocker. When the door opened, there stood a silver-haired version of his mother. His aunt is actually a year or so younger than his mother, but Thalia goes to great lengths to defy her age. "I see you found your way," Beitris said, by way of hello, then she ushered you into the drawing room and introduced you to her friend, her former tennis partner. As far as you know, Beitris has never married.

"You've timed your trip well, Angus," the guest says now. "I expect you've seen grouse on the menus, have you? Fresh grouse? Did you have it, I hope? It would be a shame not to while you're here." Angus is big and beefy and quite impossible to imagine on a tennis court.

"Uh … no, I haven't seen grouse on the menus."

Argyle looks to you, so you concur but add that you haven't been studying menus very closely, that you've been eating salad and soup mostly — food easy to digest because travel has put you a bit out of sorts. Not that travel has anything to do with your digestion problems. No, your queasy stomach is pure nerves. Argyle has fallen in love with a twenty-two-year-old intern and every indication is that he has no real interest in keeping the marriage alive. The trip had been the marriage counsellor's idea. The counselling was something you'd sought out. Argyle had tagged along for a few sessions.

"You're the picture of health, my dear," Angus tells you, "not the least bit *peely-wally*. I said to myself when you came through the door: Argyle, you're a lucky man."

Argyle laughs awkwardly. "She's not too shabby, is she? And quite a brick too."

A *brick*? What could he possibly mean? You're a wreck, have taken a leave of absence from your job at the antique shop to focus on holding your family together.

"I can't imagine grouse being hard to digest," Beitris says. She looks to Angus and he nods his agreement. They're seated on fine old armchairs with cabriole legs and scroll feet across the room from where you and Argyle sit — on a love seat, of all things.

"Excuse my ignorance, but what's so special about grouse? Isn't it rather like duck?" Argyle's question hangs there a moment.

"What's so special? Duck?" Angus echoes, his tone incredulous. "Well, for one thing, there's only one *red* grouse in the world. *Lagopus lagopus scoticus*, and it's endemic to Britain, found mostly in Yorkshire and here in Scotland."

"I'm surprised your parents haven't told you about grouse," Beitris puts in. She explains that it's the first game bird to come into season, on the twelfth of August — or *Glorious Twelfth*, as it's called — which heightens anticipation for those who hunt.

"Ah," says Argyle. To see him leaning attentively toward his aunt, no one would dream he's heard nothing but nasty things about her all his life. His visit is meant to torture her, make her feel guilty for doing his mother out of a share in the property. You hadn't wanted to take part, said you'd prefer to go for one last hike or to check out the village, but Argyle had been adamant. "First things first. We'll make it short. I'm surprised you're not curious to meet her."

In truth, you were a bit curious. Even after almost sixteen years of marriage, Argyle's family, friends, and relatives are a source of wonder and dismay, and at times entertainment. Besides, when he mentioned visiting his aunt, the trip was almost over and the quest to save your marriage seemed all but lost. It occurred to you: suppose a miracle lay in store, suppose it was about to happen at Beitris's and you opted out? You knew you were grasping at straws, but you were willing to grasp.

"We don't hunt anything — other than misplaced keys and sunglasses," you say now to Angus and Beitris, then, hoping to wean them off the topic of killing grouse, you tell them you can understand, though, the desire to be outdoors. You praise the Scottish countryside: the rolling hills, the heather, the thistles. "They're your national emblem, I believe, thistles," you say, knowing they are.

"Aye," says Angus, "the thistle is our emblem, but it's the heather shoots that are the main food source for the grouse." He pulls a pipe from his jacket pocket and waves it about. "Any objections?" he asks.

Neither you nor Argyle smoke but neither do you object.

"He does enjoy his pipe, poor man," Beitris says, and everyone watches in silence as Angus fills it to his liking. "Now what was I saying?" she asks. "I was saying something, wasn't I ...?" She looks to you, to Argyle, to Angus.

You wonder, had Beitris been saying anything? She'd said something about the glorious twelfth, but your mind had been on your children. You'd been wondering whether or not Beitris knew of Mark's and Julia's existence.

"Perhaps you were *about* to say something," Angus suggests. He assures her he was the last to speak. "I asked if I might smoke."

"I mean before that."

"Before that Marjorie mentioned thistles."

"And before that there was talk of grouse," Argyle puts in. "And I've been wondering, how do you *cook* a grouse? Marjorie would probably tell you I'm quite adept at cooking my own goose, but grouse ...?" He turns and gives you just the slightest smile, to let you know he's having some fun, he's mocking them. Is he mocking you too? You decide he's not, and while you wish he wouldn't mock anyone, he seems to be attempting to share something with you, and this ignites a tiny spark of hope.

"How to cook a grouse, the proverbial question," Angus says. "It depends on the bird, you see. On its age. How long it's been hung."

"*If* it's been hung," corrects Beitris.

"If, indeed," agrees Angus. "Like most people, I like my bird straight off the moor and very young. Damned if I bother to hang it all. I roast it: four rashers streaky bacon draped over its breast, nice knob of butter and cut-up apple or wad of watercress inside. High oven temperature. Quick in, quick out." He states that some people like chanterelles on the side, but a dab of red current jelly really can't be topped.

You resign yourself to the subject of grouse. Actually, you find yourself wondering what becomes of older grouse, so you ask this of Angus.

"You need to hang an older grouse. It helps to tenderise it," he explains.

"Hang it? What do you mean?"

"I mean it's hung from the neck, feathers, innards and all, hung for days sometimes, depending on the weather. It's actually decomposing, I suppose." He laughs. Even the thought of rot cannot dampen his love of grouse.

Beitris mentions offhandedly that she read an interesting recipe for old grouse just the other day. "You marinate the bird in beer and sherry," she says, "then cook it in marmalade, in a buttered casserole."

Angus winces, crinkles his nose.

"Another thing you can do with an old bird," Beitris goes on, "is to remove the breasts, wrap them in cling film, pop them in the freezer for thirty minutes or so, then slice them very thinly. This you serve with horseradish sauce."

"Raw?" you dare to ask.

"*Aye,* of course raw," says Angus, and he shares a recipe for young grouse that some Scottish cooking authority touts as a favourite.

Beitris lobs another recipe for old grouse his way, and he responds swiftly with another for young grouse.

Conceding, or having run out of recipes perhaps, Beitris sits quietly. Angus too. You check your watch, your head swimming with exit strategies.

"The French are known to *flambé* grouse," Beitris offers, lamely, but nevertheless you've missed your chance to flee.

"They would do, wouldn't they?" Angus chuckles, puffing on his pipe, implying what, that the French are more pretentious than they are? The hell they are, you think, and then you realise that it isn't just the silver hair that makes Beitris seem different than Argyle's mother, that actually, despite her obvious comforts, she hasn't any airs about her whatsoever. And anyway, what about you, you demand of yourself. You're hardly a stranger to pretension. Doesn't a part of you look forward to telling your folks about Beitris, the quaint cottage (*circa* 1675), the magnificent grounds, including a tennis court and man-made lake, the gentleman friend who hunts grouse? Doesn't it please you to know they'll use the story to answer the familiar question from their neighbours and friends: "Who's Marjorie hobnobbing with these days?"

You'll tell them about the trip when Argyle isn't around. He has the notion that your parents — and you, too — have no use for luxury, are at heart simple and content. He told you, in the early days of your marriage, that you were the only girl he'd dated who had no interest in what he had or had access to. He must have come to that conclusion because, lacking conviction that the dating would lead anywhere, you'd been almost indifferent to him and his display of wealth. But naturally, you had interest in what he had. How could you not? But how to separate your own interest from your parents' interest? One thing for sure, accepting Argyle's proposal had been more about raising yourself ever higher in their esteem than about money or love. You'd liked him, of course. There was charm in his attempts to win your affection. And you found him funny and attractive. Tall, fair, and blue-eyed, he was like you, only taller and fairer, his eyes a lighter shade of blue.

"Can you easily tell if a grouse is old or young?" Argyle asks.

"You can tell by the price!" Angus booms. "A young bird will cost four or five times more than an older one."

"As much as that," you say, but you're not thinking about grouse. You're wondering if Argyle realises what the long-term cost of switching wives would be, if he has bothered to sit down and calculate the expense of running two households. His father, not so long ago, put Argyle in charge of a fledgling company in order that he might finally grow up and be responsible and fully independent. He wouldn't be amused to find that Argyle has already found a distraction, nor would he approve of Argyle leaving his marriage, since he and Thalia have managed to endure theirs and believe that that's what one does, endure.

Again you take in the painting, the solidly married McInnises, their fleshy cheeks, all the velvet, silk, and jewels, the self-satisfaction. As with so many portraits, the whole point seems to be to document the status of the subjects. You find yourself wondering what's wrong with such people, what makes them need to puff themselves up and put themselves out there like that?

But are they all that different than you are?

Angus is still waxing eloquent on the subject of grouse. He explains that while the price is a pretty good indication of the bird's age, one should still look for a pliable breast bone and beak, and feet without nails, the hallmarks of a young grouse. And with that he begins to rise. "I think, old girl, I should run along now and let you have some time alone with your kin."

"Please don't, there's no need," says the old girl of sixty or thereabouts.

"Actually, we really must be on our way," Argyle tells them. "As I mentioned on the phone, it's just a hello. Our flight leaves in the morning and we have things to do yet."

"Very well then," says Beitris, unable to entirely suppress the pleasure of your imminent departure, and you can hardly blame her. How odd it must have seemed: the son and daughter-in-law of an estranged sibling just showing up out of the blue. When you had asked Thalia how long the estrangement had been, she'd been evasive, making you suspect that it went back further than the death of their uncle and the settlement of his will.

You say your good-byes to Angus, and start to thank Beitris, but having had not so much as a drink of water, you naturally flounder. "... For seeing us on such short notice," you stammer.

"Yes, well, it was quite a surprise."

Beitris excuses herself from Angus, leads the way to the foyer, and opens the door. Down the walk, an orange cat grooms itself in the sun. "I'm going to tell you something," Beitris says. "Yes, I feel I must." And then, with her back to the fresh air and sunshine that beckon you, she tells Argyle that she had known his father long before his mother had. She and Jack had been engaged in fact, but then Thalia came home from her travels and was in need of some amusement. "She had a certain flair," Beitris admits, and Argyle interjects, says his mother still has it, can even yet sail into a room and brighten it.

"Yes, well, she sailed into a lot of rooms," Beitris tells him. "She popped up absolutely everywhere. It was quite astounding how recklessly and relentlessly she pursued Jack, how publicly she humiliated me."

Tears spring to her eyes, but she does not back off or hasten the two of you out the door. She tells Argyle that his father had not been the handsomest man, nor even the brightest or wealthiest, but that he'd been the one for her, they'd had a circle of mutual friends, shared such a rapport and yes, even passion, so naturally she kept expecting him to set Thalia straight, had trusted he would.

You are startled by such frankness, the show of emotion from someone in Argyle's family. To think, this distraught lady is supposedly the notorious "Beastly Beitris," the greedy conniver who crept into her uncle's affection in order to push Thalia out.

You suspect now that the uncle had had his own reasons for bypassing Thalia and you'd like to respond to Beitris's disclosure with empathy, say something about betrayal, but Argyle would take it as personal, and indeed it would be. "It must have been very disappointing," you tell her.

"What I'm saying is, my withdrawal wasn't based on something trivial," Beitris says, touching your arm ever so lightly.

"And to think that, in the end, all that really came of their union was yours truly," Argyle says, probably aiming for a lighter mood in which to leave, but his levity feels inappropriate.

Down the garden walk, the cat continues to groom, raising a back leg high in the air as though doing Pilates, then it gets to its feet and approaches, enters the house, leaning into Beitris, brushing her legs with its tail. "What a beautiful cat," you tell her.

But Beitris seems not to have noticed the cat or heard your remark. She shakes her head in wonder, explains that she'd prepared tea when Argyle called, but forgot to serve it.

You chasten yourself for coming, distressing this woman, reopening old wounds. Still, you do not apologise as you feel you should, cannot quite bring yourself to disregard Argyle's earlier instruction not to. You shake hands and tell her good-bye, thank her again — really meaning it this time, say it was good to have met her. Then out on the walk, the heavy door closed behind you, you remark on the revelation, the relationship she'd had with Argyle's father.

Argyle looks puzzled, tells you it wasn't much of a revelation, that his parents had always admitted they'd met through Beitris.

"They met through her all right," you say in defence of his aunt, "they met right through her heart." But it's clear he doesn't care about Beitris. Quite the contrary. He says his mother will be pleased to hear how rattled she was.

You decide that he really is appalling, that a part of you hates him.

He pats his pockets, locates his BlackBerry, checks for messages, puts it away again, then actually opens the car door for you, although it's probably not a thoughtful gesture. He likely just forgot which side the driver is on in Scotland.

"No messages?" You slide in and wait for him to take his place behind the wheel. "It can't be easy for Candace to be sidelined, to know you're on a trip abroad with me."

"I explained it to her," Argyle says, "the importance of process. When you and I were weighing our options, considering divorce."

"You mean when *you* were considering divorce." You remind him that you'd considered yourself in a marriage and had wanted to maintain it, that while you couldn't force him to feel as you did, you could insist that he choose.

"At any rate, I'm not expecting messages from Candace." He explains that he's arranged to have her transferred, says it's something he'd prefer not to dwell on, that there's nothing to be gained.

"You prefer not to dwell on it? There's nothing to be gained?"

"I mean, it's over with her, so let's just enjoy what time we have left here," he says.

You can hardly believe it. His interest in marriage counselling had seemed completely bogus, and the trip, too, was more like a prerequisite for divorce than actual bridge building.

"Let's go check out the village," he suggests, taking off from the end of his aunt's driveway, the tires spewing gravel as in a high-jinx getaway. "Four rashers streaky bacon, a knob of butter," he says, mimicking Angus, grinning broadly, and in that smile you see your son, and your daughter too is there in the tilt of his head, the one raised brow.

Of course you don't *hate* him.

In the past, after his other, lesser affairs, this was the charm you succumbed to, the charm you've been hoping to encounter on this trip in order to succumb to it. In the past, too, you've tried to take comfort in having beat out the competition. You've pulled yourself together and carried on. You suppose you *have* been a brick.

You wonder what was behind Argyle's decision. Had his father got wind of things and given him an ultimatum? Had he realised how much he'd be losing? Or had the prospect of actually having a future with Candace killed his longing for her? This last possibility seems the most likely.

Is it possible? Are you really feeling a bit sorry for poor banished Candace?

A sigh escapes you.

"We'll make an early night of it, okay?" Argyle says, still smiling, his intentions there in his eyes in search of approval. But something has happened. Something prevents you from snapping up these cues he's giving you. You tell him to watch the road, offer a slight smile, hardly knowing if it's genuine or if it's meant to keep your options open.

At dinner you check the menu for grouse. *Game birds in season. Ask your server,* it says, but you don't ask. You've had your fill of grouse. You order quiche and salad. Argyle, for the fun of it, he says, orders *Carpaccio of Aberdeen Angus,* which is wafer-thin raw beef that he later blames for making him so bullishly amorous.

In bed, you resist his advances and do your best to explain that if the two of you are to continue on together you need to be sure, you can't go through this again.

He looks taken aback, insists *he's* sure, claims to be confused because you'd said this was what you wanted, stops short of saying he's been tricked, though that's what his expression conveys. But you manage to hold your ground for once, remind him to phone down to the desk for the wake-up call. You say goodnight.

Your last thoughts before falling asleep are of Freddy, a secret you have kept from Argyle. Your brother's descent into the world of drugs and his eventual overdose had been too disreputable to mention at the outset. You really had intended to go against your parents' advice and tell him when the time felt right, to share your loss. To think, almost sixteen years together, and the time has never felt right. You came close to telling him once, when he'd argued that you too were an only child and hardly in a position to call him spoiled.

Toward morning, you dream you're a grouse lying, feathers and all, on a platter. You know the grouse is you because the turquoise band around its leg is the ring Argyle bought you on your honeymoon when you stopped off in Egypt.

Looming over you in the dream is a man in hunting attire whose cap obscures his face. He prods your breastbone, tests for flexibility. You decide you'll disregard the likelihood of ruining his dinner, you'll get up off the platter and escape. You just *have* to. And then the dream segues into another. You're no longer a grouse on a platter. You and Argyle are in the back seat of his parents' car. Argyle is stroking Barbie's breasts while you search every nook and cranny for GI Joe.

"*Mmmm*," Argyle murmurs. He's breathing in the scent of you, nibbling your ear, your neck. He slings an arm over you and cups your left breast in his hand. He tries to roll you over to face him — you know the routine, he wants to swirl his tongue around your nipple, take it into his mouth — but you resist as you did last night. You know that in his mind he indulged you last night, allowed you to put him off, tolerated the reproof, and now he expects you to forgive him, engage in the rapture of making up. But the atmosphere of the dream lingers. The grouse still inhabits you. Of course you think of your children, your parents, the complications you will spare yourself if you just give in to Argyle. But no, the grouse won't let you forget how you strained and strained to get up off that platter.

Argyle is up on his elbow now. Evidently, you have taken too long to respond to his magnetism, your time has expired. He searches your face, searches and searches, and, yes, he sees you have gone.

Like robots, the two of you get up and shower; you get dressed and go down for breakfast. As you eat in silence, you think of your children, who'll be back from summer camp in a few days. You anticipate their homecoming, wonder if Argyle will muster some accord for their sake.

You try not to feel sad, but you do. You feel dismayed at how rapidly this situation unfolded, though you know it has been unfolding for years.

Argyle drinks the last of his coffee, tells you he'll take care of the tab and meet you in the lobby. "Drink up," he says.

You're about to point out that you've plenty of time, but he's gone, he's striding across the room toward the pretty young woman behind the reception counter. He says something that causes her to smile. You watch as she flicks her long red hair back over her shoulders, pauses to collect her wits before bringing your husband's account up on the computer screen. Then she glances up and meets his eyes.

Look away, you advise her under your breath, but of course she doesn't look away. She is held there by the essence of him, his place in the world, his will to mesmerise her.

You don't hurry. Determined to sit back and enjoy the rest of your scone and strawberry jam, you say *no* to that old familiar apprehension that tries to work its way into your being. You flag down the waitress making the rounds with the coffee pot, resolutely raise your cup.

Tooth and Nail

Albert's oysters come served in open shells on a bed of ice. Claire reaches across the table to salt them liberally, the way he likes them, and places the small seafood fork into his hand. "Bon appétit," she tells him, code words for *Okay, you're on your own. I won't intervene to help unless you ask me to.*

Surveying the restaurant to find something to divert her attention from Albert's progress — or lack of — she finds, at a nearby table of five, a man who resembles her dentist. He seems disengaged from the lively discussion going on around him. He fiddles with a spoon; his legs under the table are restless, as though there's somewhere else they're itching to get to. Tuning in to the conversation, Claire hears references to high finance: commodities, equities, capital gains... words she's become familiar with through reading the *Financial Post* to Albert. Like her dentist, this man is fiftyish. He has the same sandy hair and the same large mouth with a protruding lower lip that reminds her of a bass, a fish that is preserved and mounted on the wall behind him. It's hard to tell if he's as short as her dentist. Dr Clampton is probably five three or five four.

"Aren't you going to eat, sweetie?" Albert asks. An oyster dangles precariously from his fork. Claire can hardly bear to watch because he's about to lose it.

"My crab cakes haven't come yet," she tells him, and she thinks to herself that they'd better come soon. It's not that she's famished; it's just that Albert, even with all his difficulty seeing, can, with a bit of luck, go through a dozen oysters in no time, and once he's finished he's impatient to be on his way. Claire couldn't begin to count the number of half-eaten meals she's had to leave behind. She wonders again what the odds are that she could come all the way from Montreal to Florida and find herself in the same town and at the same restaurant as her dentist. And Sarasota is absolutely brimming with restaurants, making the likelihood even more remote. Why, even back home, where bumping into people she knows is an almost daily occurrence, she's encountered Dr Clampton only once, a couple of years ago at Albert's urologist, of all places. Dr and Mrs Clampton had an appointment to discuss Mrs Clampton's father's treatment on the same afternoon that Albert was in for a check-up. Dr Clampton had introduced Claire to his wife — a thin, nervous woman with frizzy hair, who sort of cringed as she smiled hello — but then he chose seats in the farthest corner of the room where, presumably, there'd be no obligation to engage in further conversation.

"Your crab cakes," the waitress says, and Claire forgets all about the man who can't possibly be her dentist and concentrates on catching up with Albert, who is zeroing in on the last oyster now draped over a lemon wedge. How anyone can eat raw oysters is beyond Claire.

After lunch, Claire drives Albert back to their rented condo so he can have a rest. "Lie down next to me, sweetie," he says, patting the bed.

Claire had busied herself by tidying up the place so he wouldn't ask, a trick that works sometimes. "Well," she says, "I think if we're going for a long walk on the beach later, you should…"

"You should come lie down," he insists, his tone that of a peevish child.

"I'll sit next to you and read you the newspaper." Claire takes up the paper and mentions a couple of articles that might be of interest.

There's a piece on President Clinton, his worries over the congressional elections, and another on the deregulation of the banking system.

Albert pats the bed next to him. "Stop messing with all that and come."

"All right, but you need to *really* rest," Claire tells him, cautioning him against the groping he's become famous for amongst caregivers in Montreal. Still, she no sooner lies down than he places his hand on her thigh. She reminds herself that he has had a stroke, which can undermine judgement, that he is old, that he has suffered so many setbacks and lost so much of the power he once had. She closes her eyes and tells herself, *So long as it goes no further.*

It is strange to think, lying there in Albert's bed, that she's actually known in various Montreal circles as the woman who has managed to "take in hand" the formidable Albert Stone. As if anyone could. It's true that since she's come on the scene Albert's temperament, his hygiene, and his general health have improved, but it would never occur to his son and daughters that these changes were the natural result of Claire accepting Albert's need to control, making suggestions rather than harping on and on about how impossible he is. Albert's doctors are pleased with his rejuvenation, but the children are another matter.

According to the woman who trained Claire (the woman Claire replaced, a bossy, charmless creature), Albert had been a womaniser who caused his wife, dead for several years now, much anguish. He'd been a domineering father too, which may be why his children are not exactly grateful to Claire for their father's transformation. Not only do they show no gratitude, they regard her devotion as suspect and treat her with veiled hostility. The fact that they've enlisted Albert's cook and his secretary to keep tabs on her is very galling indeed, as these two are robbing Albert left and right in petty ways, and possibly have been for years. The cook takes almost as much food home as what remains in Albert's household, and his secretary not only charges her own drycleaning to Albert but sometimes charges alterations on her brother's clothes. Claire would like nothing better than to expose the shady practices of these women, but it would be detrimental to Albert in the long run and rather like slitting her own throat. However much fun Albert might have firing them, he'd have a hard time replacing them because by now they know the routine so well, know his expectations and how to avoid raising his ire. And until replacements to his liking could be found (an unlikely proposition), Claire would be expected to fill in, and there's only so much of her to go around. So she tries to remain focused on the well-being of her employer who, at least, seems to value her. "What would I ever do without you, sweetie?" he'll say, just at some point when he's been most exasperating. Claire has to admit it must be hard for his children to witness an outsider getting the admiration and affection they themselves have been deprived of. She even wonders, supposing they weren't Albert's kids and she met them at a gallery, or theatre, or out walking, might they not all get along quite well?

The most disappointing thing about Claire's job as a caregiver and travel companion is that she experiences the places they go to as though she, too, were elderly. Lying down next to her employer, she feels his hand through her loose, lightweight slacks. Never mind the tropical heat, his hand is as cool as marble and seems to draw warmth from her body, to empty her of life itself. Still, this concession does seem to help him sleep better, which improves his mood, makes his mind sharper for their daily games of backgammon. Once he wakens, there's no hope of extending the quiet interlude that allows her a degree of rest too; he's keen to be "on the move," as he puts it, eager to take advantage of the sunshine he's paying for, pre-cancerous growths on his forehead and ears be damned. So once they're up, Claire applies as much sunscreen as he'll tolerate, finds his Tilley hat, and they're off.

Albert refuses to use a cane of any sort, let alone a white one, so Claire takes his arm to keep him steady on his feet, which, she imagines, leads people to speculate that they are a May-December couple — or a July-December couple, since Claire, at forty-six, is more than half Albert's age and past the point where she's mistaken for being younger than she is. When they hit the soft sand it's all she can do to keep Albert from having another of his tumbles. One thing she has to hand to him, he falls well, thanks to a lifetime of skiing. You might not think of alpine skiing as a good preparation for old age, but it is. Whenever Albert knows he's going down, his body, guided by the past, goes limp and into a roll. It's almost a thing of beauty, so in such a situation Claire lavishes praise on him to offset his humiliation. Having to give up the slopes had been devastating, and his attempt to fill the void with cross-country skiing had been a nightmare she'll never forget. She'd tried to keep up alongside, hanging on to her ski poles and Albert too, but, well, just thinking of it makes a walk on the beach seem like a piece of cake, not that it *is* one.

"Don't you just love the little sandpipers?" Claire says to Albert now. What the birds must look like through his eyes she can hardly imagine. They dart so quickly forth and back, forth and back, in rhythm with the waves. "Oh, hold on a sec," she says, stopping to pick up the husk of a sea urchin. Sometimes her beachcombing annoys Albert, but often he seems grateful for the opportunity to catch his breath, which is the case this time, so Claire intensifies her interest in the spiny globe, ponders aloud the life of such a creature. They are an obstacle, standing there, and the hordes of people taking their afternoon constitutionals — an activity as predictable and unrelenting as the tides — move around them and continue on their way.

But now a couple engrossed with one another stumbles into them. This, surely, is the man Claire had seen at Walt's, the seafood restaurant, the man who looks so much like her dentist. The woman he's with — a busty compact brunette in her twenties or early thirties — is definitely not Mrs Clampton. "Excuse us," the man says. He lets go of the woman's hand and urges her to race with him to some distant point down the beach.

Was this, indeed, Dr Clampton in swimming trunks? Had he recognised Claire as one of his patients and felt the need to escape her scrutiny? Claire dismisses the possibility that the Clamptons could have separated — not that there'd been any evidence of love between them. No, it was Mrs Clampton's extreme shyness, and Dr Clampton's active participation in his father-in-law's care that had made Claire certain the marriage was a union bound to endure. At any rate, most likely this man is *not* Dr Clampton but a look-alike.

Perhaps guilt is causing Claire to see Dr Clampton as a recurring face among the masses. She has broken the agreement she'd made with him when he took her on as a patient. His need for her to pledge a commitment to good oral health had struck her as odd, but at the time she'd been hoping to find a dentist close to public transportation and to the library, which he was, so she felt she could go along with his unorthodox approach. She'd vowed to floss daily and promised to come no less than every six months and to be on time, a feat she'd managed for several years. When she began working for Albert Stone, however, it became difficult to schedule appointments with any certainty of being able to keep them. Albert invariably grew restless in Montreal and was forever wanting to fly off somewhere. Claire tries to recall when it was she'd last had a check-up, and figures it to be ten months or thereabouts.

"Enough of this dawdling," Albert tells her now, so she brushes the last traces of sand from the sea urchin and puts it in her pocket. His tone is unusually brusque. He is glaring fiercely into the horizon as though the ground he's so determined to cover might otherwise cover him.

"Dr Clampton will see you now," says a sugary voice. Claire sets down the magazine she'd only just taken up and hands herself over to the cheerful assistant. She settles herself in the big recliner, lifts her chin so a paper bib can be clipped into place, and lowers it again to find an unavoidable view of ample breasts in a push-up bra. The assistant has not only neglected to fasten several buttons on her uniform, but her hair is piled atop her head in such a haphazard fashion that numerous curls have tumbled free, giving her a just-out-of-bed look. Yes, this is the person Claire had seen with her dentist on the beach in Sarasota. She has to wonder if the sex-kitten image is the woman's idea or if it's what she feels is required to keep her job. "You have a new assistant," Claire says to Dr Clampton, who has just appeared in the doorway, his nose buried in her file.

"Melissa has been with me for quite some time now," he replies without looking up. "You haven't been here in a long while. Not for well over a year," he adds. "A year and five months, to be exact." From the wall, his homely but fresh-faced children smile their toothy smiles at Claire — updated photos of the ones that had previously inspired her to close her eyes during the examinations and procedures. No pictures of Mrs Clampton, but then, there never had been any.

"Has it really been as long as that?" Claire asks now, knowing it has been. "My job kept me away. There was a lot of travelling involved," she adds, and with this Dr Clampton and his assistant stand perfectly still, as though suspended by what she might say next.

But Claire gives nothing away — a talent she honed during the years of dealing with Albert's bunch. "Then my employer grew ill," she says. "He was dying and needed me." Tears well up in her eyes. Maddening, inexplicable tears, considering all she'd endured as Albert Stone's ideal companion. It's just that she'd felt so much less than ideal at the end. Exhausted from the long hours — and from having to abide his children's ghoulish presence — when Albert turned to her for strength, she'd had so little left to offer. "Dylan Thomas would have loved Albert Stone," she says, as much to herself as to her dentist and his assistant. "Albert did not go gently." But it's obvious that neither Dr Clampton nor Melissa is a lover of poetry. Behind their expressionless faces is an emptiness so vast it makes Claire shiver. Or perhaps it's just the air conditioning that she finds so chilling. "I really couldn't get away," she alleges, falling somewhat short of the assertiveness she'd been striving for.

"I *see.*" Dr Clampton's skeptical tone makes it clear that in his opinion she ought to have excused herself from her bedside task and attended to her oral health, which of course she would never have done even if she'd thought of it. Not that she couldn't have come earlier, as Albert has been dead now for over two months. The thing is, she feels she is just beginning to recover from the loss of a routine she'd grown accustomed to. She'd had the rug pulled from under her, hadn't she? Her life had gone from being all about Albert to all about more or less nothing other than being unemployed. Why *had* it taken her so long to remember her teeth? Well, they'd looked fine and they weren't hurting, but this is an excuse she knows to keep to herself.

"Let's just have a look then, shall we?" Dr Clampton tells her, taking a seat. She opens her mouth, she closes her eyes.

Other dentists let hygienists do the cleaning, but not Dr Clampton. No amateurs allowed in his territory. He does all his own picking and scraping and tapping. He takes the x-rays. He gives the verdict. And what else could Claire have expected after her errant ways but bad news? She will need two teeth filled, a molar and a bicuspid. She must make an appointment for next week. "And if you don't show up, I'll kill you," he tells her as he pushes aside his tray of instruments.

The humour she looks for on his face doesn't arrive. The comment strikes her as extraordinarily inappropriate, and yet she knows that if she were to tell anyone, they'd assure her he'd been joking. He *had* to be joking. But it's not her imagination; there's something not quite right about Dr Clampton, the way he watches from the doorway as Claire makes out a cheque at the receptionist's desk. Probably he's making sure she makes another appointment. When Melissa joins him and says in a near whisper, "See, we needn't have worried," Claire stifles an impulse to say, *Oh, I recognised you in Sarasota, all right. The world is not as large as you thought it was.* It seems that not letting on she knows what she knows has become a way of life. "See you next Friday," she says, glancing in their direction on the way out.

But as she makes her way to the metro station her intuition tells her to never return. She recalls the time her train line had been temporarily out of service — a mechanical problem or someone's suicide perhaps — and she'd arrived two minutes past the appointed hour to find Dr Clampton waiting for her outside the building. He hadn't reprimanded her. He hadn't needed to. She apologised profusely, as though she'd held him up for an hour, then later she'd hated herself for having done so. She wishes now that she hadn't made the appointment to have those two fillings done. She will just have to cancel it and find another dentist.

"A little wider please," Dr Clampton tells her. He's inserting the paraphernalia that will keep her mouth open during the drilling and whatnot. Claire has put off finding another dentist for now. Aside from needing to focus on looking for work, there's the question of x-rays. She couldn't see having another set taken so soon — the expense of it, the further exposure to radiation. And she couldn't begin to imagine asking Dr Clampton to relinquish his. While it might have been preferable to never return, Claire finds there's a real sense of satisfaction knowing something Dr Clampton doesn't know: this is his final performance.

One good thing about Claire's job with Albert, it has given her so many beautiful places to return to in her mind. The olive groves in Portugal, mountains blanketed with heather and lavender on the Isle of Skye, desert flowers in the Baja region… Such lovely images to distract her from the sound of the drill, and from memories of the not-so-lovely aspects of the job with Albert: having her room searched, her pockets gone through, conversations listened in on; Albert's terrible frustration when his body no longer responded to the miracles of science. What, exactly, had he been cursing during those last, long days?

But what is this, anyway? Dr Clampton's drilling is so much rougher today than at other times, as though the drill bit is larger than in the past, the speed higher. As usual, there's no pain to speak of, such is the potency of the anaesthetic — but why so many jerky movements, such intense vibration? Is he in a hurry or what? Claire opens her eyes. Her dentist's fleshy face is just inches from her own, but he remains oblivious to her questioning look, her sense of alarm. In fact, he goes about his work with such detachment that she imagines raising her foot to his chest and sending him flying across the room. How odd to think of doing such a thing, and yet, it feels…like a *need*, almost.

And now Melissa probes Claire's mouth with the suction device. When all the debris is removed, Dr Clampton tells her how much amalgam to prepare and Claire again tries to remove herself to a place where dentists do not figure in the landscape. But words and sounds continue to prevent her total escape. When she hears Dr Clampton tell Melissa, No, no, I won't be needing that, she opens an eye just a crack to see Melissa looking doubtful and confused, as though she is, perhaps, incompetent.

The job finished, the bib removed, Claire is reminded to floss, to return in six months. She doesn't let on she has no intention of ever coming back. She pays the receptionist and leaves with a secret sense of freedom, a lovely feeling that, as the freezing subsides, is replaced with twinges of discomfort. At home the pain begins, throbbing pain that penetrates the jaw, the left eye, its grip ever-tightening as night approaches. It's Friday, no chance to call Dr Clampton to ask him what might be wrong until Monday, so Claire begins a diet of painkillers to get her through till then.

Monday finally comes and Dr Clampton agrees to see Claire on his lunch hour. His theory is that the bite is not quite what it should be. He'll grind both fillings down a bit. The pain has been so severe all weekend that Claire doubts there could be such a simple solution, but, still, she hopes he's right. It is nice of him to see her on his lunch hour. He grinds, he pauses, he asks her to bite down on little pieces of paper which he then studies before again applying the drill. He tells her that it's possible she needs a root canal on that bicuspid, that it had been neglected for too long.

A root canal. This comes as a surprise to Claire, as the tooth had given her no trouble whatever prior to her visit last week. Being unemployed now, she's concerned about the cost.

"How much might I expect to pay should it prove necessary?" she asks, and Dr Clampton tells her twelve hundred, an amount she has on hand, fortunately, but it's an expense she could sure do without.

"Let's hope it doesn't come to that," he says.

Loaded up on 222s, Claire surmises that it will take an hour or two to determine whether the touch-up work has solved the problem, but she has not even reached home when it becomes evident that the problem is far from solved. As the afternoon progresses so does the pain. It's almost as though Dr Clampton has tried to carry out his threat to kill her, despite her compliance. However unreasonable she tells herself she's being, she cannot bring herself to go ahead with the root canal — at least not yet. She calls a friend who has nice teeth — apologises for not calling sooner, for having allowed their friendship to languish, promises to make amends, then asks for the name of his dentist.

Dr Sloan is young and personable. A recent graduate, his diplomas are framed and prominently displayed, as if they were progeny. He takes x-rays of the teeth in question — a bitewing radiograph and a periapical radiograph. He explains everything he does, his voice as soothing as his hands are gentle. Studying the x-rays, he's puzzled by what he sees, or *doesn't* see. He doesn't see any medicated base in the two recent fillings. He finds it hard to fathom how such a basic part of such a simple procedure could have been overlooked by a dentist — *and* an assistant. He explains that, without the medicated base, the metal filling would transmit heat, cold, and pressure directly to the nerve, causing severe pain. Even though Claire says *yes*, yes, that's the kind of pain she's been having, he feels that the liner must be there but for some strange reason has just failed to show up on the x-ray. He tells her that, at any rate, there's probably a need for more of it to calm the pulpal tissues.

Claire recalls the moment when Dr Clampton had said to Melissa, I won't be needing that, and Melissa's look of confusion. The truth hits her as sharply as a blow: Dr Clampton had caused as much trauma as possible, then deliberately left out the medicated base knowing that pain would convince her she was in need of a root canal. Why, a mugging in an alley would be less painful — and less disturbing: the aggressor wouldn't be someone in whom she'd put her trust. And the most a mugger could hope to get from Claire would be fifty bucks and some grocery coupons. She assures her new dentist that he's *not* going to find any liner in those teeth, and he smiles and tells her that it's really quite inconceivable.

"Well, what do you know…?" Dr Sloan mutters as he drills through the first filling. He marvels to his assistant that there is, indeed, no medicated base whatever. No one states the obvious, that the omission must have been intentional. No one needs to. The question why becomes an uncomfortable presence. The only answers Claire can think of are ones she's not willing to volunteer. Dr Clampton had to have been motivated by one of two things: either he wished to punish her for not playing by his rules, or he saw her as weak and defenceless, an ideal victim from whom to extort money. His eccentric, possessive approach to his work might suggest the former, but perhaps a shrinking clientele — the exodus of anglophones out of Quebec prior to and following the recent sovereignty referendum — has forced him to take whatever profit can be found in the mouths that are still open to him. What can Claire do now but just make certain he's deterred from targeting others?

Or should she just put the unpleasant experience behind her? This is the question that comes to mind when Dr Sloan has redone the work and rid her of the pain. Claire tries not to think of all the unpleasant experiences she's put behind her in recent years, the worst involving Albert's children. Ironically, their suspicion and jealousy of her had been just the weapons against growing old and feeling abandoned that Albert needed. By the end, he had their rapt attention; he had them dropping in more and more frequently.

Claire tells herself she really must stop thinking of Albert and his family. She considers again seeking punishment for Dr Clampton, wonders if it was likely to become an all-consuming distraction, a distraction she doesn't need.

But no. She recalls Dr Clampton's face so close to her own, hears his words of admonishment. To think he'd had the nerve to blame her for the pain he'd wilfully caused.

Claire is waiting for Dr Clampton to return her call. She has never in her life felt so aware of herself as a living organism. Every nerve in her body is awake, her blood runs hot, then cold, then hot again. What will she say to him? Words rush through her mind, taking dangerous chances. No, she must guard herself against her emotions. She mustn't rant or whine, and above all, she mustn't cry. She lets the phone ring several times while she attempts to calm herself. "Hello, Dr. Clampton," she says, trembling. She thanks him for returning her call.

Dr Clampton doesn't even ask how she's doing; he tells her he wasn't surprised to learn she'd called, he'd had a feeling about that bicuspid.

Liar, liar, liar, she thinks. "I was just wondering…," she begins, "…perhaps you left something out?" She listens for sounds of panic in his silence, but hears only her own heart pounding in anticipation. Anticipation of what? A confession? Some inkling of remorse?

"Claire, don't look for excuses," he tells her. "The reason you're in pain is simple: you need a root canal. It's too bad, because had you come to me when you were supposed to have, I could've saved that tooth. As it was, I thought perhaps I could. I tried to."

"Actually," Claire says, bracing herself against the swell of anger, "you tried to sabotage that tooth, the molar too. Luckily, I sought out a second opinion and learned that you'd put no medicated liner in either filling — a most unlikely oversight." She waits for a response, but there is none. Who does she think she is that he will feel the need to confess, apologise, feel remorseful? She is going to have to make him take her seriously. "Perhaps I'd have never thought to get a second opinion," she tells him, pausing to swallow, to measure her words, "had I not kept thinking about what I witnessed in Sarasota. I figured that a man who would cheat on his wife might also cheat his patients."

"If you're thinking of blackmailing me," Dr Clampton hisses into her ear, "you can forget it. I was in Sarasota with my golfing buddies. I go every year."

Dr Clampton's fury stirs in Claire a sense of triumph, a mere taste, she believes, of what lies ahead because she intends to lodge a formal complaint against him and he's going to have to explain how both he and his assistant managed to overlook a vital step in not one, but *two* large fillings. Dr Sloan has agreed to document his findings, so it's tempting to brandish that support now in Dr Clampton's face, a face she imagines to be pale and damp with worry. "This isn't about my blackmailing *you*, this is about you *assaulting* me," she tells him. Her knowledge of his affair, she realises, isn't much of a weapon. Who would care about his infidelity except his poor wife? "Maybe you can deny your affair," she says, "but you can't deny what you did to me because I have a member of your own profession to back me up." She'd like to tell him he is nothing but a little creep, a cowardly criminal, but she prevents herself from indulging in something as desperate as name-calling by hanging up.

Claire begins the process of registering her formal complaint by writing a detailed letter to the dental association, with the understanding that they will send a copy of the letter to her dentist, who has thirty days to respond. Then comes the investigation. Understandably, members of the Complaints Committee need time to acquire and study dental records, and to consider both arguments. Perhaps they require a vacation to help put things in perspective, or perhaps Claire's file becomes buried under the files of other complainants. She can only wonder why the long wait. By the time she and Dr Clampton meet with the panel, the imagined version of the proceedings has become so fixed in her mind that the actual one feels unreal.

Her new dentist, Dr Sloan, is not present, but he has submitted a report of his findings, which the chairman of the committee reads aloud. There is no hint of the dismay he'd expressed at the time of treatment — evidently, his youth and inexperience have made him cautious, hesitant to accuse a peer. He refers to Claire's pain as *sensitivity*, and attests only that the absence of a calcium hydroxide liner *may* have accounted for her discomfort.

"There was no doubt in Dr Sloan's mind what caused my *pain*," she interjects, but it is almost as though she isn't there. Dr Clampton's explanation to panel members is swift and clinical and hard for Claire to follow. His focus is on the bicuspid, tooth #25. Tooth #25, as though it could belong to anyone. As though it might have a life of its own. He is affable and respectful and innocence personified and Claire begins to dread a possibility that had not occurred to her before: suppose they suggest he's been wrongfully accused; suppose she is made to apologise?

But no, after all the banter, the committee members concede that, indeed, an unfortunate error has occurred, an error that cannot be assumed to be deliberate because the words Claire had overheard and had found so incriminating had been non-specific. While the committee is not authorised to assess damages, the chairman mentions in passing that a refund of the money Claire has paid, plus an amount to compensate for any inconvenience, would be in keeping with other, similar, disputes. When the chairman encourages Claire and Dr Clampton to come to an understanding, Claire wants desperately to do that, to come to an understanding and put it all behind her. But then she learns that in order to receive the refund and meagre compensation, she'll need to sign a waiver — a legal document, the wording of which has been contrived to render him essentially blameless — and exempt from further litigation.

It's no wonder to Claire that people take the law into their own hands and seek revenge. The wonder is why more people don't. If only she had acted upon her instinct to find another dentist following Dr Clampton's comment that he'd kill her. If only she'd been as vigilant of her own well-being as she has been of others'.

She recalls an incident that occurred at a resort in Mexico, at Playa del Carmen. She and Albert had been swimming when her attention had been drawn to some commotion on the beach. When she turned back, he was gone. Only moments earlier he'd been floating on his back not ten feet away and yet, scanning the water's surface, she could see no one resembling Albert, no one as elderly. The waves nudged her legs on their way to the shore, rocking her, making her dizzy there in the bright sunlight. Fearing him drowned and herself responsible, she was relieved to spot him further down the beach, standing waist-deep, looking for her.

"Here, Albert," she cried, waving both hands in wide arcs over her head, as though he could see anything at such a distance. Then Claire realised he was approaching, and about to pounce upon, a woman entering the water — a woman who, although younger and blonder, had a build similar to hers, and she, too, was wearing a fuchsia swimsuit. "Albert, no, *don't!*" Claire had called. "Don't, Albert," she cried again, racing toward him, the water churning about her knees. "Here I am," she cried, oblivious to onlookers. She had so wanted to prevent a blunder that could have had serious ramifications for Albert. But even more than that, she'd felt desperate to save the woman from being accosted, this twin whose fierce resistance proved more than adequate against her amorous assailant.

A SIMPLE REQUEST

When the announcement comes, finally, that the flight from Toronto has arrived, Pru goes to stand where she's likely to be noticed by her niece and finds herself next to a man who smells faintly of wild sage and looks the type to pick up after himself. Someone's husband, no doubt. Scanning the newly arrived passengers for a woman of a certain age worthy of such a man, she locates, instead, her niece in conversation with a shaggy-bearded fellow carrying a guitar case. Karen, who must be forty by now, is wearing jeans. Anyone with so little sense is likely to have invited someone to come along with her at the last minute.

But perhaps Pru won't have to refer the fellow to a bed and breakfast after all. He has set down the guitar case and has withdrawn from his breast pocket a pen and pad. As he writes, he smiles, gestures, lingers in his farewell, as though Karen did not have a relative waiting. Pru furtively signals her whereabouts, but not until the man goes his own way does Karen turn, then she makes a beeline for Pru, whose presence she must have been aware of all along.

"Auntie Pru, you look wonderful," she gushes.

Pru bristles, but accepts a little hug. What that guitar-carrying Romeo had seen in Karen is beyond Pru. She looks haggard, as though she hasn't slept in months. Of course, he'd been no prize himself. Pru recalls the nice-looking man she'd stood next to only moments ago, checks for his whereabouts, but he's been claimed and taken away. "Shall we retrieve your luggage and get out of this madhouse?" she says, and Karen holds up a backpack. "That's it?"

Pru worries that if Lily has sent along some homemade fudge, as she generally does, it's likely to be squashed. "Wait here, it's raining cats and dogs," she says. "I'll run and get the car; it's across the way."

Karen suggests they share Pru's umbrella, but Pru tells her no, someone always gets wet. "I'll be back in a jiffy," she says, convinced that she will be, but, in fact, it takes several minutes to find the car because some baboon had parked a van alongside it, blocking it from view.

As Pru makes her way back to where she'd left her niece, she decides that if it turns out there is no fudge she will not send back with Karen the slippers she knit up in a hurry for Lily. She and her sister — her twin sister — have had another falling out and as far as Pru is concerned, Lily, having caused the rift, needs to make more than just a half-hearted attempt to reconcile. Call me when you're ready to talk, Lily said to Pru, as if that's any kind of an apology.

Pru pulls up behind a line of taxis. Now, where is that girl? she wonders. She had asked nothing of Karen but to stay put. "Well, isn't this just the ticket?" she says aloud. *"Where* did she go?"

The windshield wipers answer rhythmically, I-don't-know-I-don't-know, I-don't-know-I-don't-know.

But isn't that Karen talking to someone in the cab up ahead? Pru honks the horn lightly, and Karen looks back and holds up a just-a-minute finger. Well, heavens to Betsy, what *now*?

Now the cab door opens and out steps a man. The bearded man with the guitar, surprise, surprise. And luggage. And the alligator smile.

Karen comes and taps on the window on the passenger's side and points to the lock. When she opens the door, she says, "This is Jake. I met him on the plane." She reaches in to unlock the back door, tells Pru that Jake had been about to take a cab into Halifax, says it in a way that suggests it's outrageous, when surely it's common sense not to be meddled with.

"I'm awfully sorry," Pru tells her, "but I have a policy against picking up strangers." Her policy is really one concerning hitchhikers, but she extends it to this new-found friend of Karen's because she's determined to maintain control of this visit. It seems that whenever Karen or Lily visit, all her rules are trodden on and all her entertainment plans go out the window. Well, not this time, not if it *kills* her.

"Jake is hardly a mugger," Karen tells her in a lowered voice. "He's a well-known musician." She gives the name, but it means nothing to Pru, who has to wonder if Karen had previously heard of this fellow, or if he's just told her he's a somebody. Would he dare to appear in public looking this scruffy if he has any kind of reputation to keep up?

Karen goes ahead and opens the door to the back seat — is about to actually disregard Pru's wishes when the fellow says to never mind, then the two of them murmur things to one another that Pru cannot quite catch. When Karen finally gets in the car, she tosses the backpack recklessly onto the floor. If the fudge wasn't squashed before, it's bound to be squashed now.

"Ever since that prime minister of ours married a flower child, it seems anything goes," Pru says, easing the car through a gaggle of jaywalking pedestrians, "but some things don't change. A girl is still wise not to be too accommodating."

"Keep in mind, this girl is forty-one, Auntie Pru."

"And this one is sixty-five, or close enough to it. But let's not argue. Can you really blame me for wanting you all to myself?"

However resolved Pru is to hold the reins, the visit must go well, otherwise Karen is bound to report back to Lily what a vexing time she had. Oh, yes, Pru knows how it goes. Karen and her mother may have a brittle relationship, but there are certain things they see eye to eye on and Pru is certain she's one of them.

"I'm going to take you out for lunch to a new place," Pru says to Karen, and she mentions a charity auction they might attend afterward. "That is, if you don't have other plans," she says. "*Do* you have other plans? You didn't mention any specific reason for your visit."

"Uh, no... I suppose I don't have other plans."

"There's no conference or anything this time?" Pru asks. Karen's visits have always coincided with conferences or research of some kind, and had occurred once or twice a year until three years ago or so, when they dried up with no explanation.

"No, there's no conference, just a visit."

"Well, aren't I lucky?" Pru says, still unconvinced.

The restaurant Aunt Pru takes Karen to for lunch is in a shopping mall. It's been decorated to resemble a tea room, the type one generally finds in old restored houses. On the walls are cheap prints of Victorian homes. Cascades of fake ivy tumble from plastic pots suspended from the ceiling. The tablecloths are vinyl, a blue gingham pattern. Karen peruses the plastic-coated menu in search of something simple, contemplates backing out of the charity auction, can't imagine how she could possibly endure the hubbub.

"I'm having the chicken pot pie," Auntie Pru says decisively. "Right in front of your nose, dear girl, under Lunch Specials."

"You know, I think I'll just have a bowl of the vegetable soup," Karen tells her. "And a nice glass of milk."

Her aunt removes a coupon from her purse and dons her glasses. "I feared as much," she says, then she reads aloud: "Buy one entrée from our daily specials, and receive a second one free." She peers across the table at Karen. "The soup is not an entrée, and it's no bargain either. You'll get the same vegetables in a pot pie. Plus dessert and a choice of tea or coffee."

Karen explains to her aunt that she isn't very hungry and really would prefer soup and milk, that she doesn't mind paying for lunch, would like, to in fact.

Aunt Pru fingers the cutlery. "You mentioned on the phone that you'd like to take me out for supper to that same place you took me to last time, remember?"

Karen assures her aunt she hasn't forgotten her offer, and argues that it's all the more reason to partake of a light lunch.

"Hopefully, the menu won't have changed much," Aunt Pru says. "It's been such a long time since we were last there. Whatever happened to your conferences? You used to come every year."

The truth is, the conferences do take place annually in Halifax and Karen has continued to attend, sneaking in and out of town, feeling hardly any guilt at all, just vulnerable to discovery. She had not, for a long time, perhaps ever, enjoyed the visits with her aunt, who goes ahead and plans things she has no interest in, obsesses over everything, and can't leave Karen's mother out of the conversation. "The conferences go on as usual," she explains, "here and elsewhere. I can't attend them all."

She has avoided an outright lie. Her aunt needn't know that it's the elsewhere ones she rarely attends. Her aunt seems satisfied with her explanation. She tells Karen that, anyway, it wouldn't be right for her to pay for both lunch and supper.

Karen doesn't mind paying for both, but knows she won't be allowed to.

"So will it be two pot pies then?" Aunt Pru says, and Karen relents, anything to improve the chances of delivering her aunt to her dying mother.

Her aunt's demeanour brightens — must be the thought of two pot pies, the thrift, the victory. She looks quite youthful, but then, Karen has grown accustomed to her mother's emaciated state. Yes, one could say her aunt is even cautiously attractive. Her grey eyes dart around the room now, alighting here and there, as if trying to find something about the decor worthy of praise, a hopeless proposition. Karen asks how her garden is doing, thus inviting a report on plants under siege, which is, by and by, mercifully interrupted by the waitress.

"Ready to order, ladies?" the woman says, and Aunt Pru plunges in, ordering one pot pie. "And my niece — who's just arrived from Toronto for a little visit — will have the vegetable soup and a large milk. Can we assume a bread roll comes with the soup?"

"Crackers."

"Well let's make it a nice warm roll if you've got one. With butter."

"Why, thank you, Auntie Pru," Karen says, truly thankful. She wonders why her aunt had argued against soup only to order it, but of course this is classic Aunt Pru behaviour.

Prudence removes her shoes, gets Karen and herself some slippers from the closet, indicates the usual guest room and tells her niece she should feel free to take her things there straight away — a subtle hint that she retrieve the backpack from where she plunked it in the vestibule, but never mind that the girl has a master's degree in sociology, she's as thick as they come in some ways. "You probably have things you'll want to hang up right away," Pru suggests, but it turns out the girl has brought nothing but jeans and sweats. *Sweats*, thinks Pru, doesn't that sound lovely? "I'm just thinking we might trip over that satchel of yours where it is. Perhaps I should give you a moment to arrange your things. Then we'll have some tea. I have regular or decaf."

"Decaf, please, Auntie Pru. Just let me use the john and I'll be right with you."

Pru hauls the backpack into Karen's room and sets it on the bed. In an outer pocket is a book whose title is obscured by the plane ticket that really ought to be in a zippered compartment, not where it could be easily lost. The name of the book, Pru sees now, is *On Death and Dying*. Talk about taking your work with you on vacation! Pru would love to put the ticket where anyone with any sense would put it, but she settles for pushing it deep into the pocket the book is in, after which she goes to put the kettle on. "I took the liberty of putting your bag in your room," she says when Karen appears in the doorway.

"Oh, you needn't have bothered." The girl's offhand tone and not a word of thanks renders Pru absolutely speechless, but really, it should come as no surprise, because, after all, this is Lily's child, so what can you expect? And now Karen has actually taken it upon herself to peer into one of the boxes Pru had brought up from the basement earlier to sort through. (What a huge ordeal it is, deciding what to throw out and what to keep.) "Ah, Freddie," Karen says, holding up a greeting card of sorts and waving it. "Mom's mentioned him, I believe."

I'll just bet she has, thinks Pru, first dashing to pull the screeching kettle off the heat, then snatching from Karen the battered and forlorn card — something Freddie had fashioned from next to nothing while serving overseas. She puts it back in the box and slides the box into a corner, asks Karen if she'd mind stacking the two remaining ones there too. She apologises for the mess.

Karen insists that the place is as sparkling as ever, and she urges Pru not to bother trekking the tea things to the living room, but Pru knows by now where she prefers to serve tea. When the tea is poured, she gives the plate of cookies a nudge in Karen's direction, cookies she made especially for the occasion, running all over town for the macadamia nuts the girl has fancied in the past. "I've been meaning to mention, you seem to have lost a fair amount of weight," she ventures.

"I've been under a lot of stress lately," Karen says. She takes the smallest cookie and nibbles without comment. Pru might as well have used almonds or walnuts.

Lily has always painted Karen's life as a charmed one, so it's hard for Pru to imagine what could be stressful. Even Karen's divorce from her husband (a mannerly, pleasant enough man with a steady job) was amicable — all part of "mutual growth," if you can believe it, which Pru does not, because who would throw away a perfectly good marriage? Perhaps Karen's son, David, has fallen in with a bad crowd. Or perhaps there are money problems. "I'm not one to pry," Pru says, "*but…*"

Karen, seated on the sofa, draws her legs up under herself like a youngster might. "As a matter of fact, there *is* something I need to talk to you about, Aunt Pru. But I think it would be better to wait until tomorrow, if you don't mind."

So this visit isn't just a visit. "We all have our trials and tribulations, I guess." Pru shares a few of her own, exaggerating about the upkeep on the house and car to warn Karen against asking for a loan, because she has a sneaking feeling that there's a false impression that she's sitting on a big pile of dough. The loan, if there *is* a request for one in the offing, might not be for Karen herself. Pru has often wondered how Lily, who is impulsive and irresponsible, has been making ends meet since Les passed on.

Karen remains silent, is perhaps nurturing resentment about the charity auction, which turned out to be an ordinary rummage sale — the auction being next week. There are always numerous announcements to keep track of, but still, Pru, being an organised person, was surprised by her mistake and embarrassed not to have arrived at the church earlier to help set up. Of course, the ladies of the Women's Auxiliary assured her that everything was well under control, but knowing better, and despite a sullen look from her niece, Pru had insisted on helping out. Once a clergyman's daughter, always a clergyman's daughter. There are things you simply have to do or as soon as your back is turned, people gab about what a disappointment you'd be to your parents. Anyway, with the weather being so miserable and all, what in heaven's name else would she and Karen have done to pass the time? Pru hadn't put a gun to Karen's head. She'd only stated that a glad hand makes for a happy heart.

She tries to enliven Karen now with recollections of the old days, when her parents had gone backpacking in Europe, leaving her, Karen, in her auntie's care — Auntie being Pru's own younger, livelier self. She laughs, "I remember you said to me once, after I'd pushed you on the swing, 'Mommy always gets tired, but not you, Auntie Pru.'"

Karen smiles wanly and shakes her head as if to deny Pru's account. And to think that Pru had essentially given up her own summer vacation to babysit because otherwise Lily wouldn't have been able to go, or so she claimed, but of course she'd have roped some friend into duty, if not Pru. Almost anyone other than Lily would have left their child with the child's grandparents, but Lily had been certain they'd emotionally scar the girl for life. (Les's folks were never an option, being on the other side of the planet, in New Zealand.) It had been quite a sacrifice for Pru to abandon her cute wee apartment to return to the manse to care for Karen — the manse being roomy and close to a playground. She'd also sacrificed the independence she'd only recently won, thus subjecting herself once again to daily parental reprisals. As for that swing ride, Pru's arms had felt about ready to fall off, but she'd been determined to somehow win Karen's affection before Lily and Les returned. Such a recalcitrant girl at times, even back then.

"I guess it's almost time for bed," Pru says, rising to draw the living room drapes. "Bedtime for me, I mean. You'll want to read a bit, I suppose." She thanks Karen for the lovely supper, worries aloud that she, Karen, having had only a salad for supper, and soup for lunch, might not be properly nourished.

"I'll be fine," Karen tells her.

"I could coddle an egg for you," Pru suggests, wanting to at least get a little protein into the girl, some iron, but Karen claims to have had enough to sustain her. "I find when I'm not quite up to snuff I can generally get down a coddled egg," Pru says, but all she gets is silence.

Pausing at the window as she does each night before retiring, to check the neighbourhood for anything suspicious, she sees that the rain has finally stopped. The street glistens in the lamplight. There's something eerie about the row of houses tonight, something solemn about the deep narrow lots on which they sit. Freddie, the fellow whose greeting card Karen had brandished, had had the dream of getting into real estate once the war was over, but both he and his dream had been blown to bits in France. How unfair that Freddie, such a decent sort, should perish, whereas Lily's beau at the time, a rascal if ever there was one, came home with nothing more lamentable than some new card tricks.

It seems awfully early to be getting into pyjamas. Karen dawdles with her night-time preparations, a luxury after a month of caring for her mother. She recalls the long-ago time her aunt had mentioned, the time her parents went to Europe, not the swing incident, but when she and Aunt Pru played hide and seek. Karen had curled up in the back of the cupboard under the stairs and listened with delight as her aunt, unable to find her, grew more and more frantic. "Karen, did you stay in the house like I said?" Aunt Pru cried. "Okay, I'm gathering up your toys then, and taking them to the harbour. Oh look, here's Dolly. I hope she knows how to swim."

Of course her aunt hadn't just been weary of playing the game, she had to have felt powerless and frightened of the possible consequences if Karen had ventured outdoors and wandered off.

Still, it had been no way to relate to a child. During this moment of reflection, it seems to her that her mother's absences and seeming indifference to her as a child are easier to forgive — not that she has quite forgiven her mother, either.

Karen can see herself yet, storming out of her hiding place to rescue her toys, only to find them right where she'd left them. How well she remembers the sickening feeling of having been tricked.

She shakes the past from her mind, takes her book from her backpack and crawls into bed, but no matter how much she tries to concentrate, her thoughts turn to Jake, the man she'd sat next to on the plane. He'd been such a good listener. She worries that she may have burdened him by confiding in him her conflicted feelings toward her dying mother, wonders if maybe she should call and apologise. After all, he'd given her a number, invited her to call.

Pru scrambles from bed in alarm, hastens into her robe. 8:15 am! How could she have slept through the clanking of her neighbour's garage door — her usual reveille? Pulling her bed into some semblance of order, it occurs to her that Karen could be up and waiting for breakfast. Suppose she takes it upon herself to snoop in the boxes? Not that there's anything in the boxes to be truly ashamed of, given Pru's uneventful life, but there have been a few items Pru's come across herself — long-forgotten mementoes from friends and office colleagues — that seem of questionable taste now, were of questionable taste then too, though she used to laugh along rather than raise an eyebrow.

The bathroom proves empty. The door to the guest room is closed, a good indication that Karen has slept in as well — unless she's just shut the door on her unmade bed. No sign of her in the kitchen.

Pru exchanges her slippers for the pair of gardening shoes by the door, and takes the boxes one by one to the garage — where she'd have put them yesterday if time hadn't crept up on her and sent her off to the airport without a backward glance. She feels relieved, and ready now to put in a nice day with her niece, who, under the circumstances, should be allowed to sleep in a bit longer. Pru is fairly certain of the circumstances. She had lain awake half the night putting two and two together: Karen being so gaunt, toting around that grim and awful book, reluctant to explain her trip, the fact that there is no conference. The girl is dying. She has come for one last trip to her birthplace — and, indeed, to see her Auntie Pru.

There's something quite profound about setting the table for someone whose days are numbered. Pru tries to make the table extra special by using her silver and her best linen napkins. She'd had a good cry during the night, but the thought of losing Karen has her tearing up again. She peers into the depths of her china cabinet and fishes out a precious crystal dish — real crystal with 24k gold trim — for the grape jelly.

And now it's 8:45 and still no sound of Karen up and about. Pru decides to go ahead and eat, not because she's hungry, though she is, but this way she'll be free to rustle up anything her niece might like to have. She has second thoughts about the linen napkins, grape stains being a real devil to get out, is tempted to replace them with some patterned, quite-nice polyester ones, but no, this is no time to hold back. Karen had been such an adorable child, blonde curls, round blue eyes and long lashes, ordinary words tripping off her lips and made brand new somehow, wondrous. Not that she didn't have her ugly moments. My, my, the ruckus she made if you tried to put her in a high chair.

9:05. Pru has been quiet as a mouse out of sympathy, but for Karen to be sleeping away her precious time… Unless she's suddenly lost ground in there, is unconscious...or worse. She really should have stayed home. She ought to be near her mother, not that Lily would be much help, but she ought to be nearby.

Now who can *that* be calling?

Prudence hurries to answer the phone. If it's someone from that blasted church asking her to bake something when they know very well she has a house guest... "Hello?" she says.

"Hi, Auntie Pru, I hope I haven't got you out of bed."

"...*Karen?* I thought you were... Heavens, where *are* you? I've been waiting..."

"You didn't see my note?"

"No," Pru tells her, her eyes falling on the note right in front of her on her own notepad: *Couldn't get back to sleep. Gone for a walk with Jake. Don't wait breakfast.*

Gone for walk with Jake. And here Pru has been tiptoeing around and knocking herself out... "Why, I might have called the police," she tells this most exasperating girl, who says *Oh well, you didn't* in a way that forces Pru to acknowledge to herself the emptiness of her threat.

"I'm on my way," Karen says. "Thought I'd better call because I don't have a key."

Pru inquires whether Karen has had breakfast and learns that, yes, she has, so all those thoughtful efforts were for naught. Hanging up, she decides the call had not come from a phone booth, rather from Jake's hotel room. Being office manager, Pru is familiar with deceit. *The flu*, the girls will claim, straggling in late to work, their necks marked with love bites not entirely concealed under foundation cream. When Pru addresses them about some task or other, she has to struggle to keep her eyes from drifting to the soft violet smudges that seem such an affront to the workaday world.

Returning from a walk with Jake, Karen finds her aunt silently hostile. By now, she knows it's a mistake to try to appease her; better to just give her time to come around. She heads for the washroom, and over her shoulder tells her aunt she's just going to hop in the shower, if that's okay.

She's also learned not to linger in the shower as she does at home, so after a quick bird bath she wraps herself in a towel and retreats to her room. She dresses leisurely, plotting the best way to broach the subject of her mother's request, and the illness itself. She decides she'll present her aunt with the fudge before saying anything — the fudge being significant somehow, but then... what to say and how to say it?

She spies a photograph on the bureau, one of her aunt that looks familiar and yet different somehow, familiar because it has been around since Karen was a child, different, Karen sees now, because her mother is no longer in it too. Yes, Aunt Pru has cut Karen's mother out, has placed herself into a smaller frame, alone. Seeing this prophetic image sends a chill through Karen. She wonders what prompted the vandalism, then recalls a misunderstanding of some sort that her mother and aunt have had, obviously something not so trivial after all, at least not in her aunt's eyes.

She hears the vacuum cleaner start up and decides to lie down for a bit. Her thoughts turn to breakfast with Jake. Something about his easy manner reminds her of her father. Taking care of her mother, rather than letting others do it entirely, is something her father would have wanted her to do. It is in his memory, really, that she has persevered. He'd always been so understanding of her mother, even when she least deserved it. Her mother had authority issues, was all, according to him. The problem was, or so it seemed to Karen, her mother imagined that everyone was trying to exert power over her — not just bosses, government officials, police officers and such, but "uppity" store clerks, Karen's "know-nothing" teachers, and anyone mentioning, even casually, a spiritual bent.

But her mother *has* mellowed. Even before the cancer, she'd begun to vent less. She'd had some counselling following the death of Karen's father, grief counselling it had started out as; a pity it hadn't been undertaken sooner. Karen's father had been understanding of Aunt Pru too, said she was coping as best she could, avoiding relationships, yes, but that's what it took for her to remain in control. He said that while Karen's mother and Aunt Pru weren't identical twins, they were more or less the same. They just didn't look alike.

Pru has driven far along Purcell's Cove Road to a place Karen's parents had fancied, a place where the ocean dashes itself against great slabs of rock day in and day out. Unknown to tourists, it is, supposedly, the perfect place to clear one's head, though Pru much prefers Point Pleasant Park. She'd had no choice but to give in to Karen's request, though, her niece's illness being so sad and all.

Gazing along the jagged coastline, Pru sees not a soul but Karen. To think: only yesterday Karen was a child. Pru remembers how Les would sweep the girl up onto his shoulders and the two of them would stand on the very rock Karen stands on now, looking out beyond the harbour to the sea, and Lily would join them eventually, leaving Pru to finish setting out the picnic things, to wait and wonder when in heaven's name they'd come to eat, the uncertainty and annoyance making her more ravenous by the minute. She supposes that Lily had, back in the early days of her marriage, been a fairly good wife and mother. At least she wasn't stirring up trouble. Later, any job she embarked upon ended in conflict with management, which was probably why Les started that business he worked himself to death in. Lily could meddle to her heart's content with only him to deal with, and she'd had him wrapped around her finger.

It occurs to Pru now that Les, and her parents, of course, will soon have company in the hereafter, if there is one. Her faith has become the kind her parents railed against: the kind that needs whipping into shape on a regular basis.

She proceeds to remove the lids from the Tupperware containers and to help herself to a tuna sandwich and pickle. "Come and get it," she calls to Karen, who is, anyway, coming. Karen has been *very* closed-mouthed about Jake and the night-time rendezvous despite all the opportunities Pru has given her to come clean. And Karen's promise to talk about what she hadn't wanted to talk about last night — her illness, presumably — seems to have been forgotten. "Dig in," Pru says, offering the container of sandwiches with one hand and shielding her eyes from the sun with the other. "…What's that you have there?" she asks, because Karen has ignored the sandwiches and is taking a small box from the drawstring bag she borrowed from Pru for her shoes and sunscreen.

"Fudge," Karen tells her, placing the package into Pru's hands.

Fudge. So her sister is feeling remorseful, as well she should: telling Pru that she should see a shrink — just because she herself had seen one. Well, the very fact that Lily had found a doctor that she hadn't regarded as a quack, or worse, was progress, Pru supposes. Therapy made perfect sense for Lily. She's blamed everything under the sun — even her monthly cramps, back before menopause — on their parents, who, Pru has come to realise, had no easy time of it. Oh, how their father had slaved over his sermons, their mother too, typing them up for him, both of them so diligent when it came to preparing members of the congregation for the day of judgement. No need? Lily had howled when Pru balked at therapy. Then she went on to imply that Pru's tidiness — which she referred to as hyper-fastidiousness — was misdirected energy loaded with repressed anger and hurt.

Pru sets her sandwich down and removes the plastic wrap from a small piece of the candy that is looking none the worse for wear, after all. She is still thinking about Lily, wondering when it was Lily had gained the upper hand. Perhaps she'd always had it, being the prettier — the older too by four minutes. Who but Lily would have taken those four minutes and tried to make them relevant? Lily, the self-proclaimed adventurous one, the leader, the one to figure everything out for her know-nothing sibling.

"Is there something wrong, Aunt Pru?" Karen asks.

The colour of the fudge seems lighter than Pru remembers it being, and, taking a nibble, she discovers that the texture is as grainy as her own attempts.

"What?" Karen asks.

"Well, my dear, it's not smooth and creamy as it usually is. I'd say she's losing her touch, but don't tell her I said so... It really is the thought that counts, isn't it?"

"Actually, Aunt Pru, *I* made the fudge."

Well, Pru might have guessed her sister would withhold the olive branch.

"Mom told me which recipe to use, which pot, which spoon even... and she warned me against all the pitfalls."

My heavens, but the girl can be dim. "Well, maybe your mother didn't *like* the fact that you were set on making fudge for me. Maybe it wasn't exactly your fault it didn't turn out."

This comment elicits a look from Karen that Pru can't begin to fathom. Her face has gone flat, empty of all expression. She sits down and gazes out over the water. "Mom's very ill, Aunt Pru. She's been in the hospital, but she's home now. She's come home to die."

Suddenly the rock they're seated on seems like something adrift. "...Cancer?" Pru hears herself ask.

Karen nods, says it may have started in a lung, that doctors did what they could to buy some time, but now it's a matter of keeping her comfortable.

"And is she...?" Pru asks. "...Is she aware of things?"

"Oh, yes," Karen says, her eyes welling up with tears, which she swipes away.

In the last few years, cancer has claimed several close acquaintances of Pru's — which is why she has been anxious to rid her house of junk. When she passes on, people will come poking around, won't they? But not Lily. It had been Lily Pru had previously imagined poking around. She replaces Lily with Karen in the nightmare, and it's an improvement to be sure. But knowing Karen, she'll bring David with her; it'll be a field trip of sorts. They'll examine the evidence and draw all the wrong conclusions.

Karen draws a tissue from a pocket and blows her nose, swipes at tears again.

"It can't be easy taking care of her," Pru thinks aloud. To herself she thinks that it's no wonder Karen has aged so: Lily is running the girl ragged. "Make sure to mind your own health," she cautions. "Your grandmother literally killed herself tending your grandfather."

Karen assures her she has lots of help, that friends are taking turns filling in while she's away, and there's David, of course. She blots her face with her shirttail and tries to smile, her eyes so like her mother's, Pru sees now. "Actually, we're *all* hoping you'll fly back with me," she says, as though Pru had met these friends.

"But you know I don't fly," Pru tells her. The gulls echo the alarm in her voice, swoop and glide overhead, filling the air with melancholy.

"I *do* know." Karen shifts her attention from the waves, the bobbing fishing boats, to Pru, forcing Pru to look away. "But I thought, perhaps, with someone next to you… I thought that under these circumstances…"

Pru does hate it when people spring things on her. "Is your mother *expecting* me to come back with you?" she asks. "Or is this an idea you and these friends you mentioned came up with? Maybe she'd like me to remember her the way she was." Pru imagines her sister, not glowing with health, but shrivelled and grey the way the others were. "Anyway, I can't just run off. I'm still a working woman, for a few months yet." She'd almost forgotten this most convenient fact.

Karen insists it's her mother's wish and argues that even if Pru weren't due to retire soon she'd surely be able to arrange for a few days off. Then she goes on to describe her mother's situation as not in the least grim, the bed being in the living room, which is spacious and bright and so convenient for visitors. In the silence that follows, Pru stares into the water, mentally slips below the surface, and begins to drown. She decides death is not so bad really. Her ocean is tepid and as clean as tap water.

"Okay, so flying is out," Karen says. She begins to replace the lids on the Tupperware containers. "How be I cancel my ticket and we drive back together?"

The suggestion sounds too much like a one-way offer to interest Pru, and besides, she cannot think out here with the noise of the waves. "I tell you what you *can* do; you can drive me back to my place now," she sighs. "This sun has given me a splitting headache."

They arrive at the airport and find the parking lot nearly empty. "Well, I'm not going to miss the plane, that's for sure," Karen says.

"Better to be a bit early than a bit late," Aunt Pru tells her. "Do you have the slippers I knit for your mother?" she asks.

"Mm-hmm." Karen doesn't bother to explain that her mother, being completely bedridden now, has no use for slippers.

"You have your ticket handy, I guess?"

"Mm-hmm."

"Well, come then. Shall we see if we can find a spot of tea?" Aunt Pru opens her door, hanging on as the wind snatches at it. "Watch your ticket," she says.

"You know, Aunt Pru, you don't have to come with me into the terminal."

"Oh, but I want to."

"No, really, I have a book I'd like to finish."

A look flits across Aunt Pru's face, one that says she resents playing second fiddle to a book. "I think that once you have a chance to think about it," she says, "you'll see that my having a little visit with your mother on the phone is really the perfect solution — especially since you're planning to have a memorial service here in Halifax that I can be a part of." She tells Karen that it's not that she doesn't care, it's just that she doesn't fly, isn't keen on travel of any sort, and then there's work.

Karen tells her that there's no reason to go over it all again. She gets out of the car, tolerates a hug, tries to reciprocate. "Thanks for… everything," she says, remembering her manners, swiping at yet more tears. What can this crying mean? Exhaustion, it has to be exhaustion.

Aunt Pru strokes Karen's arm. "Well, good-bye until…then. Oh, I almost forgot." She opens her handbag, removes a paper bag. "Cookies for the trip. The macadamia nut cookies, although maybe you're not as fond of them as you used to be?"

Karen feels burdened by the cookies, but she takes them, says good-bye again, heads for the terminal, but she hasn't gone far when she hears her name. She swings around. "Yes?" she cries. Perhaps her aunt has had a change of heart...?

"It's nothing, really," Aunt Pru apologises. "I was just wondering... Do you suppose you'll see him again, the musician?"

Karen feels absolutely mystified by this woman. She tries to explain, rationally, that despite his acclaim, Jake finds touring lonely, that he was glad to share some time and be of help.

"It's probably wise not to get your hopes up in that case," her aunt tells her, waving tentatively, then actually blowing a kiss.

Gusts of wind buffet the car on the drive home. Other drivers seem to have no problem whatsoever holding the road. They whiz by, some of them glaring in at Pru as though *she's* the menace. She tries not to let thoughts of Lily distract her, but it's hopeless. It's like an episode of *This Is Your Life* playing in her mind's eye, the life being not just hers, but Lily's too. ...Those wintry days in their youth when they were snowed in, Pru knitting socks or a scarf, Lily making fudge, the radio playing old songs: "The Sheik of Araby"..."Hello, I Must Be Going," the kitchen filled with the sweet smell of caramel, and best of all, their parents gone for the day, out checking on elderly parishioners, picking up prescriptions, shovelling doorsteps. But now Pru has to caution herself, because feeling torn and miserable and full of nostalgia may have been Lily's objective; after all, she had to know Pru wasn't going to get on a plane. In any case, Karen can't be blamed for trying to sway her. She was duty-bound.

Pru feels sort of sickened by the way she and Karen parted. But how could she have explained to her niece the dread she feels at the very thought of travel? She recalls her one trip to Toronto after Lily moved there with Les and Karen — a train trip. She recalls the public washrooms: dribbles of people's urine on the toilet seats, refuse containers spilling over with used paper towels. And the trip home had been even worse: she'd discovered a spent condom on the washroom floor. You must have had a good look, Lily said later when Pru told her about it on the phone, told her about the fly that had been examining the contents. What I did was, I walked the length of the train and used another washroom, Pru told her in no uncertain terms.

In Pru's last conversation with Lily, almost a year ago now, Lily was full of advice. She reminded Pru that their parents were dead now — as if Pru needed reminding — and told Pru she should stop being anxious over trivialities, and that she should definitely stop playing the role of a widow since she'd only dated Fred a half dozen times at most. Pru has forgotten the exact wording of how Lily put it, but the word *crazy* was in there.

The nerve of it!

Still, she'd no sooner slammed down the receiver when she'd been awash with memories of how her parents had gone from disapproving of Freddie, when he was calling on Pru, to encouraging the relationship after he'd shipped out. While their unexpected, very public pride in her sense of patriotic duty pleased her — her patriotic duty involved writing letters and sending care packages and encouraging others in the church to support their troops — some part of her realised, even then, that they'd created her sense of patriotic duty themselves.

But did that really matter? The fact was, she'd grown very fond of him during their correspondence — more than fond, she'd grown to love him, and it was not crazy to miss him yet, not to herself anyway.

A few weeks after she'd hung up on Lily, Lily called back and said, "I think we ought to be able to talk about our youth together like normal people do. After all, we shared a womb." But Pru hadn't wanted to listen to any more of Lily's versions of past events. She liked her present-day life well enough and didn't need advice from someone who'd cheated on her devoted husband and hadn't even attended their parents' funerals. Perhaps Lily already knew she was dying when she phoned, but how was Pru to have known? When Pru had finally resigned herself to maybe engaging in a conversation for the sake of peace, she could not quite bring herself to call. Lily's last words, *Call me when you're ready*, had not felt inviting. In fact, they felt like yet another directive. And besides, there'd been no apology.

When Karen arrives home she finds her son waiting to be relieved from duty, eager to depart for some sporting event or other, and her mother on the phone in conversation with Aunt Pru, presumably, the dismissive tone being the main clue. She hears her mother say, "Well, we're all dying, essentially, it's just a matter of *when*, isn't it? In my case it's disease, but, sadly, accidents happen daily."

Karen is glad her aunt has called, glad she herself won't have to break the news that she failed in her mission. She sits on the sofa and waits for whatever might come of the conversation. The voices of the little girls next door waft through the open window. Something has been broken or ruined or lost. One claims that she didn't mean to; the other insists she did so mean to. "Did not," the one says. She takes up skipping, her rope rhythmically tic-ticking against the driveway.

There are other sounds too: the roofers a couple of houses down tacking shingles into place, their lighthearted banter, their radio playing; someone further down the street trimming a hedge; the backdrop of traffic. All the crackle and drone of an ordinary day, while inside this room death is standing by. It's unlikely to come today, or even this week, but it could. The doctor had said that oftentimes the final stage plays out very quickly, that she, Karen, should be prepared for that possibility. He also conceded that sometimes life persists even when all will is gone; there's simply no way of predicting with any certainty. She hears her mother say now, "Well, thank you for calling, better you than a stranger. Yes, I'm sure Karen will make arrangements to come as soon as possible."

"What's all this?" Karen takes the receiver from her mother and places it in the cradle. She is definitely not going back to Halifax. Aunt Pru can bloody well get on a plane herself.

"That was Elaine Prescott. We went to school together. She thought we'd have heard about Pru by now, was terribly sorry to learn about the state I'm in. Anyway, she just happened to arrive at the scene." Karen's mother motions for Karen to sit by her side on the bed. "Please, don't stand over me, dear. Sit." And when Karen does, she quickly takes up her hand in her own.

"The scene? What *are* you talking about?" Karen asks, and her mother tells her that Pru has been in an accident, that Pru apparently lost control of the vehicle and is, according to Elaine, in pretty bad shape, and that there's bound to be official word soon. "God, I can't believe it," she says. Karen, too, is stunned, expresses disbelief. "All this just when you thought you were nearly home free," her mother says softly, as if testing, nudging a horrible truth, checking to see if it has expired.

Karen turns away, tells her she shouldn't even imagine such things, and her mother claims to have been kidding.

"To think Pru just may beat me to the golden gates," she says, her eyes misting over. "I wonder how she lost control? …Between you, me and the bedpost, having driven with her numerous times, I wouldn't be surprised if she was distracted by litter on the side of the road, the nerve of some people, etcetera. Fate is such a funny thing," she goes on. "Perhaps I shouldn't say it, but I was just thinking, if she'd come to see me like I wanted her to, this wouldn't've happened, would it? Such a simple request, really. Maybe our father looked down and didn't approve of her not coming, sent her to her room, if you know what I mean." She frees Karen's hand and gives her a nudge, asks her to close the window, then to please call and find out about poor Pru, get the prognosis. "Those brats," she says of the squabbling girls in the driveway, "hardly a day goes by…"

Karen had spent the flight home from Halifax resenting her aunt more than ever, but now, as she contacts a phone operator for information, she recalls Auntie Pru ordering vegetable soup, a warm bread roll with butter, offering to coddle an egg, rifling through her purse for homemade cookies. She sees her there in the barren airport parking lot, the wind playing havoc with her hair, snatching at her voice too when it crossed her mind to ask about Jake. She stands there in Karen's memory as if in a dream of someone departed, waves tentatively, blows her a kiss.

CASTLES IN THE AIR

Standing amid coats, boots, and a decrepit assortment of houseplants, Phil taps softly on the sun porch window, whistles under his breath to the sparrow on the other side of the glass. The bird — perched on a lilac branch — cocks its head in response, or maybe it's questioning the racket, the slamming of cupboard doors and drawers coming from the kitchen. Phil tells the bird not to be alarmed, that the noise is just Vera in her search for the photos from Gran's last visit.

Suddenly it's quiet, like in all the world there's just Phil and the bird, then Vera's right there beside him. "I see you had no trouble shaving for your mother," she says, running a finger along the sill, drawing his attention to the caulking he hasn't got around to replacing yet. He stumbles back, out of her way. The bird takes flight.

"Dad, what's with her, anyway? Can't we just go?"

Mary-Beth is in the doorway, freshly scrubbed, hair combed neat as neat.

"Well, now..." he begins.

When Mary-Beth was little he used to say, Well, now, aren't you a pretty picture? And she'd answer *Yeth*, looking pleased and self-conscious. Today, like him, she's altered her appearance for Gran's sake, removed the lip stud, nose ring, and eyeliner, but unlike the old days, he doesn't dare voice his approval for fear it'll be taken as criticism of the other look, the one that will be back tomorrow.

Vera sniffs the air. "Something in here smells."

Phil tells her it's the plants, that he'd watered them and the soil is musty.

Her face becomes pinched in bitterness as though she's remembering that he had bought all these plants as gifts for her, that once upon a time he'd been full of surprises, which he had been, though he'd stopped buying plants because he felt he was essentially burdening Vera and condemning the plants to a premature death. "These have got to go," she says of the ragged survivors, then she turns her attention to Mary-Beth, pokes her and tells her to change into the outfit on her bed.

"No fucking way," Mary-Beth says, proving she doesn't require the hardware, heavy eye make-up, and provocative clothes to become a stranger. "The blouse is prissy and the skirt is actually peeling. I mean, the vinyl is, like, separating? ... From the backing?"

"Right. It should prove quite effective."

Phil isn't sure what Vera is getting at, and Mary-Beth seems just as perplexed.

"Go the way you're dressed now," Vera explains, her tone suggesting she's dealing with a half-wit, "and you'll be sent home with an old lace hanky or something. Wear what I tell you to wear and you'll get money for a new outfit. Trust me on this."

"Ohhh...," says Mary-Beth, a light going on.

Phil picks up his cap and puts it on. "Do you really have to dream up ways to scam my mother?" he asks, and Vera says yes, she does. "Well, I wish you wouldn't," he tells her, and she snaps back that she wishes she didn't have to.

"Where do you think you're going?" she wants to know, as he edges toward the door to the backyard, and over his shoulder he tells her he's just going to back the car out of the garage.

"I'll only be a minute," she yells after him. "Don't you dare disappear."

"Now there's an idea I hadn't even thought of," he calls back, but he's only trying to lighten the mood. He flashes a grin so she knows he's kidding, but her sour look doesn't fade in the slightest.

The woman next door is on her sundeck, playing deaf. A church secretary and volunteer in the high school cafeteria, she's behind the slander presently circulating about Mary-Beth, has nipped Mary-Beth's babysitting career in the bud. She unpins a dishcloth and slips back indoors. Phil hears Vera mutter *cockroach* and is unsure if it's the neighbour she's referring to, or him.

When he first told her that he'd been given the pink slip, he'd felt what was left of her regard for him die. Oh, she said some nice supportive things initially, that it was just a bump in the road, that he'd easily find another job, given all his experience, that good things frequently spring from disappointment. It was sort of touching, really, that she even tried to sound convinced of what she was saying, things being what they were between them, even then.

They've scarcely pulled out onto the highway that leads to Gran's when Vera rummages in her purse, takes out her eyeglasses and the letter that had delivered the news of a man in Gran's life, news she finds alarming. It seems to Phil, though, that his mother is deserving of a little happiness. His father had been a hard man to live with, impossible to please.

"When she says this guy is younger, I wonder just how much younger she means," Vera ponders aloud. "Let's say he's sixty-five or even sixty, surely you ought to be able to intimidate him, though I guess fifty-two isn't exactly young either. I keep forgetting how old you're getting to be. Geez, another eight years and you'll be sixty. Maybe the guy is only a year or so younger than Gran. If he's seventy... "

The number in Phil's head is one hundred, not the possible age of a man named Cecil, but the number of kilometres per hour the law allows him to go, the number he's going. Phil likes being on the open highway, keeping the needle steady, gliding along. He could drive all day were it not for the price of fuel.

Vera continues to read, pausing now and then to stare out across the flat fields, her face as empty as the landscape. During such moments, he sees his wife not only as the mother of his only child but as someone who has been let down, by him and life in general, someone who might have softened under kinder circumstances. But maybe not. Hadn't he, as an older man — he'd been thirty-nine to her twenty-six — offered those kinder circumstances? When they married, he really believed in transformation, that with their union both their lives had become shiny and new, full of possibilities. They had only to be vigilant of corrosion and add to the lustre. But even early on she was not willing to give up her tendency to be aggrieved about one thing or another. Of course he had noticed back when they were dating that she hadn't any natural sense of humour, but he believed his would rub off on her over time. It had to. Hadn't he risen to the rank of assistant to the assistant manager mainly because of his ability to get along with others and smooth tensions? But right from the start, any attempt to apply his talent at home was met with a stare. "Are you *trying* to be funny?" Vera might say. Or, "Is that supposed to be some kind of joke?" Ten years into the marriage, Phil, on occasion, toyed with the idea of separation, but he'd had the feeling that Vera was contemplating the same thing and he figured it would be better all around if she made the move. The very idea of *him* wanting to leave *her* was bound to stir up all her old insecurities and consequently strike her as an outrage.

Phil recalls a dream he had not long ago in which he came home from his deliveries and found Vera stretched out on the sofa reading a magazine, an article on how to get blood from a stone. She looked at him and said, "Don't act surprised."

"Presenting himself as a handyman, what a con artist," Vera says now. And then further down the road — after a good half hour of silence save for the hum of the engine, the whish and drone of passing cars and trucks, the fluid, languorous sound of Mary-Beth turning magazine pages in the back seat — she says: "For Gran to invest in a dinky house that's close to an ugly water tower…why, she might just as well have thrown her money out the window!"

Phil has no intention of getting into a debate with Vera, but he knows that while the tower might put some people off, his childhood home is a solid little bungalow that was built back when contractors didn't cut corners, and such houses are enjoying a comeback. If truth be told, he sort of hopes this new man will turn out to be the fatherly type, worries that Vera will ruin things and embarrass poor Gran. He says to her, "Why not at least meet him before you judge him, Vera?"

"If he's spent all Gran's money," Mary-Beth grumbles from the back seat, "then I've gone and dressed like a dweeb for nothing."

Eyes still fixed on the letter, Vera tells Phil that Cecil is not the only crafty one, that during Gran's last visit there wasn't a hint about what had to have been going on for some time. "…Why are you stopping here, Phil? We can't be low on gas yet."

"I'll just top it up. I need to stretch my legs," he tells her, supposing there's some truth to the fib. What he needs is to get away from her misery for a moment, get out into the fresh air and sunshine. He tells the young pump attendant that eight dollars should do it.

The attendant squeezes out the fuel to exactly eight dollars, then produces a squeegee and washes the windshield. There's something about him that harkens back to Phil's own generation — eager, conscientious. But when the boy moves along to the side windows, staring in on Mary-Beth, the sense of affinity is lost. Phil would never have been so brazen, especially with a girl's father right there.

"Did you have to tell him eight dollars, Dad?" Mary-Beth says, as Phil settles back into his seat. "Why not say to fill it up? It sounded like we're broke."

Phil looks at her in the rear-view mirror but she's peering off in the direction of the boy. "Do you suppose that Gran is actually sleeping with the guy who's been fixing up the house?" she asks, which recalls to mind Vera's account of Mary-Beth's recent sexual activity with that scoundrel, Darren. Only fourteen, Vera told him, and going at it like a couple of pros, a phrase Phil has had to push from his thoughts again and again. He himself had been twenty-three when he lost his virginity, older than average but not so very uncommon then. Fourteen. His Mary-Beth.

"That boy at the filling station had hustle," Vera says when they're back on the road. "He's got a real future ahead of him, unlike that scum you hang out with, Mary-Beth."

Phil cringes at the word *hustle*, a word his father used almost daily. He'd say, Nothing comes to those who wait. Nothing. You've got to have hustle, you've got to get out there and take what you want.

What his father wanted were deals on the side, women on the side, fast cars, and the excitement of flirting with death and possible jail time.

"I hated him," Mary-Beth says of the boy. "Didn't you see how he looked at me? ...That smirk he had? Of course, thanks to you, Mom, I'm in this ridiculous get-up, so who wouldn't smirk?"

"Shut up for once," Vera tells her.

Phil keeps his attention on the road. The word *future* seeps through the knot in his stomach and begins to burn.

It has always seemed to Phil that the car could find the way to his mother's all on its own, so it's surprising to find they've gone through the main intersection — they've actually passed Gran's place.

He circles the block. It's easy to see now how such an error was possible. Gran's house has undergone dramatic changes. New roof, new siding, new windows — with shutters yet — new porch railing, new brick walkway.

"We're too late," Vera wails.

"Too late for what?" Mary-Beth asks, but her question hangs there unanswered, because Vera isn't explaining herself and Phil wouldn't know what to say. "I'm not going to just sit here," Mary-Beth says opening the door. "I'm going in to see Granny."

"Just stay put for a minute," Vera tells her. "He has taken advantage of your silly old mother," she says to Phil, her voice quaking with emotion, "and you have *got* to be a responsible son and do what you can to rectify the situation. And if you don't, well then…I guess *I'll* have to, and don't think I won't."

The door to the house opens and Gran steps out onto the landing, all smiles. Mary-Beth says, "This is nuts," and Phil watches as she flees from the car, dashes across the lawn into her grandmother's outstretched arms. He extracts himself from the car, leaving Vera to stew on her own.

"My, you must have missed me," Gran is saying to Mary-Beth. She studies Mary-Beth so intensely that Phil is filled with the dread that Vera has blabbed about the sexual episode. "Aren't you blossoming into quite the young woman all of a sudden?" she says. "You're going to have a fine figure like your mother and make heads turn." She strokes Mary-Beth's back. "I know, I know," she coos. "You're too young for all that yet."

Phil cuts in to have a turn in his mother's arms. She smells like always, like roses — perhaps it's the soap she buys from Vera. "Son," she murmurs.

Usually it's Phil who pulls away first, but this time it's Gran. "This is Cecil," she tells him, her voice surprisingly boisterous, maybe to include Vera in the introductions. Vera's slow journey up the walk is probably meant to worry Gran, let Gran know acceptance of this outsider is not going to be automatic, but Gran is too excited to pay any mind.

Phil and Mary-Beth shake hands with Gran's boyfriend. A short, wiry, bald man dressed neatly in slacks and a cardigan — with a gentleman's way about him, to be sure, but he's certainly not Phil's idea of a ladies' man. He may be younger than Gran by five years or so, but there's nothing strange about them standing side by side as a couple.

"So very pleased to meet you all!" Cecil's jovial attempt to establish immediate rapport reminds Phil of the school counsellor Mary-Beth has to visit every week until the end of term — unless she'd rather be expelled from school, which she said she'd rather be, but Phil had begged her not to dash all his hopes and dreams for her. He'd been crushed at the thought of her selling copies of an exam Darren had stolen from the principal's office, and had been greatly relieved when she agreed to co-operate and provide details of the theft. He remembers the look she gave him when he reminded her that honesty is the best policy, a look that said, *Oh yeah, and where has that gotten you?*

"Cecil's responsible for all this work here, the siding, the eavestroughs," Gran tells them. "You must have noticed the new roof, the uh…matching shutters." Her enthusiasm seems to ebb into embarrassment. "It's a lot to take in all at once, I know."

Phil thinks to himself, The man has been one hell of a busy beaver. "We didn't recognise the place," he admits. He steps aside so Vera can bestow one of her feeble hugs on his mother, something she does while at the same time deliberately turning her back to Cecil, or so it seems.

"I'm surprised you didn't mention any of these changes until the recent letter, Gran," Vera says. "Not a peep during your visit or during our phone conversations." She asks, "The weather's more noteworthy, is it?" but her little chuckle has a tension running through it that even Cecil must have picked up on.

"Don't blame Florence," he puts in. "It was my doing. I wanted to prove myself before having to pass muster with family."

He's so eager to take the blame it's hard to imagine him guilty of anything, but Vera doesn't seem at all appeased. "You're looking well, Gran," she says. "The house is not the only thing to get a makeover. That's a new dress, isn't it?" She helps herself to the sleeve, rubbing a bit of it between her fingers. "*Feels* like silk."

Gran admits the dress is silk but says it isn't new. She doesn't remind Vera it's the dress she bought for Gramp's funeral, the one she's to be laid out in whenever her time comes, or at least that had been her plan, a plan she'd shared with Phil when his father died, one that had registered as a sudden and very real pain in his chest.

"Silk for everyday use," Vera says. Again she laughs a little laugh, and this one says she's not amused by such a lifestyle.

"You look very nice, Mother," Phil says. He's happy to see the dress somewhere other than in a casket.

Cecil opens the door and steps to one side. "Well, it isn't every day family comes, is it?" He urges everyone in and Vera flashes a look at Phil that says, *Who does this man think he is? The master of the house already?*

"What will you all have to drink?" Cecil asks, and he recites an amazing list of options — every soft drink imaginable, plus Scotch, rum, gin, beer.

Phil takes a seat in the recliner by a window that looks out on the backyard. He tells Cecil a beer would be dandy.

"Scotch for me," Vera says. "Gee, you've made a lot of changes in here too." Again, her voice is strained and accusing. And when Gran tells her she's had the sofa and love seat since Phil was a boy, Vera strokes the eggshell brocade and says in disbelief, "It's just your old stuff reupholstered?"

Gran surveys the room as if dazed by the changes herself. "We got rid of some things too — things I'd been hanging on to for no good reason."

"What about the lamp with the amethyst glass shade?" Vera wants to know. The lamp is an item she routinely hints for, which dismays Phil, but he knows his mother doesn't hold it against her. His mother knows as well as he does that Vera grew up with so very little. Phil wouldn't be surprised if Vera has suffered more from his job loss than he has. He's been humbled, to be sure, but it seems that Vera, lacking imagination, can't escape the situation for even a moment.

"The lamp is in the bedroom," Gran assures her.

Vera's eyes sweep from object to object, into every nook and cranny. "I see you have the grandfather clock up and running. That must have set you back."

"Cecil has your drink ready, Vera," Phil tells her. He watches her take it, sees the look of pleasure on Cecil's face when she's overwhelmed by the size of the tumbler, the depth of amber within. The man is clever. He's intuited Vera's love of a good stiff drink.

Reaching for her glass of ginger ale, Gran almost spills it. "Thanks, lovey," she whispers. She hangs onto it with both hands and cautions Mary-Beth to do likewise, but Mary-Beth, perched on the armrest next to her, takes the tall glass of Dr. Pepper from Cecil undaunted.

"What do we say, dear?" Gran prompts ever-so-gently, and Mary-Beth accommodates her by murmuring thanks. She studies Cecil a moment and tells him that he sounds American, which makes him laugh. He puts his hand on his heart as if to pledge allegiance, and says, "Guilty as charged," a quip that endears him to Phil, makes him understand why his mother might take to the man. Then Cecil explains, not just to Mary-Beth but to Phil and Vera too, that he'd come to Canada after the post office returned a letter he'd written to an old friend — a coin dealer — the envelope stamped *deceased*. Unfamiliar with any of the man's relatives, he thought he'd come up and speak with the neighbours.

"Guess whose doorbell I rang first?" he asks, his eyes twinkling at Mary-Beth, and she guesses *Gran*. "Right-o," he says, raising his mug, winking at her. "I guess you could say it was fate that led me here, but not entirely so. I like to think of myself as a man of action. Cheers," he tells her. He says cheers to Phil and Gran, then turns his gaze upon Vera, clinking her glass in a languid way that suggests he's trying to woo her out of her present mood, and indeed, her mood does seem to brighten.

"American, not Canadian, so aren't there limitations to how long you can stay?" she asks.

Cecil doesn't flinch. "I dare say there are even worse characters than yours truly allowed to linger on." His tone is one of amusement.

Vera takes a good swig of her drink. "That's quite the chair," she says, referring to the throne-like seat he occupies, and he explains that it had been in his wife's family for three generations and was one of only a few things he bothered to bring up from Vermont.

"Your wife has passed away."

Phil assumes that Vera has merely stated the obvious, but from the look that passes between Gran and Cecil, a complicated answer must be in store.

Cecil explains that his wife of almost forty years has had a series of strokes and is totally incapacitated. Gran murmurs sadly that the woman is, unfortunately, a vegetable.

Someone might just as well have dumped a wheelbarrow-load of potatoes into their midst. Everyone stares in silence at the carpet. The grandfather clock counts off the seconds. A good long minute passes. Phil tries to think of something to say. He is surprised, amazed, really, that his mother would become involved with a married man.

"My wife's getting the best care money can buy," Cecil assures them by and by.

Vera crosses one leg over the other and points an agitated foot in Phil's direction. Perhaps she's concerned that Gran may be providing the care. She ought to have figured out by now that the guy is flush, that if Gran had paid for even half the renovations, her nest egg would be non-existent. But that's the way it is with Vera, her emotions take over.

"Is she conscious, your wife?" he asks to satisfy his own curiosity.

"Her eyes open from time to time, but she doesn't respond," Cecil tells him. "It isn't something I like to dwell on."

"Do you go back to the States often?" Mary-Beth asks. "Because CDs and DVDs generally cost less there, so I could tell you what I want, and you could maybe pick some items up for me if it isn't too much trouble."

"He will do no such thing," Vera tells her — although it is Gran she seems to be addressing. She stresses that there are plenty of things *urgently* needed and that entertainment purchases will just have to sit on the back burner indefinitely.

Mary-Beth takes this rebuff as her cue. "If I don't get a new gym suit I'm probably going to get a detention...or maybe I'll have to do about twenty laps a day, because our teacher is a real Nazi when it comes to appearances."

"Well, it doesn't seem fair that you'd have to do more laps than others." Gran tells Mary-Beth that she's been wanting to get her something anyway, and she'd like nothing better than to cover the cost of the gym outfit. "We'll settle the matter before you go, dear," she says.

"Okay," Mary-Beth murmurs. "Thanks," she adds, as if in response to Phil's telepathic reminder. He doesn't understand why his daughter's manners have to be constantly resurrected from when she was a child.

"I hope you'll let me treat you to a new skirt and blouse too," Gran goes on.

"Mother, you needn't…"

"Oh, but I'd like to," Gran insists, and Mary-Beth again murmurs thanks, basking in the love of her granny.

The conversation prompts Vera to mention that she's brought along Gran's Avon order. "It comes to $36.13 with tax," she says. "I looked high and low for the photographs you asked about, but they seem to have just disappeared."

"I'm sure they'll turn up by next time," says Gran, but they won't be turning up because Phil, in a moment of anguish, put them in the garbage, something he ought to have owned up to doing, and he would have if Vera's scorn hadn't seemed certain. The film had been in the camera for so long that by the time it was developed life was no longer as it had been back when the pictures were taken, back when he had a job that allowed them to have a reasonably comfortable lifestyle, back before they'd had to sell the split-level Mary-Beth had grown up in and move to a cottage that had been listed with the realtor as a handyman's dream.

"I never was one for taking pictures," Cecil tells them. "I bought a digital camera when they first came out, but I haven't used it except to document my coin collection. I guess I prefer to not spend a lot of time looking back."

"It can be painful," Vera says, nodding in agreement. She fingers the rim of her glass pensively, as if maybe she's getting set to tell the story of her life, how she'd been raised by an aunt not much better than the parents who'd abandoned her. But she spares them. "You started to tell us before about how you and Gran met," she says to Cecil. "You mentioned that you came to find out about a coin dealer — a friend or associate, whatever — and wound up on Gran's doorstep…and *then* what?"

Cecil's attention, Phil notices, is riveted to Vera's legs, something Gran appears to have taken in too. "Tell them how we met, Cecil," she says, and he begins an account that mustn't be romantic enough because she interrupts to say she'd opened the door and found him standing in the rain looking like Gene Kelly but without the umbrella.

Or the *hair*, Phil muses to himself. *Singing in the Rain,* now that was a good movie, he continues to muse. He can hear the song in his head clearly, envisions himself leaping nimbly over a puddle to the curb.

"Anyway, I'd made some biscuits that morning," Gran recalls wistfully, "and Cecil and I talked for hours while his jacket dried off. Then, next day…" A look of panic replaces her smile. "He didn't stay *here*; he stayed over at the Holiday Inn up on the strip there, as you come into town."

"I was home and back many a time before we got familiar," Cecil offers as corroboration.

"Who cares if you were or not?"

This from Mary-Beth, whose legs straddle the sofa armrest. She rocks back and forth.

Phil gives her a look of disapproval. "Why not take a proper seat before you fall from there?" he says.

"I'm not a child," she tells him. "I'm not going to fall."

Gran explains that the other armchairs are in the TV room they fixed up, and Cecil apologises for not thinking to arrange better seating for the visit.

"Mary-Beth can sit right next to me." Vera pats the middle cushion. "Come," she says. "Gran doesn't want to have a great big girl like you looming over her."

Gran murmurs that she hasn't minded a bit. "But you'd better do as your parents say, dear. You'll still be right beside me, love."

And now both women pat the cushion, urging compliance from Mary-Beth, who finally obeys. Only now does Phil really notice the ill-fitting skirt and blouse Vera had her wear as a means to wheedle money from Gran. No wonder she'd been embarrassed earlier, when they'd stopped at the filling station.

"Kids these days," Vera says. Then, as though she'd been reading Phil's mind, she launches into a description of the attendant, an exceptional young man in a world of hopeless cases.

"Your mother told me about your setback, Phil," Cecil states, as if to say, *Speaking of hopeless cases…* "I understand you're in distribution now."

He's referring to the part-time job Phil managed to acquire before his unemployment insurance ran out, delivering advertisement flyers door to door.

"Must be good exercise."

"It is, yes." Phil doesn't mind the job, actually, being out and about, connecting with people he normally wouldn't, like the distressed child he happened upon yesterday. In just a few moments he was able to disentangle the lad's pant leg from a bike chain and set him back on his way.

When Cecil tells him what a tragedy it is, all the downsizing, good men reduced to taking anything they can get, Phil doesn't know how to respond. He turns away to gaze out the window. "What happened to the willow?" he asks.

"The willow?" Vera says, choking, spilling the last of her drink down the front of her blouse. "We were talking about your employment and you ask about that ragged old tree." She turns to address Gran and Cecil. "If this so-called *good man* doesn't find a better job soon," she says, "we'll have to re-mortgage the house we just bought."

She shares with them her fear that Phil is settling into the wretched delivery job, tells them he comes home with stories of helping disabled folks in and out of wheelchairs and cars — goddamn wheelchairs and cars is how she puts it — stories of helping people retrieve goddamn plastic bags from rooftops and trees, helping people push their cars through goddamn snow during winter months, and now he's helping people move rain barrels and whatnot, and it's clear from her account that she has failed to grasp that these small gestures over the course of many months kept him from losing his mind. "The dogs run to meet him," she goes on disparagingly. "Cats too, apparently. He comes home covered in cat hair."

"Please, Vera," Phil says. He acknowledges that of course the job is meant to be a second job, to pay for extras, not the one and only job. Again he turns to the window, gazes out upon the spot where the willow had stood. He had spent several summers of his youth up in its boughs, pretending to be Tarzan, surveying from his lofty vantage point an imagined jungle and deep dark river, grasping the tree's reed-like branches and swinging over the heads of alligators to the far shore. Back then, the far shore of his imagination was a place where he demonstrated his talents for survival, oftentimes rescuing distressed maidens from marauders and other dangers. He'd had a slight build and a stammer, was a colossal disappointment to his roaring, barrel-chested father, but up in that tree and with his father gone to wherever it was he went on weekends, he'd felt invincible — like thousands of other Tarzans, he supposes, timid fellows like himself. He wonders how many of them remained timid, unable to truly compete out in the real jungle, unable to push others out of the way to scramble higher up the ladder, unable to even negotiate with a hostile spouse.

"The tree lost a main limb last week in that storm you got the tail end of," Gran says apologetically. "Cecil decided to take it down. Cecil dear, maybe now would be a good time to share your idea."

"I was just thinking the same thing." Cecil leans forward in his chair. "But how to begin?" He places his hands on his knees, and seems, for the first time, unsure of himself. "I like to keep active. And as I've told Florence, I'd like nothing more than to have the pleasure of fixing up your place."

Vera thanks him for the offer, her tone dismissive, explains that the exorbitant cost of materials makes it out of the question. "Even if you were to work for free," she says, "it would…"

"He wouldn't work for free!"

Phil assures Cecil that if they were able, at some point, to put together some money to have a few things done, he'd be paid for his time and expertise, assures him too that there's no real emergency, something that causes Vera to drop her jaw dramatically. "Ha," she says.

Cecil chuckles softly and explains that he's not looking to do business. He tells them that undertaking renovations is his hobby, it helps him relax. He confesses that he hadn't done all the work on Gran's place himself. "I hired a few local boys...to do the risky work," he jokes. "My passion is carpentry, not masonry, shingling and the like. Hell, at my age I'd be a fool to be up on the roof."

"You were up on the roof," Gran says mischievously.

"That was just to check the progress."

There's such merriment in his words that Phil can almost see him scampering across beams, and sure enough, he admits to being fit and agile for his age — admits this to Vera in a way that causes Gran's smile to fade. He tells Vera that while he's not a rich man, not in the Bill Gates sense, anyway, he has, nevertheless, ended up with more money than he's likely to spend in his lifetime. "If I had children it would be another matter, but I was never blessed that way."

"This is very kind of you, Cecil," Vera murmurs, her speech slurred by the Scotch. "*Very* considerate."

"What I had in mind," Cecil goes on, "is to make the house comfortable and functional, and bring it up to date."

"Do you think I could have a window seat in my room?" Mary-Beth asks.

"That's not functional," Vera tells her. "And anyway, you shouldn't interrupt. Just listen, or go find something to do. You could take a walk, if nothing else."

"Oh, now," says Cecil, winking at Mary-Beth, "I wouldn't rule out a bay window, a bench with maybe some storage space under it. I think it would be a good place to sit and do homework."

Aside from the mention of homework, it's as though Cecil has suddenly become Mary-Beth's fairy godfather. Phil tells him that, however kind the offer, having someone come into their lives and wave a magic wand just wouldn't be right.

Cecil and Vera are in such perfect unison asking *Why not?* it sets them laughing.

Mary-Beth doesn't join in, is perhaps resentful having been told, more or less, to take a hike.

"I know what Phil means," Gran ventures. "There's just something about it..." She explains that it wasn't until she realised just how much enjoyment Cecil got from planning and keeping busy that she was able to give the go-ahead on her place.

There's something about this little speech of hers, the helpless flutter of her hands, that reminds Phil of when they first arrived, his mother's lapse into embarrassment when enumerating all the changes. She hadn't wanted such an extensive overhaul, he would bet on it. Cecil had had his way. There's no question the man has money and skills, but it seems to Phil that this self-proclaimed man of action is about as adrift as anyone could be.

Vera — enunciating each word carefully — tells Cecil that she thinks it's just marvellous that some men are so productive. She describes her house, the crazy layout, ramshackle porch, the outdated plumbing, tells him the place could sure use some TLC. "But couldn't we all?" she giggles, whisking her hair back from her flushed and glowing face. It's hard to believe she's the same person Phil brought to Gran's.

Cecil asks her if the wall between the dining room and living room is a load-bearing wall, and when she shrugs he says, "Phil, is the wall..."

"Oh *he* wouldn't know," she tells him, laughing.

Phil studies Gran's ceiling, the broad swirls in the plaster that, he supposes, his wife and daughter will want on their own living room ceiling. "None of this is for sure yet," he says, but Vera's enthusiasm isn't at all deflated, such is her faith in Cecil.

"You'll have to excuse me for a bit," Gran says rising. "I'm just going to go and get a head start on dinner."

Behind closed eyes, Phil climbs the tree of his childhood, looks across to the far shore, the real world where he's lived all these many years. Along the bank, alligators bask in the sun. One of them smiles at him and slides into the shadows. He lets his mind drift south to Cecil's wife in Vermont, a woman dead to her husband's whereabouts — unless she's lying there fully conscious of the wreckage that is her life. From the woman's bedside, Phil hears Vera drumming her nails on the sofa arm. "This is what he does," she says to Cecil. "Even with things really looking up for a change, he sleeps. ... Phil, Phil, are you with us? See what I mean? He's drifted off to fantasy land again. My god, the ideas he comes up with for employment! An animal bed and breakfast, for Christsake. All of them just ... castles in the air."

Back in the upper boughs of the willow, Phil catches sight of a clear day and an open road, a road that promises to just keep unfolding, through forests and valleys, over the green hills and beyond, and he's gone, gone a long way before he applies the brakes and comes to a halt. "Mary-Beth ...?" He opens his eyes and trains them on his daughter. "I'll bet your grandma would enjoy your company in the kitchen. I want you to go now, run along and lend a hand. I mean it."

Mary-Beth sits there, testing perhaps, then, casting a hateful look at her mother, gets up and saunters toward the kitchen. Phil hears her fiddle with the lock on the new sliding door in the dining room that exits to the patio, hears her cop out of helping with dinner: "Can I put some water in the birdbath, Granny?"

Gran says of course. She says isn't it nice that Mary-Beth has acquired her father's love of birds. "Is that door giving you trouble?" she asks. She takes a turn tugging and working the lock that must be jammed. Phil rises, hoping to be of help.

"Never mind, I'll just go out through the kitchen," Mary-Beth says, but Gran doesn't back off, not even to let Phil have a try. She continues to fiddle, saying *goldarn it all,* and *blast.* She informs Mary-Beth that the door off the kitchen no longer exists, tells them both she's sorry for causing such upheaval in the family, that without meaning to she's gone and wrecked everything. Her eyes fill with tears. "It's really just hit me now," she sobs as the lock gives way, "how much I miss my old back stoop, the willow, everything. You know, Phil…the way it all was."

Mary-Beth becomes misty-eyed too. She embraces her grandmother. "It's okay, Granny," she says. "Nothing's wrecked, not really."

Phil tries with all his might not to break down. He reaches out, slips one arm lightly around Mary-Beth's shoulders, gently drawing her to him, the other around his mother's waist. It's such a relief to hold them, and such a pretty picture in his mind.

"Like I said before, whatever it takes," Cecil tells Vera, his voice distant and yet resonant, profound. "There's nothing that can't be changed," he says. "Just leave it to me."

ARTHUR'S FIRST WIFE

When Violet was in grade ten she broke the school record for the running broad jump. She hadn't tried to, particularly. She simply took her turn as every student was required to do, running and hurling herself toward the far end of a sandpit. She leapt as if crossing the creek on a shortcut home from school, and in doing so, she propelled her scrawny frame farther than any other grade-ten girl ever had in the academy's sixty-year history. Her teacher and the two other adults officiating the event were completely floored, and in an instant Violet had gone from feeling like the shabby girl who hadn't a clue how to fit in socially, to an athlete capable of who knows what.

Her other two jumps — everyone had had three jumps and only the best one counted — were disastrous, but never mind, the teacher, Miss Nugent, was certain that Violet's self-consciousness could be overcome before the provincial meets. As it turned out, however, the provincial meet didn't include Violet because, during the interim, her father failed to find another job as he'd said he'd do when he quit the one he had, and she was roused from bed one night to slink out of town — out of the province, in fact — leaving behind her dream of medals and glory, leaving behind Miss Nugent, who'd made clear her intention to "exterminate the mouse" that was Violet's whole being.

And now it was many years later, Violet had married Arthur, and their tenth anniversary was at hand. A friend had led her to believe that some kind of celebration was called for, that it was not unreasonable for Violet to expect her husband to pull himself away from business to treat her to, say, a weekend, or at least an overnight stay at a bed and breakfast snuggled in some hillside. This had sounded logical to Violet, and yet implausible too, and indeed, she found herself assuring Arthur that really, she hadn't forgotten how busy he was; key people, she knew, had to be accessible, not off somewhere taking moonlit walks. Dinner out would be fine, she told him, more than fine, it would be great. "Shall I make the reservation?" she asked, and he told her to go ahead if she wanted to, but it was hardly necessary. He had obviously assumed she'd make the reservations at one of the places they always went to, where a table, reservation or not, would be found, pronto.

He was such a creature of habit, Arthur was: sex every second Saturday night, movies on the first Friday of every month — not any movie but the one most talked about in the media to prepare him for whenever a little chit-chat with employees was called for. Not that there weren't variations to the schedule. Sunday brunches May through August, for instance, were more hurried than during the rest of the year to accommodate Arthur's sessions with a golf pro. His interest in golf had nothing to do with the game or with exercise or relaxation; rather it was to further establish business ties, something everyone did, or so he claimed, but Violet doubted it very much. She figured that any other man with as little aptitude for golf as Arthur had would give it a pass.

On the evening of the anniversary, Violet, half-expecting Arthur to go berserk, confessed that she'd not made a reservation at one of the usual places, but at Calico's, a place she'd heard people mention most favourably, a place that had been given five stars by the newspaper food critic. "No problem," he said, "I'll just phone and cancel."

"But surely after ten *years*, Arthur...!" she cried.

Arthur glanced with surprise at Violet, then toward the door to the family room behind which was their daughter and the babysitter. "Very well," he murmured tersely, then he asked which sitter Violet had hired, Cindy or the other one, and Violet told him Cindy, without bothering to explain that there were actually *two* other ones, university students, two brunettes to call upon when need be, and Cindy, the redhead, the aspiring model/actress/singer/dancer — the oldest at twenty-two, but the least mature.

Violet probably would have let Arthur cancel the reservation at Calico's were it not for Rita, who lived next door. She'd popped by earlier to help Violet with her hair and make-up and, taking hairpins from her mouth, said, "You listen to me, Violet. You can be sure he didn't dare treat Suzanne as he treats you," Suzanne being Arthur's first wife, someone larger than life to Violet, and now to Rita, too, through Violet. Suzanne had been someone who knew how to get what she wanted. Banished from Arthur's life, but still… "And I doubt very much that Suzanne had a green thumb as you do, or knew how to operate a backhoe, for god's sake." Rita had been in some kind of fury, and Violet, sitting on the vanity stool in the washroom and looking at the reflection of her own apprehensive self, had realised it was entirely possible that Rita might wash her hands of her if she didn't soon show a bit of gumption. Rita, who did a lot of charity work for destitute women, had told Violet that there was a certain kind of victim she had little sympathy for, and even though Violet did not regard herself as a victim of any kind — being full to the brim with aspirations — she had a feeling Rita might think otherwise.

Now, as Violet and Arthur were about to depart for their anniversary dinner, Cindy and Ginny appeared from the family room to see them off. "Oh, my God, I just *love* your dress, Mrs Wyatt," Cindy gasped. She went on to praise Violet's hair and shoes and earrings. "Seriously," she said, "you're red-carpet awesome, super-glam, you know what I mean?"

"Me too, Mommy," Ginny said, "I think you're totally glam."

Arthur took a closer look at Violet. "You've really done yourself up," he conceded. "I could pass you on the street and not recognise you."

Violet's little black dress wasn't new. It was, in fact, the dress Arthur agreed to when her mother died, but she'd made some alterations — lowered the neckline and raised the hem — that made it seem less like death. Still, if there was a sight to behold in the room it was not Violet but Cindy, whose red hair stood up like a hedgehog's, the effect ethereal, not bristly. Her skin was luminous too, her eyes bright as stars. It occurred to Violet that if this were a movie and not real life, Cindy might, at this moment, burst out of her torn jeans and faded T-shirt into a ball gown and dance away with Arthur. "Have fun, eh, you guys," Cindy said.

Arthur stroked his tie, repeated the word *fun* as though the word was a sweet but vaguely obnoxious candy. He said he'd try to. He told Cindy he'd be making a short night of it, and she shrugged and sang "…Mmmm, whatever." As fantasy material for Arthur, Cindy fell a bit short sometimes.

Violet gave the girls some last-minute instructions, then swished out the door into the early evening, feeling, all in all, more like a bride than she ever had. Her wedding had been a very solemn affair consisting of oaths and signatures. Afterward, Arthur had had to run off to some meeting or other, but he'd given Violet money to take her mother to a café near the courthouse.

"I'm not sure you fully appreciate what you've stumbled onto here," her mother told her over coffee and five layers of *gateau citron*. "I hope you don't continue to mope around like you've been doing." Her mother reminded her that she herself had been crazy about Violet's father when she'd married him and things had gone sour within the month, and downhill from there, down and down, year after year.

"I liked Pop," Violet said, and she had. She had loved him. It was true he'd gone from job to job, but with each one he learned a new skill. "Come, Vi," he'd say, "let's make a little welder out of you." Or, "Put on your rubber galoshes, Vi, we're going to rewire the joint." Things like that, always with a big grin. He'd been struck by lightning several years prior to Violet's wedding, but still she felt he'd been ripped from her life just yesterday. If only he'd been wearing rubber boots when he'd been struck by lightning, not steel-toed ones.

"And it's not just about money," her mother went on, expansive in her praise of Arthur. "There's a great deal to be said for living with a man who is honest, or at least smart enough to keep track of his lies, and the smell of expensive after-shave is far better than the reek of oil and perspiration."

Vi's mother had been smitten with Arthur's grooming habits too. "Even better-looking men couldn't have cleaner hands," she stated. "That imaginary friend you had as a child, the girl with everything going for her, well, you've managed to become her, haven't you? So be nice to Arthur, is all I have to say." And it was more or less all her mother had had to say, but she said it over and over until she died, always mentioning Violet's imaginary childhood friend, Caroline, someone Violet had never told anyone about, not even her dad. Her mother must have overheard conversations that Violet had carried on with Caroline when she and Caroline thought they were alone. One thing Violet remembered and cherished about her companion: she seemed to really care when Violet was hungry, when no one was home and the fridge was all but empty. At such times she'd arrive in Violet's thoughts with a huge cheeseburger or a fried drumstick, a chocolate sundae or strawberry pie, eager to share.

At Calico's it took no time at all for Violet to state what she'd have: the duck breast with red current compote.

She found it disconcerting the way Arthur viewed the menu, looking down his nose, shaking his head and muttering something about embroidery.

"What was that, Arthur?"she asked, aware of a light cadence to her voice that must have sprung from the ambience of Calico's.

"The flowery prose, that's what," he said.

She sipped her aperitif and tried to relax and enjoy the setting. The music was not piped in, but live, the rippling piano pieces ebbing and flowing, merging, continuing on anew. The decor, too, was soft, elegant, the table linen of a fine quality, the flowers fresh — most likely changed daily. There were clusters of greenery to break up the dining space, and mounted high in each corner was a long, lean ceramic cat. These cats had a strange presence. Like butlers or sentinels, they seemed to know far more than they'd ever let on. All in all, Calico's seemed very deserving of its quick rise in popularity.

While Arthur continued to study the menu, Violet noticed that, without exception, other couples were at least moderately engaged with one another. "It all looks so very good, doesn't it?" she said of the food choices. "The rack of lamb sounds exceptional. Or swordfish maybe," she went on. "Why look, they even have elk!" She bet to herself that Arthur would settle on the pork tenderloin since there was no halibut, these two dishes, pork tenderloin and halibut, being what he ordered at his usual haunts. It was a bet she won, but without satisfaction.

"How's the tenderloin?" she asked part-way through the meal, and Arthur had to think before supposing it was fine. He thought to ask, then, how the duck was, and upon hearing it was absolutely sublime, he said he was, in that case, glad she went all out.

The dessert menu was like a fantasy, but Violet chose the fairly simple but rich chocolate mousse and cappuccino. Arthur had tea only, his digestion troubled as it was by the red cabbage that had come with the tenderloin medallions. Chocolate mousse was, Violet knew, something Arthur's first wife adored. Over the years, Violet had developed a keen sense of Suzanne, her likes and dislikes, and how she behaved in all kinds of situations. Early in her marriage Violet had done her best to be as little like the former Mrs Wyatt as possible, and she excelled to the point where she could do nothing but stand in awe of Suzanne, her ability to be herself, her blatant willingness to fall out of favour.

When the waiter came with the bill, Arthur checked it thoroughly for possible errors. As he added the columns, Drs. Robert and Buffy Ingersoll, friends of Violet's friend, Rita, and the parents of one of Ginny's friends, stopped by to say hello. "We didn't recognise you,

Violet," Robert said. "We thought Arthur was up to a bit of mischief. We were relieved to realise it was you and that you were having a night out on the town, so deserving after all that landscaping you've done recently, not to mention the beautiful gazebo you built this spring. Rita had us in to view it from her kitchen window, most extraordinary. Anyway, you look lovely, doesn't she, Buff?"

"She surely does. You *do*, Violet. Don't you think so, Arthur?"

It was most alarming, Arthur being confronted like that, and Violet feared what he might come out with. "I'm sure my wife knows by now what I value most," he said, his tone good-natured enough, a relief, although she wasn't certain what he meant. What *did* he value most about her? But there was no time to become distracted by the possibilities or impossibilities. Their daughter had developed a little crush on the Ingersoll boy and Violet wanted this chance encounter with his parents to go well. She confessed she hadn't noticed *them* at all, so they indicated where they'd been seated, at a far table partially obscured by plant fronds.

"You're just back from Dubai, I understand," Robert said to Arthur, and Arthur looked blank for a moment then nodded in agreement. "Quite the place, Dubai," Robert went on, as though he had a hope of getting conversation out of Arthur, whose trip to Dubai was probably not much different than a trip to, say, New York or even Calgary: a swift transport from airport to hotel, from hotel to some office tower or other, some verbal wrangling, then the paper exchange, back to the hotel for a bit of halibut or tenderloin and a bad night's sleep, then an early morning flight home. Mission accomplished.

When Violet and Arthur were first married, Violet always asked about his trips because she'd thought it so exciting to actually know someone who went to the far reaches of the world, but he'd set her straight and asked her to please stop jumping on him and grilling him, as though she ever would dare to jump or grill. She had, in fact, always broached the subject over Sunday brunch, even if he'd been back nearly a week by then.

"What's the occasion?" Robert asked, his voice still expressing the surprise of seeing Arthur and Violet. Thanks to Rita's lack of discretion, Arthur's uncompromising dining habits were known, or so Violet presumed. She mentioned the tenth anniversary, hoping Arthur wouldn't mind, which he didn't seem to. Oftentimes he minded things that were of absolutely no consequence to her.

Buffy looked sort of puzzled, doing the math, most likely, because her son Nigel was twelve or thirteen, and Ginny was only one grade behind.

"Ginny was nearly two when we married," Violet said, folding her napkin and placing it on the table. She wondered if she should mention that she and Arthur had been more or less involved for a few years prior to their marriage so the Ingersolls would know Arthur was, indeed, Ginny's father, but such a statement could be awkward for Arthur, and anyway, surely they could see the resemblance between Ginny and her father.

The Ingersolls launched into an account of their own courtship and unplanned wedding, an account that was so much more upbeat than her story, were she to tell it, which she wouldn't, ever. She and Arthur had only dated on and off. He seemed to keep forgetting about her between the times he came into the print centre where she worked. He'd come in every three or four months to have some promotional material done up, material that for some reason he hadn't entrusted to one of the underlings that generally came. Despite their using condoms whenever Violet was in the middle of her monthly cycle, she became pregnant. "You must have miscalculated, and now this," Arthur had said when given the news, even though he'd been the one to convince her it was, as he put it, safe to ride bareback sometimes if one knew what one was doing.

He made it clear he had no interest in marriage, having been badly burned by Suzanne, he said. And Violet, too, by the time her pregnancy was confirmed, felt she was way out of her league. Also, he was kind of old and no fun at all. Even the sex had seemed different than any she'd previously had. He arrived at her apartment bearing flowers or chocolates or wine, or all three, handing them to her or plunking them down with barely a word. Yes, they'd felt like bribes, and he'd tried to bribe her into having an abortion, too, but she wasn't tempted. It turned out he wasn't nearly as generous when it came to her keeping the baby, but, as her mother was quick to point out, at least he'd been gentleman enough to make an offer, and didn't have to be dragged into court. Her mother thought highly of anyone whose cheques never bounced. Then, after almost two years, Arthur dumbfounded Violet with the marriage proposal.

He was very grave about the matter, claiming Ginny was at a terrible disadvantage not having a proper home and two parents. Violet had said she'd think about it and then made the mistake of telling her mother. She'd only wanted to impress her, but it had been like igniting a grass fire and then trying to stomp it out. Afterward, a year or so into the marriage, Violet wondered if Ginny's well-being had been Arthur's primary concern. After all, Arthur was Arthur, and by this time she realised that in the circles he moved in, image counted. Being a family man was far preferable to being someone paying child support and having to dream up things to do with a child all on his own — although, it may have been that Ginny charmed her father into wanting to take parenthood seriously. Not only was she a sweet-natured, imaginative child, but when he looked at her he was bound to see himself staring back at him, and Arthur being Arthur was not likely to regard this as unfortunate. Rita was certainly of another mind and had already broached the subject of nose work and chin work, though she agreed with Violet that Ginny was still too young to go under the knife.

Violet thought to ask the Ingersolls if anything special had brought *them* out for the evening or if they came to Calico's often, and together they assured her that a couple of GP's such as themselves were too busy, and besides, not quite flush enough to frequent the likes of Calico's often. They explained that they were rewarding themselves for finally doing something they'd been putting off for ages: getting their estates in order, redoing their wills, drawing up lists of special wishes regarding funeral arrangements, etc., etc. The two of them, in their late forties at the most, looked the picture of health. A proper will was paramount, Buffy asserted, wishes needed to be spelled out. She and Rob had drawn up lists of far-flung friends and relatives, anyone they thought ought to be notified, even ex-spouses who might like to attend a memorial.

It was the first Violet had heard that Robert and Buffy had both been married before. "My," she said. "Well, I guess we ought to think about doing all that too, one of these days. I'm only thirty-six, but Arthur's fifty-five."

"It's done," Arthur said. "Long ago."

"Really? Mine too?"

"Your *what*?"

Arthur chose a credit card, snapped his fingers at a passing waiter who failed to respond on the first pass — on principle, most likely, as Violet used to at the print shop. She'd pretended not to see or hear Arthur, and he'd puff himself up and drum his fingers to let her know she ought to excuse herself from the other customer and rush to serve him. He was really so awful right from the start that she could hardly believe she was there with him now, celebrating, or at least collecting a bit of recognition for ten years.

"Tolerance is key," her mother used to say in a most exasperated, intolerant manner whenever Violet expressed disenchantment in her marriage. "You will drive me to an early grave, girl," she'd gasp, and then she went ahead and did it, dropped dead the day after Violet finally worked up the nerve and left Arthur. Rita had been ecstatic, saying "Bravo, girl" and such, but the bold move had been too much for Violet. Her mother's death was overwhelming enough, but experiencing the death during a crisis as unnerving as separation, well…

Fortunately, Arthur had been away so Violet had had no trouble returning with him none the wiser, and at the time she'd been glad she'd chickened out because he treated her mother to the kind of funeral he said he'd give his own parents, not that he was close to his parents. In fact, he hadn't spoken to them since he was twenty-two.

"We really must be off," Robert Ingersoll said, and his wife nodded vigorously and wished Violet and Arthur a happy anniversary.

With the Ingersolls gone, Violet's mind turned to Arthur's ex-wife, somewhere on the west coast. Would Suzanne travel such a distance to pay her respects to someone who loathed her? It was too complicated a question for Violet to, just like that, find an answer for, but once she got settled in the car for the drive home, she decided that if Arthur were to die, she'd absolutely insist that Suzanne come for a visit. Ginny would want it too. Ginny had a blossoming interest in fashion and was very impressed that her father's first wife was a successful designer.

Violet thanked Arthur for the lovely evening, and he made a little sound and kneaded the steering wheel in that odd way he had. He didn't mention the red cabbage again, which probably took a great deal of restraint, an acknowledgement of the occasion, perhaps, something Violet appreciated. At such moments, she felt superior to Suzanne who, Violet just *knew,* had been too impatient an individual to value such a simple thing as restraint. Violet's thoughts of Suzanne were secret thoughts now, ever since Arthur threw a fit saying he was sick to death of Suzanne and Violet's endless prying into his previous life. She shared Suzanne with Rita still, and Ginny, of course.

"Did you have the duck?" Ginny asked the minute Arthur and Violet stepped through the door, and Violet murmured yes and hurried to hang up her wrap.

"Get your things, dear," she said to the sitter. "Mr Wyatt will drive you home."

But Arthur had not been as tuned out as he usually was. "How did Ginny know there'd be duck? Oh, *Rita,* I suppose. Still running with the wolves, are you, Violet? I guess you know how I feel about that."

"The duck was featured in the newspaper article," Violet said, though Rita, too, had recommended it and Arthur was maybe right to view Rita as some kind of adversary. She did, as he often said, meddle.

Rita had said to Violet not long ago, "You remind me sometimes of the women I see at the shelter, but you're not like them. You're the best car mechanic I've ever had, for one thing. And you're not poor. Everything here — this big house, the cars, any investments he's made — fifty percent belongs to you, you do understand that, don't you?" And Violet had nodded at the wonder of it, because even living in the midst of it all, everything, even the things she herself built, felt like Arthur's. "Of course," she said, "I'm not the type that needs much."

Rita had looked at her long and hard. "Don't be an idiot," she said.

"I guess you'll be going to the office for a bit," Violet said to Arthur, who held the door open for Cindy.

"Yes," he said, and that was the last she saw of him for the next couple of days because he was late-to-bed and early-to-rise and their paths just didn't cross. Still, the dishes she covered and left in the fridge at night were empty and on the counter in the morning, so all was well, or as well as ever it had been. Then one afternoon, just as she was getting set to sew buttons on the outfit she was making for Ginny, her own creation, Arthur appeared in the doorway to the sewing room, a cosy room on the top floor, a maid's room, the realtor had called it, assuming wrongly that they'd have a maid. "Can you spare a minute from that, Violet?" Arthur said, looking even more serious than usual.

Violet's mind scrambled to think what she might have done. After installing the new garage door, had she left it open? Had she left the electric hedge trimmer outdoors? His mail, what had she done with it? She'd had it in her hand when the phone rang, the poor chap selling frozen meat, and then what … ? "What is it, Arthur?" she asked.

"It's nothing of importance, really. I just stopped in to pick up some paperwork and there's something I've been meaning to mention, since the, uh, other night…"

"Oh, me too," Violet said setting the sewing aside. "I hope you don't think I'm sick of those other restaurants we go to because, really, how often do we go?"

"The first Tuesday of every other month."

"Right. Not often enough to grow weary. And I like halibut as much as you do."

"This is not about restaurants."

"It isn't?"

"First of all let me say how impressed I was with the way you managed to pull the whole thing off the other night. I never would have thought you capable, even with someone like Rita as a mentor."

"What?" Violet asked. "Pulled what…?"

"No, really, it's okay. Naturally, you want to know where you stand, so I intend to tell you, then we can carry on without you setting up chance meetings and conversations about estates."

"I never— I hardly know the Ingersolls." But even as she was protesting she had to wonder if Rita had set things up. Rita seemed to really dislike Arthur and enjoyed pulling strings more than anyone Violet had ever encountered, except, maybe, for Arthur.

"I don't have time to argue, Violet," Arthur said. He pointed out that he had a meeting in forty-five minutes and had a few things to go over yet, but still he wanted her to know that if he were to kick the bucket first, she'd be well taken care of. "I'm not such an egomaniac that I'd cut you out and give my money away in exchange for immortality of a sort," he said. "Besides you have rights, and, for the most part, you've been a…a good wife, and you're Ginny's mother, and I've become genuinely very fond of the girl, although I wish you'd give her more grounding in reality." He suggested to Violet that she start by changing the wallpaper in Ginny's bedroom. "She's way too old for unicorns," he said. Returning to the previous conversation, he told her that in the event of his demise, she could count on his secretary to organise everything. Loreen had the key to his safe deposit box, and at her fingertips the lawyer and accountant. There'd be papers for Violet to sign, of course, but she needn't worry; she'd be notified when everything was in order.

"Oh," said Violet. "But I really hadn't thought about it."

"I'm sure." Arthur checked his watch again. "And one more thing," he said. "About Suzanne…"

"We weren't going to talk about her, remember?"

"I just want to make it absolutely clear that I wouldn't want you to trouble yourself to get in touch with her."

"Oh, it wouldn't be any trouble."

"What I'm saying is: *don't*. It is my wish that you do *not*, is that clear?"

"Yes, Arthur, you've been very clear." Violet took up her sewing. "Don't let me keep you," she said.

She listened to him descend the stairs, heard the door close, smiled to herself just thinking how tortured he must have been imagining she might discover what she'd known almost from the start: that he'd never been married to anyone but her. He was, back when she met him, one of those men who'd rather admit to a failed marriage than try to explain why he'd remained single past the age of forty. Most likely, his other dates had been satisfied with very little detail. But she'd asked a lot of questions about Suzanne, making it necessary for him to invent a viable character profile, which proved so viable that however fictional Suzanne had been at the outset, she became, after a time, real to Violet, very real, a friend, like Rita, only nicer and more accessible, always on the sidelines, silently coaching, silently cheering her on, and now fervently urging Violet to once again unleash that great, long leap constrained within her, spring into a new life and leave all fear behind.

Violet took a moment to admire the garment she was working on, a sample for a line of dresses Rita had commissioned, then, choosing the perfect set of buttons, licked the thread and deftly slipped it through the needle's tiny eye.

Mary Hagey grew up on a dairy farm in Southern Ontario near Cambridge and Kitchener-Waterloo. A long-time resident of Montreal, she attended Concordia University, majoring in studio art and taking a minor in creative writing. She graduated with distinction in 1985. She has earned a living primarily as a personal support worker, caring for the elderly and people with disabilities, but also as a housepainter, a clerk in retail books, a copywriter for a mail-order house, and as an instructor at Concordia. She received her M.A. in English in 1994 while employed as a travel companion, a job that allowed her to see some of the world, including much of Canada. Her stories have appeared in various literary journals including *Prism international, The New Quarterly, Descant, Rhubarb,* and *Room of One's Own*. A story published in *Grain* was nominated for the Journey Prize and a National Magazine Award, and a work of creative non-fiction was short-listed for the CBC Literary Award. She now writes and paints in Ottawa. She has two grown children.

Eco-Audit
Printing this book using Rolland Enviro 100 Book
instead of virgin fibres paper saved the following resources:

Trees	Solid Waste	Water	Air Emissions
2	126 kg	8,330 L	328 kg